She Sings of Old,
Unhappy, Far-off Things

Books by Caren J. Werlinger

Currently available:
Looking Through Windows
Miserere
In This Small Spot
Neither Present Time
Year of the Monsoon
She Sings of Old, Unhappy, Far-off Things

Coming soon:
Hear the Last Unicorn
Cast Me Gently

She Sings of Old, Unhappy, Far-off Things

— by —

Caren J. Werlinger

CORGYN
Publishing

She Sings of Old, Unhappy, Far-off Things
Published by Corgyn Publishing, LLC.

e-Book ISBN: 978-0-9960368-0-1
Print ISBN: 978-0-9960368-1-8

E-mail: cjwerlingerbooks@yahoo.com
Web site: www.cjwerlinger.wordpress.com

Cover design by Patty G. Henderson
www.boulevardphotografica.yolasite.com

Book design by Maureen Cutajar
www.gopublished.com

Dedication

To Beth
From the beginning, you were my happy ending

Acknowledgements

The seeds for this story were planted so long ago, I can't really remember its beginnings. I wanted to write a story about a middle-aged woman reluctantly falling in love, something she thought she was too old to experience again. Of course, by the time I got around to writing this book, it became easier to write as I myself am now in that age category... I owe a huge thank-you to Marty and Marge, my main beta readers, who always give me honest feedback and help me make my books better than they could ever be without their input. As always, I owe a tremendous debt to my partner, Beth, for her encouragement and support through this process of getting my stories launched out into the world. And to my readers, thank you, thank you, thank you. Your support makes all the difference in the world.

She Sings of Old, Unhappy, Far-off Things

Chapter 1

MARGARET BRAITHWAITE STOOD AT the bedroom window, staring out at the brooding August sky, wondering if those low clouds promised a downpour. A raincoat would be a good idea today. Her attention was caught by movement down below.

"Gavin," she said, half-turning from the window. "There's someone in the garden."

"Oh, yes," he said from his chair where he was struggling to put his shoes on. "It must be the landscaper. Fitz somebody. I hired him to come and do some pruning."

"Really?" she said in surprise. Gavin had never wanted anyone else working in his garden. She turned from the window and saw that he was still trying to stuff a grotesquely swollen foot into his well-worn wingtip.

"Damn it," he huffed in frustration.

"Gavin," she said, coming to kneel beside his chair, "why don't you wear slippers today?"

Grudgingly, he agreed and allowed her to help him. She noted that he had dressed in his typical attire of khakis, button-down shirt and tie, though his bloated body strained the buttons and made it look as if his tie were threatening to strangle him. Pushing off from the arms of the chair, he got heavily to his feet and shuffled from the bedroom. Descending the stairs one at a time, he was out of breath by the time he got to the breakfast table.

"Aren't you eating?" he asked as she placed a bowl of warm oatmeal and a cup of coffee in front of him.

"I've already eaten," she said, giving him a kiss on the forehead. "I drew the short straw this semester – an early lecture. I'll be home sometime this afternoon. There are sandwiches already made in the refrigerator."

Remembering to pull her raincoat off the peg in the mudroom, she gathered up her purse and briefcase as well.

"Tell that landscaper I want a nice square edge on the boxwoods," Gavin said as she stopped with her hand on the door to the garage.

Sighing, she turned instead to the back door. "Yes, Gavin," she said, stepping out onto the flagstone patio. "Like I have time to deal with the gardening help," she muttered. "Who probably don't even speak English."

Looking around impatiently, she saw no sign of the person she had seen from the window, but there was a large white pickup parked at the end of the driveway beside the garage with "Fitzsimmons Landscaping" painted on the door.

She heard a rustle and a snap overhead, and realized there was a figure some twenty feet above her up in a tree, lowering a cut branch to the ground with a rope.

"Mr. Fitzsimmons," she called, adjusting the strap of her briefcase on her shoulder, "I'm Margaret Braithwaite. Dr. Braithwaite wanted me to tell you to trim the boxwoods with a square edge."

A long handsaw was lowered by rope to the ground also and the figure began climbing down from the tree.

"Wrong and wrong," said the tree-climber, dropping lightly to the ground from the lowest branch.

Margaret found herself looking into the amused eyes of a slightly built young woman with short dark hair that stood up scruffily. Margaret couldn't tell if the scruffiness was accidental or deliberately made to look accidental. She blinked as she realized the woman was speaking.

"The name is Wyck Fitzsimmons or Ms. Fitzsimmons if you prefer, but not mister. And I won't use hedge trimmers to give him a square edge," she said with a nod toward the kitchen window where Gavin's head was visible, haloed in silver hair. "So if your father is going to insist on that, you'll have to find another landscaper, Ms. Braithwaite."

Margaret raised one eyebrow in an expression that usually indicated to anyone who knew her that she was displeased, but this Fitzsimmons - *what kind of name is Wick?* she wondered - was busy coiling the rope knotted to her tool belt and wasn't looking at her.

"Wrong and wrong," Margaret said coldly. "Dr. Braithwaite is my husband, not my father. I am Dr. Braithwaite as well, not Ms. Braithwaite. And I suggest you speak with him about how you will or will not trim his hedges."

Wyck watched in amusement as Margaret gave her one more disdainful glance up and down before letting herself through the back door to the garage, closing it with a slam.

"Well, I guess that's me told, isn't it?" Wyck said with a grin.

Margaret found herself scowling as she escaped the lecture hall after her third class that day and made her way to the inner sanctum of her office where she closed the door firmly. Sinking into her chair, she pulled her reading glasses off, rubbing her eyes tiredly.

"God save me from undergrad English classes," she said as she sat back with her eyes closed. She knew she was just irritable after another night of practically no sleep. Gavin's breathing was getting worse, but he refused to take the fluid pills the doctor had prescribed - "I'll be up ten times to pee," he complained. But Margaret didn't sleep no matter what. Either his getting up and down all night disturbed her, or she lay listening to his labored breathing – "no, it's the not breathing I listen to," she corrected herself. "Wondering when it will stop for good."

She groaned at the sound of light raps on the frosted glass of her office door. "Come," she called apprehensively. "Close the door," she said in relief as a well-dressed, slender man entered and quickly shut the door behind him.

"Hiding already and it's only the first day of the semester?" he quipped as he sat, adjusting the knot on his tie. "God, you look terrible."

"Thanks."

He tilted his head, scrutinizing her. "When are you going to move to another room?"

"I know, I know," she said tiredly. "I'm going to have to. I'll never get through the year like this. But he wants me near."

"And what Gavin wants..." he said archly, leaving the rest unsaid.

"Don't be a bitch, Taylor," Margaret said. "What did you come by for?" she asked, changing the topic before he could take another jab at Gavin.

"I was sent to see if Gavin is going to be at the dedication tomorrow," he said in a bored tone that clearly indicated he didn't care whether Gavin was there or not.

"Of course he will be," Margaret said, but she looked worried. "I just don't know if he can walk that far, and it will kill him to have to come in a wheelchair. He's so disappointed that he's had to go on medical leave this year, but I suppose it was inevitable..."

"A little humility will do him some good," Taylor said. "Or humiliation. Either would do."

"Why do you dislike him so?" Margaret asked.

Taylor brushed a hand over his carefully highlighted hair, making sure it was still in place, and sniffed, "I don't dislike him. I just won't kiss his ass like everyone else here does."

"I didn't think there was a man whose ass you wouldn't kiss," Margaret said.

"Now who's being a bitch?"

"Well, you'd better be careful," Margaret warned. "Gavin Braithwaite is an institution unto himself. Talk like that could get you branded as a heretic."

"He's a professor, not Jesus, for God's sake," Taylor insisted waspishly.

"At St. Aloysius University, he's both," Margaret said wryly.

Wyck sang along with the radio as she drove home. She'd ended up spending most of the day with the old man, touring the gardens. She guessed him to be in his eighties, scuffing along with his cane as he showed her around. He'd had to stop at almost every bench or seat to rest – fortunately, there were plenty of them – thus, the all-day tour.

He hadn't bothered hiding his surprise and displeasure upon meeting her. "A woman!" he had scowled when he came outside to inspect her work. "You were operating under false pretenses when we spoke."

Wyck laughed at his consternation, something Gavin Braithwaite was obviously not accustomed to. "I was perfectly frank with you on the phone. It's your fault if you made an assumption that I was a secretary. This business is me, just me." She picked up her rope and saw. "But, if you'd rather hire someone else, it's also fine by me. I'll write up an invoice for the work I've done this morning."

"Not so hasty," Gavin said, surveying her work. His eyes were still sharp – "Thank goodness something still works," he often grumbled – and he carefully looked to see where she had made her cuts. Grudgingly, he had to concede that she seemed to know what she was doing. He looked her up and down, much as Margaret had done a short while ago, and suggested they tour the garden.

He refused to use the electric scooter sitting in the garage – "Margaret's idea, but I'm not an invalid," he insisted gruffly – preferring to walk along the wood-chipped paths that meandered through the property. "I did all of this myself," he puffed, and even through his breathlessness she could detect the note of pride in his voice.

"Justifiably so," she muttered to herself as she took in the dry-stacked stone walls, many of them now in need of repair, the bluestone terrace where sat a wrought-iron table and chairs, the beds of peonies and rhododendron, roses, azaleas and hostas, the crabapple and dogwood and cherry trees. He pointed out patches of ground – "those will be covered in a sea of crocus and daffodils, come spring," he said. There were a few leftover blooms on some of the plants, but mostly at this time of year, it was variegated shades of green. "The entire property is nearly twenty acres," he informed her, though over half remained untouched woodland. "I'd better get working on the other half," he said, chuckling at his own joke.

"This reminds me of Winterthur," she said during one of his rests, and he glanced at her in such a way that she knew he was re-appraising her.

"This is better," he said, allowing a smile as she laughed.

As they walked and talked, he quizzed her on her knowledge of the various plants and trees, her grasp of features such as hardscape and water drainage, and she realized this was turning into an interview. The plants were in need of serious pruning and cleaning up and she could see that some of the walls had started to crumble or collapse from the pressure of the earth behind and inadequate drainage.

He invited her inside for a sandwich and drink as they talked.

"Now this is a mudroom," Wyck said admiringly as she swiped her boots on the brushy scraper and stepped into a slate-tiled room with a drain set in the floor, and another slate countertop against the wall with a farmer's sink set in.

"I started most of my seedlings and grafts in here. I haven't been able to do much the last few years," Gavin admitted as they sat at the table. "It needs someone to look after it." He squinted at her from across the table. "I think you'll do."

"Do?" she asked, feigning ignorance.

"To take over here," he said with a sweeping gesture.

Wyck sat back and crossed her arms. "I'm sorry," she bluffed, "but I have other clients, and the amount of work this place would take..." She paused, looking through the large windows to the gardens. "I don't think you could afford me."

He squinted at her again, his gray eyes sharp under his bushy eyebrows. "Try me."

She considered. She had only been in the Asheville area a couple of seasons, and, though jobs were coming her way, this contract could be enough to carry her all by itself. Gavin was clearly used to getting his way. Even Wyck had heard that St. Aloysius was preparing to re-dedicate one of its buildings to Gavin Braithwaite, who was something of a local Asheville celebrity, and she was beginning to understand why.

Still, she didn't want to be pushed into a commitment she couldn't handle. She stalled, saying, "Let me put some figures together, and I'll get back to you by the end of the week."

As they finished eating, Margaret Braithwaite came home, clearly displeased to see Wyck still there.

"I have good news, my dear," Gavin said as Margaret came into the kitchen. "I have found someone to take over the landscape and garden work."

Margaret's mouth tightened in disapproval as she took in Wyck's mussed hair, her t-shirt and carpenter jeans, the knees permanently stained with dirt, her scuffed leather work boots. "How lovely," she said.

The fact that Wyck clearly caught the sarcasm in her inflection, and was amused by it, only irritated her further.

"I haven't agreed to take the job," Wyck reminded Gavin.

He waved a hand as if shooing away a gnat. "You will, you will," he said confidently. "Sit down, my dear," he said, pulling a chair out for Margaret. "You two will get to be great friends," he said even as the expressions on both women's faces clearly indicated their doubt that his statement would ever prove true. "You already have something in common."

"What's that?" Margaret was forced to ask.

"Ms. Fitzsimmons' first name is Wyckham. She goes by Wyck."
Gavin chuckled. "Right up your alley, my dear." He turned to Wyck.
"Margaret's expertise is Regency and Romantic literature," he explained.

"I'm sure 'Wick'" – *is there no end to this woman's sarcasm?* Wyck wondered – "neither knows nor cares about Regency literature," Margaret said as, rather than sitting, she gathered up the sandwich plates and carried them to the sink. "I would guess that 'Wick' is more likely an homage to Frances Hodgson Burnett."

"Wrong again, Dr. Braithwaite," Wyck said cheerfully. "*The Secret Garden* is one of my favorite books, but Wyckham is my middle name, not my first, and it is spelled with a 'y', not an 'i'. So, although I am as charming as Jane Austen's Mr. Wickham, I assure you, I am of much better character."

Gavin laughed heartily as he tried to heave himself to his feet, falling back into his chair. Margaret and Wyck both came to his assistance, each taking an arm, and helped him to stand.

"As I said before," Wyck said, "I will crunch some numbers and get back to you. And now," she said with a mock – *or was it mocking?* Margaret asked herself – bow, and let herself out the door.

The truck rumbled along a road shaded by an avenue of trees with old split-rail fences on either side and cleared pastureland visible beyond the trees. Wyck turned onto a gravel lane that ended at a turn-about in front of a large barn. In a clearing nearby were the remains of the stone foundation of a house abandoned long ago. A blond golden retriever galumphed from somewhere behind the barn, wagging her whole body as Wyck slid out of the truck.

"Hello, Mandy," Wyck said as she rubbed the wriggling dog. "How was your day? Hmmm?"

Mandy responded by talking back with soft little barks and whines and yowls that blended together until they sounded like conversation.

Wyck unlocked the front door that had been framed into the opening of what had once been the barn's sliding door and flipped on the lights. The continued overcast skies, still threatening rain, brought an early twilight to the barn's cavernous interior. Inside, the edifice looked like a cathedral with exposed posts coming up through the main floor's open space like tree trunks, supporting beams that extended up to the lofty spaces above.

One wall contained a chimney, the stones salvaged from the dilapidated farmhouse next door, now serving as the flue for a large soapstone woodstove that provided heat in cold weather. The living area was littered with a mishmash of objects masquerading as furniture: an upside-down half-barrel serving as a side table, an up-turned apple crate passing as either a seat or a table, depending on the need of the moment, one dilapidated but comfortable armchair and a camping cot set near the woodstove.

Mandy, lying on her bed, moved only her eyes as she followed Wyck's every movement.

"I think we have time to get some more wire pulled upstairs before we eat," she was saying as she went to a post with old, hand-cut nails pounded into it, each nail holding a different tool belt. She plucked the one loaded with electrical tools and climbed the wide wooden stairs to the upper level where a large coil of wire lay waiting to be run through the holes she had already drilled through the studs of what would become bedroom walls. The only finished room in the entire barn was the bathroom up on this level, which was also furnished with a washer and dryer.

"I can live with unfinished space for as long as it takes," Wyck had defended her odd priorities to Mandy, "but I've got to have a hot shower and clean clothes."

For the next couple of hours, she worked, pulling wire and making connections to the junction boxes and outlets mounted at regular intervals. Mandy kept an eye on her progress and listened attentively while Wyck explained Gavin Braithwaite's proposal. As she talked, Wyck weighed the pros and cons - "talking to Mandy always helps me figure things out," she would have said had anyone wondered why she was talking to her dog. At last, she stood stiffly, rubbing her sore knees.

"That's enough for tonight," she said tiredly, looking around with satisfaction at how much she'd gotten done. "Let's eat."

Mandy followed her downstairs to the kitchen – "well, not much of a kitchen yet, but it will be," she often reminded herself, seeing the completed room in her mind's eye – where she dished out a bowl of kibble garnished with green beans and carrots for Mandy and opened a can of soup for herself.

The kitchen had already been plumbed and wired so that a sink and stove, connected by a plywood countertop, were at least functional. She heated her soup on the stove and sat at a makeshift table fabricated of yet another piece of plywood supported by two sawhorses. While she ate, she scratched figures on a pad of paper.

"I kind of want the job," she said to Mandy, who looked up politely from her bowl as Wyck talked, "but I'm not sure I can put up with the Doctors Braithwaite." She looked over at Mandy who tilted her head as she listened. "I should charge triple just for the aggravation."

Chapter 2

THE FOLLOWING AFTERNOON, MARGARET made sure Gavin was in position early, using a wheelchair to get him to the dais that had been erected on the quad. She helped him up the steps and got him seated while she stashed the wheelchair out of sight. She had instructed someone to collect a chair with arms so that Gavin would be able to get to his feet on his own.

"Jim," she said quietly to the university president. "He's struggling. Try to keep it short."

Dr. James Evans looked over at his old friend and colleague. "Don't worry, Margaret," he said. "I've known him longer than you have. Gavin will bull through. He always does."

"Yes, he always does, and then I always have to deal with the aftereffects," she nearly retorted, but, with a resigned sigh, Margaret took her seat in the front row of folding chairs that had been set up for the ceremony. Looking up at the overcast sky still threatening rain, she hoped it would hold off. At least the cloud cover had arrived with cooler temperatures. She'd been worried about Gavin sitting, wearing a jacket and tie, in the heat and humidity that would have been more typical for August. There had been discussion of holding this ceremony as part of next spring's graduation festivities, but Gavin's last bone scan had made that impossible.

She was soon joined by Gavin's children from his first marriage. Just four years younger than Margaret, Jeffrey was an earlier version of Gavin. Looking at him was like seeing Gavin back when Margaret had first met him – handsome, professorial. He had also inherited his father's arrogance and his tendency toward pretentiousness. Jeffrey was a PhD in history and taught at UNC. Margaret remembered an incident many years ago in which Gavin had proudly introduced Jeffrey just so to a confused woman who asked, "Don't you mean he *has* a PhD? Not he *is* a PhD." The poor woman was completely bewildered as Jeffrey had haughtily replied, "You, madam, most obviously are not." Margaret had understood early on that Gavin would never have considered marrying her if she hadn't also had her Doctorate, the equivalent in his mind of being on his intellectual level, even if he never quite considered her his equal. To Gavin, the degree and the person were one and the same.

Amanda, Gavin's daughter, though she held a Master's of her own in education, had married her PhD in the form of Matthew Sikes, a medical researcher at Duke.

"Matthew couldn't get away," Amanda murmured as she settled into her seat, leaning across Jeffrey to talk to Margaret. She waved at Gavin. "He doesn't look good, does he?"

Jeffrey squinted at the dais, adjusting his glasses on the bridge of his nose as he frowned. "Have you been making sure he takes his medicine?"

"You try living with him and making him do something he doesn't want to do," Margaret longed to retort, but instead said, "Nobody makes your father do anything. He takes his medicine when he feels like it."

Barely registering Amanda and Jeffrey's continued conversation, Margaret scanned the crowd that had gathered. Most of these students, she realized, had never had Gavin as a professor, but his presence at this university was still so powerful that she knew the administration had pushed the faculty to "encourage" their students to attend.

Her eye was caught by a person standing on the edge of the crowd wearing a waxed cotton rain jacket and jeans. It took her a moment to realize it was Wyck Fitzsimmons. Her face burned a little as she realized that her immediate reaction to Wyck's androgynous good looks had been one of attraction. Her embarrassment became more acute as she saw that Wyck was watching her.

"You must be careful about the image you project," Gavin had schooled her when she first joined the faculty at St. Aloysius. "In academics, there is a very fine line between the relevant and the ridiculous," he'd said seriously. "Your predecessor, Dr. Tandy, was so engrossed in all things Jane Austen it seemed after a time that she believed she was Jane Austen. She became laughable."

Under Gavin's tutelage, Margaret had abandoned her preferred grad student uniform of jeans and sweatshirts for his preferred tailored clothing – though she stopped short of dresses and rarely wore skirts. "Just be careful not to get mannish," he had warned repeatedly.

Now, Margaret self-consciously smoothed her slacks and adjusted the collar of her jacket. Her jewelry, bought by Gavin of course, was tasteful – diamond studs in her ears, a simple gold bracelet on one wrist and a Rolex on the other. Fortunately, she'd always been slender – she was under no delusions that Gavin would have kept quiet if she'd gained weight as she aged. Not that it hadn't become more difficult to keep extra weight off as she passed through her forties and even more so now in her fifties. Recently, she'd noticed more streaks of silver beginning to show in her dark hair and her skin was beginning to sag in places, facts that bothered her more than she had expected they would.

Over the continued murmuring of the voices around her, she became aware of a loudly whispered conversation taking place behind her.

"I wonder how much the old goat promised the university to buy this honor."

"Shhh, that's his wife.

"Where?"

"In the front row. The dark-haired woman."

"You're kidding. She must be, what? Thirty years younger than him?"

Gritting her teeth, Margaret stared resolutely ahead. This wasn't the first time she'd heard similar sniggers. She knew some people assumed that her every promotion, her every accomplishment had been solely due to Gavin's influence. Those who knew them best understood the deep respect and compatibility they shared, despite the difference in their ages – twenty-seven years, not thirty – and knew, too, that the respect had blossomed over the years into love, even if it wasn't a romantic love, "but who needs that at my age?" she might have said if there had been anyone in her life with whom she could discuss such things.

Dimly, she registered that Jim had begun speaking, outlining Gavin's years of service to the university, his best-selling books and innumerable papers on the Civil War and Carolina history, the impressive numbers of his students who had gone on to pursue postgraduate studies.

I wonder where Julia is? she thought and immediately wondered what in the world had prompted that thought. Julia Vargas hadn't crossed her mind in years, at least not consciously. Only in occasional dreams, like the one a few weeks ago....

"Kiss me," Julia had whispered, rubbing her velvet-soft cheek against Meggie's – not Peggy as she had been to her family, nor Margaret as Gavin had insisted on calling her, but "Meggie, like the Meggie in *The Thornbirds*," Julia had murmured. "Wild and beautiful and irresistible," she said, kissing her deeply and passionately, arousing her in ways Gavin never had....

Her attention was snapped back to the present by applause as Gavin stood and tottered to the podium while Jim dramatically whisked the drape off the easel holding the new bronze plaque for Braithwaite Hall, soon to be affixed to the building behind the dais.

Margaret joined the standing ovation, glancing back to the edge of the crowd. Frowning, she realized Wyck Fitzsimmons was gone.

Gavin was exhausted by the time they got home. He went straight to bed while Jeffrey poured himself a Scotch and Amanda helped herself to a glass of wine. Margaret, who rarely drank, put the kettle on for tea.

Jeffrey sighed as he sat in an armchair in the adjoining sunroom, putting his feet up on an ottoman. "What are we going to do with this old place when he's gone?"

"Sell it, of course," Amanda said as she settled in a neighboring chair.

Margaret stood in the kitchen as they began reminiscing about growing up in this house. She'd been a part of this family for so long, that it was sometimes a shock to be reminded that there were parts of their history that didn't include her. Jeffrey and Amanda had been in high school when their mother was killed in a car accident. By the time Gavin had announced that he and Margaret were getting married, Jeffrey had been in grad school and Amanda was a senior at Duke. If they were bothered by the fact that their father was marrying someone only a few years older than they, it had never come up, but... sell the house? Since when was that a decision "we" would make?

The kettle whistled. As she made her tea, Margaret was struck by a startling realization. *I have no idea what Gavin's will stipulates.* The house had been his when they married – adding her name to the deed had never come up, not even when his lung cancer had first been diagnosed seven years ago. Their focus had been on the surgery, and then the chemo and radiation that followed. But last year, when they found it had metastasized to his spine... *why have I never asked him?* she wondered as she absently sipped her tea.

It wasn't until Friday of the following week that Wyck had the opportunity to return to the Braithwaite house. She rang the front bell,

15

but after a minute or two with no response, she stepped off the front porch.

"Stay," she said to Mandy who was watching her from the truck's open window.

As she rounded the back corner of the garage, she and Margaret nearly collided.

"I'm sorry," Wyck stammered. "I rang, but -"

Margaret shook her head. "Sorry, Gavin is napping and I... I just needed some air," she said.

Wyck looked at her more closely. "Are you all right? You look upset. Is he -?"

Margaret shook her head again. "He's fine - well, as fine as he can be these days. You've probably heard that he has cancer." She paused, taking in Wyck's close-fitting polo shirt and seemingly ubiquitous carpenter jeans, though these were clean - *I don't think I even still own a pair of jeans,* she thought.

"Dr. Braithwaite?"

Margaret blinked and realized Wyck had been speaking. "Sorry... what?"

"I have the figures your husband asked for," Wyck said. "My estimate for cleaning up and maintaining the yard and gardens, plus my ideas for some new projects. May I go over them with you since he's sleeping?"

"I don't really deal with the grounds," Margaret said. "That's always been Gavin's territory."

Wyck watched her closely, her sharp eyes probing Margaret's. "Excuse me if this comes across as insensitive, but... it seems likely that this will all be your territory before long. And then you will have to deal with it."

Margaret's eyes filled with unexpected tears.

"I'm so sorry," Wyck apologized, cursing herself for being so blunt.

"Damn," Margaret hissed, clearly embarrassed. She walked a few steps away from Wyck. "It's just that... I don't know... after Gavin is gone..."

16

"Of course," Wyck said, misunderstanding Margaret's meaning.

They were startled by a sharp rap on the window. Gavin waved them inside.

Margaret turned away, quickly wiping her cheeks dry as she composed herself and led the way to the kitchen door. "I didn't realize you were awake," she said as Wyck followed her inside.

"Yes, yes," said Gavin. "Sit down, Ms. Fitzsimmons."

"Please, call me Wyck."

"We may as well all be on a first-name basis," Gavin said genially. "Could we offer you something to drink?"

"Iced tea if you have any," said Wyck.

"I'm sure we have some sweet tea," Gavin said.

Wyck tried not to grimace. "Thank you, no. Ice water would be fine."

Gavin chuckled. "You live in the South and don't drink sweet tea?"

Wyck shook her head. "I grew up in New Hampshire. My drinks are the only thing I like straight." She glanced up at Margaret who was blushing slightly as she handed her a glass of ice water. "Thank you." She took a sip. "Congratulations on the dedication of the building," Wyck said as Margaret went back to get two glasses of iced tea for herself and Gavin. "That's quite an honor."

"Yes, yes," Gavin nodded. "Of course, my work has brought more grants and more notice to St. Aloysius than all the others combined."

Margaret tried not to smile as she pictured Taylor's reaction to Gavin's statement.

"I assume you have figures for me?" Gavin said. "Let's see them."

"Margaret, if you'll move around to that side of the table, I can show both of you what I've come up with," Wyck said.

"Oh, Margaret has no interest in this," Gavin said dismissively.

Wyck glanced at Margaret. "That may have been true in the past when the gardens were your outlet, your sanctuary," Wyck acknowledged, "but that is changing now."

"How is that?" Gavin asked with a frown.

17

Margaret took a quick drink. Gavin wasn't used to being challenged or questioned.

Wyck leaned both elbows on the table, her hands lying protectively on the sheaf of papers she had brought. "Gavin, I could pick up all the work I want just hiring myself out to prune and clean up or designing landscape plans for strip malls. This," she said, peeling back the top page to reveal a beautifully rendered sketch of the garden from the patio, "requires commitment and vision to continue what you started."

Margaret leaned closer, looking at the sketch.

"I'm only interested in this if the work is to be ongoing."

"What do you mean?" Gavin asked.

Wyck sat back, meeting his sharp gaze, and said carefully, "It's public knowledge that you have cancer. At some point, you will not be able to confer with me about what you would like to have done. It seems important to me to involve Margaret now, so that she can continue to guide things the way you would want. Of course, if the plans are to sell, or maybe donate the property to the university, then I am not interested at all."

Margaret couldn't help staring at Wyck. No one spoke to Gavin Braithwaite like this, and, *how could she know?* she wondered. Ever since Jeffrey and Amanda's comments about selling the house, Margaret had felt as if her entire world stood on a faultline, just one tremor away from slipping into a void.

"Of course it's going to Margaret," Gavin blustered indignantly. "I've given that university my blood and sweat for decades. They're not getting all the blood and sweat I've poured into this place, too."

With a quick smile at Margaret who sank into a chair next to Gavin, Wyck said, "All right, then," and peeled away her top sketch to reveal other drawings with proposed structures and changes: a patio with a pergola near the roses – "There are too many ants in the peonies," she said, "They'll drive you crazy." – with replacements for some of the stone walls that had been collapsing for years; vine-covered archways over some of the paths. She slid her estimate for the various projects out next to the drawings.

Margaret, reeling a bit from her relief at learning the house would remain hers, was only half-listening as Wyck and Gavin talked. She watched Wyck's hands as they moved across her sketches, pointing out certain features, and it struck her that these were an artist's hands - long-fingered and delicate - and clean, she noticed with surprise. She smiled to herself as she recalled her initial impression of Wyck Fitzsimmons as a grubby gardener. *Wrong again.*

She held her breath as Gavin looked the drawings and figures over for several minutes. "Agreed," he said at last.

Wyck stared at him for a long moment. "Really?"

Gavin narrowed his eyes as he regarded her. "You expected me to haggle? I would have if you were only talking about upkeep, but you clearly have a vision that is in keeping with my own, and that is worth something to me."

He raised his tea glass and said, "To our partnership."

Wyck raised her glass also and took a drink.

"You know, Wyck," Gavin said, appraising her, "you're a good-looking woman."

Margaret closed her eyes with a silent groan.

"If you would just dress more like a woman," he continued.

Wyck allowed herself a smile and said, "Well, Gavin, if I gave a damn about your personal opinion of me, I guess I'd be absolutely devastated right now. Luckily, we're good."

She sat back looking at him as Gavin laughed heartily.

"I won't be able to start until later next week," Wyck said. "The Biltmore is getting ready for their fall garden display and I'm scheduled to work there over the next several days."

"You work at the Biltmore?" Margaret asked in surprise.

"Only part-time, usually when they need extra help setting up seasonal displays. Do you ever get over there?" Wyck asked.

"Rarely," Margaret shook her head.

"Well, the chrysanthemums are going to be spectacular this year," Wyck said. "You should go." She slid her chair back. "Thank you for the water. I'm looking forward to working with you," she said, holding her hand out to Gavin.

"I'll walk you out," Margaret offered, leading Wyck through the house to the front door.

Wyck took in the fine furnishings, rich fabrics and numerous built-in bookcases. The walls were covered with paintings, mostly Civil War era landscapes and portraits, and a few framed maps.

Wyck paused at one of these, scrutinizing it. "Jedediah Hotchkiss?" she said in surprise.

"You know Hotchkiss?" Margaret asked, equally surprised. "Gavin will be impressed. He insists the war would have been over within two years if Lee and his officers hadn't had Hotchkiss's maps to guide them."

Mandy whined a greeting as Wyck emerged from the house. "Good girl."

"She waited for you all this time?" Margaret asked. She stepped closer to pet the soft head. "Do you always bring her with you?"

"Not always, but she gets lonely waiting for me at home," Wyck said.

"Well," Margaret cleared her throat a little as she stepped back to allow Wyck to open the door. "Feel free to bring her with you when you come here."

"Thank you," Wyck said, a trifle uncertain as to why Margaret was suddenly being so accommodating.

"And," Margaret stammered, staring at the truck door, "thank you... for... in there," she gestured toward the house. "I've not known what Gavin's plans for the house were..."

Wyck looked at her, a stab of pity momentarily mixed in with all her other more negative feelings toward Margaret Braithwaite. "You're welcome."

Wyck backed the truck around and, as she pulled away, she glanced in the rear-view mirror and saw Margaret still standing there.

"Stupid people," she muttered.

Mandy whined and shoved her nose against Wyck's arm. Wyck laughed and cradled Mandy's head. "I didn't mean you," she said, kissing Mandy on the muzzle.

By the time they got home to the barn on the outskirts of the Pisgah National Forest south of Asheville, there were still a few hours of daylight remaining. She parked the truck and went inside to change into running clothes. Mandy, recognizing what the change signified, danced around impatiently.

"Ready?" Wyck asked, propping the door open as Mandy bounded outside, startling a pair of squirrels who scampered up a tree. She jumped at the tree with a playful bark and then waited for Wyck to indicate which way they would go. Together, they jogged along a trail that led them to a dirt logging road.

"Stay close to me," Wyck said as she ran, keeping a wary eye out for shooters. It was not yet hunting season, but that didn't stop some of the rednecks in the area from getting out for some target practice.

Within an hour, they were circling back home, both pleasantly tired. Wyck cooled down and stretched, using the time to move some more split firewood from the large wood shed to the wood rack on the barn's covered back porch, while Mandy stretched full out on her side in the shade, her tongue lolling.

"Who's gonna do all the other work for ya?" the stone mason had asked as he rebuilt the stone chimney for the woodstove.

"No one," said Wyck. "I'll need help for a few things, but I'll do the rest of the work myself."

All those summers as the grunt in her uncle's construction company were finally paying off now as she did her own electrical, plumbing and carpentry work. She'd called on buddies to help with some of the larger windows – there was no way to do those jobs alone, even with hoists and jigs – and she'd hired out the new roof, but "all the rest is mine," she said proudly, looking over what she had accomplished thus far.

Wyck went inside to shower, Mandy following through the dog door a few minutes later. She quickly dressed, running her hands through her still-damp hair. Stifling a yawn, she said, "Rest later. Got work to do."

Mandy dutifully traipsed after her into what would become the master bedroom as she continued the electrical work.

"You'll be dead and buried 'fore ya git this done," the stone mason had drawled, looking at the empty shell of the barn as he shook his head.

"I'm not in a hurry," she'd said. "I like to stay busy."

No, you need to stay busy, she corrected herself now as she recalled that conversation. She sat on the floor, pulling wires into a junction box. Soon, she knew, the telephone calls would start - "Aren't you coming home for Thanksgiving?" and soon after, "You need to come home and be with family for Christmas." Sometimes, they would put Michaela on the telephone, pleading, "Please come home, Aunt Wyck."

"Damn," she muttered, twisting the insulation off a wire too vigorously and breaking the wire short. She snipped the end off and began again, concentrating on what she was doing, twisting the bare wires together with a wire nut and pushing them securely into the junction box, and then running wire up the stud to the mounting box for a wall sconce near where the bed would be.

Giving up on getting any more done for the evening, Wyck sat on the plywood subfloor and pulled a guitar out of a case resting there. Leaning her back against the wall, she plucked at the strings, the fingers of her left hand moving up and down the frets of their own accord.

"Things are better," she murmured to Mandy, "when you don't rely on other people."

Chapter 3

"I FEEL LIKE I should genuflect," Taylor said as he caught up with Margaret and held the door to the newly christened Braithwaite Hall.

"Hi, Dr. Braithwaite, Dr. Foster," said a good-looking male undergrad whose name Margaret couldn't recall.

Taylor stopped to allow himself a look back. "What? Just enjoying the view," he protested as Margaret took him by the elbow and propelled him through the second set of doors.

"You're still on probation from the last time," she reminded him. "Students are off-limits."

"They only jumped on me because I'm gay," Taylor pouted. "You can't tell me they haven't looked the other way countless times with our illustrious colleagues," and he began ticking off names of other faculty rumored to have had affairs with colleagues or students.

Margaret rolled her eyes. She had heard this litany many times before. "They jumped on you," she interrupted, "because you jumped on an eighteen-year-old whose parents went to the administration. And just in case you've forgotten, you signed a morals clause when you were hired. They may not use it often," she said quickly as Taylor opened his mouth to protest, "but it gives them the right to enforce it when they want to. We work for a private, religious institution that does not include sexual orientation in its anti-discrimination clause. And even if it did, it wouldn't protect you from having sex with a student and you know it."

Taylor allowed himself a wistful sigh. "It was so worth it."

"Was it worth your career?" Margaret snapped.

"I don't know why you remain friends with that milquetoast," Gavin often grumbled. "He offends me."

Sometimes, he offends me, too, Margaret thought now.

"I'm in here," she said, indicating a small classroom. "See you later."

"Bye, sweetie," Taylor said, blowing her a kiss.

Margaret shook her head as she closed the classroom door where seven graduate students were gathered. This writing class was so much more gratifying to her than most of the undergrad courses she taught. *At least these students read real books and know how to put together complete sentences.* For the next hour and a half, she enjoyed a stimulating session during which each of the students read from something they had written while the group offered feedback. Occasionally, Margaret read some of her own work – usually passages from her debut novel, published over twenty-five years earlier to wide critical acclaim....

"But nothing since."

"What a pity."

Sometimes, the whispers were from others, sometimes they were echoes of her own thoughts.

Not that she hadn't tried. The beginnings of six separate novels sat locked away in her desk at home, but she had never been able to complete them.

"Well, since you're not working on anything important," Gavin had gotten in the habit of saying, "you can be my research assistant," as he churned out book after book about various players and scenarios in the Civil War - "the Clive Cussler of the Civil War," reviewers called him - a topic for which there was apparently an insatiable appetite.

Through osmosis and repeated exposure, Margaret had become something of an expert on the conflict herself, though, as a Northerner, the South's continued fascination with the war escaped her.

It's as if they think if they reenact it enough times, one of these days the outcome will change, she often thought, though she had learned early on to keep such thoughts to herself.

When her writing class was over, she headed home. As she pulled into the drive, she saw that Wyck's truck was still there. She parked her Audi in the garage next to Gavin's black Lincoln, rarely driven these days, and let herself out the back door onto the patio, looking out into the yard to see if either Wyck or Gavin was there.

Guided by the sound of someone singing, Margaret wandered along one of the paths toward the hedges. Without warning, Mandy came bounding toward her. The fluffy blond dog sidled over to her, wagging her tail so hard, her whole body wriggled as Margaret reached down to stroke the luxurious coat.

"Mandy, where -?" Wyck stopped short as she emerged from the tall hedges.

"Hello," Margaret said, giving Mandy a final pat. "Was that you singing?"

Wyck immediately turned scarlet, even her ears. "Oh, that. Bad habit of mine when I'm working. I'll try not to disturb you."

"Not at all. You have a fine voice," Margaret said. She looked around. "What are you working on?"

Wyck swung a gloved hand back toward the boxwoods. "Pruning."

"No hedge trimmers, I see," Margaret smiled wryly, pointing to the pruners in Wyck's hand.

Wyck laughed. "No. No hedge trimmers." She invited Margaret to follow her. "If you keep lopping the ends off," she said, holding a branch, "all the new growth extends out from the cut and the interior of the shrub will be nothing but woody stems. But, if you prune by

25

hand, some on the outer edge, but mostly deeper in, you can stimulate new growth that keeps the hedge full and green and healthy."

Margaret, who knew next to nothing about plants or gardening, found herself watching Wyck's animated expression as she talked.

"Do you use them?" Wyck asked, pointing to the pile of clipped box-wood branches lying nearby. "For flower arrangements? Decorating?"

"Uh, no," said Margaret.

"I'll mulch them then, if that's okay," Wyck said.

Margaret shrugged. "Whatever."

Wyck laughed. "You really aren't into plants, are you?"

Margaret shook her head. "No, sorry."

"Listen, I have two passes for Biltmore, for the Fall Festival. One of the perks of working there. It's beautiful. I guarantee, you cannot tour those gardens and that house and not want to come home and do more with your own place."

Margaret blinked. If she really was going to have to take over the yard and garden at some point, perhaps she ought to learn a bit more. "All right."

"Can you get away on a weekday?" Wyck asked. "It'll be less crowded."

"I don't have any classes on Thursdays," Margaret said.

"Next Thursday at nine, then?"

"Next Thursday would be fine."

"Great," said Wyck. "I'm just going to do a little more here before I quit for the day."

Margaret turned and walked back toward the house, waving at Gavin who was watching from the sunroom window.

Margaret, in spite of herself, found herself staring in open-mouthed delight as they approached Biltmore House. She had been relieved to see Wyck emerge from her truck wearing khakis and loafers, but when Wyck gestured her toward the pickup, Margaret had hesitated.

"I could drive," she suggested hopefully.

Wyck grinned. "Not a truck gal, are you?" taking in Margaret's suit and dress shoes.

"It's not that," Margaret protested, "it's just that you got the tickets, so it's only fair I should drive."

Wyck raised her eyebrows at the feeble reasoning, but said, "That's fine," following Margaret into the garage where she slid into the passenger seat of the Audi.

"I hope Gavin doesn't mind that I didn't include him," she said, "but there's no way he could walk, and –"

"Good Lord, no," Margaret said with a sarcastic laugh. "He would never have agreed to come unless there was some politically advantageous function involved."

She backed the car out, saying, "He's had breakfast and is settled with a new book. He'll be fine."

Because they had arrived early on a weekday, there were smaller crowds than typical. Margaret had forgotten the massive scale of the château, the two huge stone lions guarding the entrance. The morning was chilly, typical for mid-September, as they bypassed the house and wandered the gardens first. Wyck pointed out features of the different gardens, most of which were still laid out as originally envisaged by George Vanderbilt and Frederick Law Olmsted in the 1880s. Turning to look back toward the house, Wyck showed Margaret how the architect, Richard Morris Hunt, had worked with Vanderbilt and Olmsted to frame certain aspects of the architecture with some of the garden features so that the whole blended seamlessly.

Margaret found herself listening intently and had to admit a certain grudging admiration for Wyck's knowledge.

"Have you trained as a docent here?" she asked.

Wyck grinned sheepishly. "Sorry if I get carried away. I'm just a tremendous admirer of the vision that created so much beauty. I took as many architecture courses as I could when I was studying. It didn't make sense to me to be a landscape architect if I didn't have a good grasp of building architecture also."

"So, if we were to visit..." Margaret searched for a name, "one of Frank Lloyd Wright's houses –"

Wyck snorted derisively. "The most over-rated name in American architecture."

"I thought he was an icon? A visionary?" Margaret said in surprise.

"To some, maybe," Wyck said, shaking her head. "But to me, a true visionary would have figured out how to find a compromise between design and function," Wyck said. "Nearly every building he ever designed leaked or started to fall apart within a few years of being built."

"Are you always so frank?"

Wyck looked askance at her. "You mean, I give my opinion very decidedly for so young a person?"

It took Margaret a moment, but then she laughed. "Something like that."

Wyck swept an arm around them. "This... this has stood the test of time. Monticello, Winterthur, the Greene and Greene houses, great houses like Highclere, Powerscourt –"

"Highclere?" Margaret interrupted. "In England?"

"Yes," Wyck said. "I studied in England and Ireland."

"Architecture?"

Wyck's expression changed. "No, literature," she said as she ambled along one of the gravel paths. "Although I was already interested in architecture at the time."

Margaret stared after her. "Wait."

Wyck paused, looking back at her.

"You studied literature?"

"I was a Rhodes scholar," Wyck said.

Margaret stood staring at her for so long that Wyck laughed and walked on.

"Why didn't you say anything before?" Margaret demanded, hurrying to catch up.

Wyck shrugged. "You didn't ask." She smiled drolly. "Believe me, it doesn't come up in everyday conversation."

"But..." Margaret blustered, "but you studied at Oxford. You could be doing anything. Teaching, writing. Anything."

Wyck stopped abruptly. "I am doing something," she said coolly.

"I'm sorry," Margaret said. She pressed her fingers against her forehead, feeling as if these revelations had left her reeling. "I didn't mean it like that."

"Yes, you did," Wyck corrected her. "You meant that I could have had academic success, been published, been lauded in my field of study, been successful as the world defines success." She shrugged again. "You're right. I could have done those things, and probably would have..."

She walked on again. Margaret walked beside her. "But?"

"But I decided I liked making things grow better," Wyck said in a lighter tone. "Plants and animals - give them enough time and attention and love, and they'll never let you down."

She turned and gestured back toward the house.

"Shall we head in?"

Wyck took over again as tour guide as she escorted Margaret through the château. She watched Margaret taking in the magnificent fireplace and fresco in the library, her eyes shining, her face looking happier - and younger, Wyck realized - than it was at home. Allowing her to gaze and explore as long as she wished, Wyck noted with some surprise what a good-looking woman Margaret was. *When she's not being pissy,* she thought. *But, maybe living with Gavin and his illness has taken something out of her.* Margaret turned suddenly and caught Wyck watching her.

"We go back this way," Wyck said, leading her through the tapestry gallery to the entrance hall. "Have you had enough or shall we go upstairs?"

Margaret's eyes lit up as she said, "I'm not ready to go home. Let's go up."

Chapter 4

THE CHANGES AROUND THE Braithwaite house over the next few weeks were dramatic – *or are you just noticing for the first time?* Margaret asked herself.

Hedges were thinned out, beds were weeded, mulch was put down on the beds and leaves were raked as autumn settled in in earnest. "Wyck is working wonders," Gavin had commented, but instead of making him feel better at seeing order restored in his precious garden, it seemed to trigger a deeper despondency at the realization of how little he could do now.

Margaret hadn't actually seen Wyck since their day at the Biltmore. By the time she got home in the afternoons, Wyck was usually done for the day. She sat now in her campus office, trying unsuccessfully to concentrate on grading midterm exams. Swiveling in her chair, she gazed out the window at the October foliage, just beginning to turn shades of crimson and gold.

"So what's your first name?" Margaret had asked unexpectedly when they'd had lunch at one of the Biltmore's restaurants that afternoon.

"Excuse me?"

Margaret watched Wyck as she said, "You said the day we met that Wyckham is your middle name. What's your first?"

Wyck grimaced. "Mary," she replied ruefully.

"Mary Wyckham Fitzsimmons," Margaret said slowly, testing it out. "Mary is a lovely name."

"Yes, it is," Wyck agreed. "For a lovely woman. That is one adjective no one has ever applied to me. You certainly wouldn't have."

Margaret laughed. "You are correct." She pushed at the salad on her plate. "I apologize for calling you Mr. Fitzsimmons that first morning."

It was Wyck's turn to laugh. "It's not the first time. And I'm sure it won't be the last. Occupational hazard of being a dyke in a mostly-men's profession."

Margaret looked up, shocked. "Doesn't that bother you, though?"

"What? Being a lesbian or being mistaken for a guy?" Wyck asked in amusement.

Margaret glanced around, clearly uncomfortable at the thought of being overheard discussing this. "Both, I guess," she said in a low voice.

Wyck just looked at her quizzically for a second and said, "I never really thought about it. It's happened my whole life. People just don't look closely. They see what they want to see. I am what I've always been. As far as I'm concerned, if it's a problem, it's their problem, not mine." She saw the doubt in Margaret's eyes. "It would bother you, wouldn't it?"

Margaret frowned. "I... maybe."

"You care so much what people think?" Wyck asked, a small smile tugging at the corner of her mouth.

Margaret, interpreting the smile as ridicule, said coldly, "You think that makes me weak?"

Wyck, somewhat taken aback by her reaction, said, "Not at all."

"No," said Margaret harshly. "You're right."

She signaled for the check, leaving Wyck frowning in complete puzzlement.

Margaret closed her eyes now, remembering that conversation.

How freeing it must be to be like her, she thought enviously. *You are such a coward.*

Her thoughts were interrupted by Taylor, popping in uninvited and taking a seat after pushing the door shut.

"You look like a new woman, darling."

"I'm finally getting some sleep," Margaret said with a wan smile.

"The king let you abscond to a room of your own?" Taylor asked in surprise.

Realizing she wasn't going to get any more grading done, Margaret sat back. "He wasn't happy about it, but the doctor insisted he take his fluid pills. The steroids are causing so much fluid retention that he's on the verge of heart failure. I told him I simply had to get some rest."

There was a knock on the door.

"Come," Margaret called, expecting to see a student.

The door creaked open to reveal Wyck standing there.

"I'm sorry," she said quickly. "I didn't realize you were with someone."

"Uh, no," said Margaret. "It's all right. This is Taylor Foster, one of my colleagues. Taylor, this is... Ms. Fitzsimmons, the... our..."

"I'm the gardener," Wyck volunteered, shaking Taylor's hand, a slight flush to her cheeks. "I apologize for dropping in unannounced, but I was near campus, Dr. Braithwaite. I know it's only October, but I'm taking orders for Christmas trees and wreaths and wondered if you might want me to supply them for the house?"

"Uh," Margaret stammered, her face very red. "I... I hadn't really thought about it."

"Well, let me know," said Wyck. "I deliver for most of my clients, but I only harvest what I've pre-sold, so there won't be extras. If you want one, it's no problem." She backed out of the office. "Nice to meet you, Dr. Foster," she said.

"Oh, you have no idea how nice it was to meet you," Taylor said, smiling delightedly at her.

With a curt nod, Wyck turned on her heel and pulled the door shut.

Taylor turned slowly back to Margaret, looking as if Christmas had come early. "Oh, my God!"

"What?" but Margaret couldn't meet his eye.

"Are you looking better because you're getting some sleep or because you're finally getting some?" he asked, a look of utter glee on his face.

"Don't be crude!" Margaret said sharply. "I told you, she's the gardener. And why would you –?"

Taylor backed off the line he had crossed, but only just. "She's gorgeous, if a little young. Those blue eyes and little boy face... and what a nice ass –"

"Stop it!" Margaret stood and reached for her coat. *Why are you getting so angry?* This was Taylor. This was what he did. She just wasn't used to being his target. She realized with some shame how many times she'd laughed along when he did this to others, even when she knew it was wrong.

Taylor was watching her shrewdly. "All right," he conceded, but she could tell he wasn't done with this.

"I have to go," she said, swinging her purse over her shoulder and sweeping by him. "Lock the door."

Out in the parking lot, she slammed the car door and sat, fuming. She knew part of her anger at Taylor was because his jibes had hit too close to home. Just two nights ago, one of her dreams about Julia – dreams which had been occurring more frequently lately – had morphed so that it was Wyck who was making love to her. She had awakened panting, aching, throbbing... "Stop!" she said, hitting the steering wheel with her palm. But no one, absolutely no one, knew about that part of her past. Why would Taylor even suspect...?

She turned the ignition and pulled out, heading home. Part of what was making her feel even worse was picturing the look on Wyck's face as she had stumbled over how to introduce her.

"You hurt her feelings," said Margaret to Margaret.

"I know," she replied irritably.

"She's been nothing but nice to you."

"I know," more angrily this time.

"What are you going to do about it?"

Wyck checked her voice and e-mails. Though she preferred to draw up most of her designs out at the barn where she found more inspiration, she'd discovered it was necessary to have an office in town for meeting clients. Cell phone and Internet coverage were sketchy and unreliable at home, and the convenience of this downtown location made it worth the extra expense.

Shaking her head, she jabbed angrily at her computer keys. It had been a stupid whim to stop by Margaret's office, uninvited and unannounced. She wasn't even sure why the idea had taken hold. *Yes, you are,* she admitted to herself unwillingly. She'd wanted to see Margaret. Plain and simple. She couldn't have said why, even later when she thought back - Margaret was annoyingly snobbish and condescending, but there were moments... moments like in the back yard when her eyes had filled with tears... or at the Biltmore when she had turned to look back at Wyck with wonder - it was those unguarded moments, Wyck realized as she sat there, that's when she felt like she was really seeing Margaret, not Gavin's wife.

She was still berating herself when she was startled by the ringing of the telephone.

"Fitzsimmons Landscaping."

"It's Margaret."

"Dr. Braithwaite," Wyck said, the chill in her voice clearly audible.

"Wyck, I'm sorry," Margaret said. "I just -" She sighed. "Taylor is such a gossip. I wasn't prepared -"

"I shouldn't have dropped by unannounced," Wyck conceded.

"No," Margaret objected. "You can come by any time you like -"

"And next time you'll remember to introduce me as the gardener?" Wyck suggested helpfully.

"No." Margaret paused. Wyck could hear her breathing. "Next time I'll introduce you as my friend."

Wyck sat back, somewhat amused despite her continued irritation at being treated so dismissively.

"We... we are friends, aren't we?" Margaret asked hesitantly.

"I'm not sure," Wyck said. "If Foster is typical of the kind of friends you keep, I'm afraid I'll disappoint you repeatedly."

"I can't imagine your disappointing me," Margaret said. A ringing silence followed these words. "Besides," Margaret said at last, "you only met him for a few seconds."

"Sometimes you only need a few seconds to take the measure of someone and see that there's no moral fiber in him," Wyck said perceptively. "Jane Austen should have taught you that."

She could hear a muffled chortle from Margaret. "Jane's characters were often mistaken in their initial impressions," Margaret pointed out.

"True," Wyck admitted. "But I'm not. Am I?"

Margaret laughed. "No. You're not." She paused for several seconds. "I would be proud to call you my friend."

"Even if I'm only the gardener?" Wyck teased. She knew she shouldn't prod, but she was enjoying this newly discovered humility in Margaret Braithwaite.

"You're much more than that," Margaret said.

"Not to the rest of the world," Wyck reminded her.

Margaret cleared her throat. "Well, anyway... I wanted to apologize."

"Apology accepted," Wyck said. "And I meant what I said in your office. Let me know if you would like any trees or wreaths and I'll get them to you after Thanksgiving."

"I have been thinking about that since your visit," Margaret said. "We haven't done much for Christmas the last few years, but I was thinking, this might be a good year to do a bit more..."

Wyck understood the unspoken, "...since it might be Gavin's last Christmas."

"Good," she said. "I'll get together with you closer to the holidays to talk about what you would like. We'll make it beautiful."

"Thank you, Wyck," Margaret said in such a warm tone, that it made Wyck smile as she hung up.

Chapter 5

GRUNTING A LITTLE, WYCK loaded yet another bag of leaves into the bed of her truck to be hauled to the landfill. The truck wouldn't hold much more. As much as she loved autumn, the cleanup seemed never-ending. This was the last of the leaves from the Braithwaite property and she was definitely looking forward to a cold beer – *or two* – tonight.

She went back to where she had left her rakes and was surprised to see Gavin standing there, leaning on his cane, wrapped in a heavy wool coat with a scarf to ward off the November chill.

"What do you think?" she asked as she gathered her tools.

He nodded, looking around. "It looks good," he said. "Everything will be ready for the new projects in the spring." He made to go back inside and as he turned back toward the house, Wyck heard a sickening "crack" as Gavin cried out and collapsed.

"Gavin!" She dropped everything to rush to his side. "Stay still," she urged as he writhed on the ground.

"It's my back," he said through clenched teeth. "Help me up."

"No," Wyck said. "I am not going to move you."

Trying not to panic, she cursed as her trembling fingers fumbled with her cell phone.

"No ambulance," he gasped.

"Gavin," Wyck said, trying to sound calmer than she felt. "You have to get to a hospital, and I cannot carry you. I have to call an ambulance."

She made the call, Gavin yelling in pain every time he moved.

"They're on their way," she said as she finished. "What is Margaret's number?"

His eyes squeezed shut, Gavin gasped numbers that she punched into her phone, but there was no answer.

"She's not in her office, but I'll find her," she promised. She tried to keep him calm until she heard a siren. She ran around to the front of the house to flag them down and guide them back to where Gavin lay.

Several minutes that felt like hours later, the EMTs wheeled Gavin away on a gurney and got him loaded into the ambulance.

Wyck went into the house to do a quick check that Gavin hadn't left anything on in the kitchen and then let herself back out the mudroom door, taking the chance on leaving it unlocked in case she needed to get back inside for anything.

Fighting to stay near the speed limit, she drove as quickly as she could to campus. Parking illegally in the faculty parking lot, she left a note on Margaret's windshield in case she missed her somehow, and then went to her office which was still locked and empty. She found the department secretary and quickly explained that there was an emergency involving Gavin. The plump woman consulted a schedule and told Wyck which classroom Margaret was in. Wyck sprinted down the hall, nearing bowling over Taylor Foster as he stepped out of another room into the corridor.

"Excuse me," Wyck said, and without waiting for a reply, pelted off again for the neighboring building. She found Margaret in a lecture hall holding perhaps eighty students.

Margaret glanced over and, through the glass door, saw Wyck standing out in the hall. With a frown and a slight gesture, she signaled Wyck to wait as she concluded her lecture and dismissed the class. Wyck pushed her way against the tide of exiting students to where Margaret was waiting.

"It's Gavin," Wyck panted. "Something happened – I don't know what. He fell and was in horrible pain. The ambulance is taking him to Mission Hospital."

Margaret's mouth tightened into a thin line. "I need my purse," she said, gathering up her notes and books.

"I'll drive you," Wyck offered.

Margaret accepted with a grateful nod. Together they walked hurriedly back to Braithwaite Hall where Margaret got her coat and purse from her office, stopping only long enough to ask the secretary to cancel her remaining class that day. Wyck escorted her out to the parking lot and helped her up into the pickup. They were silent as they drove to the hospital, Margaret's fingers nervously drumming a regular rhythm on the armrest.

Wyck found the parking lot for the emergency room and they hurried inside. She stood back while Margaret went to the window, asking after Gavin. A nurse came to take her back to him. Margaret turned to Wyck who nodded and said, "I'll be waiting out here."

She took a seat in an empty row of hard plastic chairs, grateful that the waiting room was nearly vacant. Nearly an hour and a half later, she was pacing when Margaret came out to find her.

She sank into a seat and Wyck sat beside her. "It's his spine," she said tiredly. "Two of his vertebrae collapsed. His doctor had warned us that this was likely to happen at some point."

"Can they do anything?" Wyck asked. "Operate?"

Margaret shook her head. "They said not. The bone is so fragile, there's nothing to anchor any hardware in." Her eyes filled with sudden tears. "The scan also showed shadows on his liver now. It looks like it's spreading."

Without thinking, Wyck reached for Margaret's hand. Margaret held on tightly as she struggled to get her emotions under control.

Her voice cracked as she said, "All they can do is try to keep him comfortable."

Wyck didn't know what to say to that, and so didn't say anything.

After a long while, Margaret released Wyck's hand and reached for her purse. "I should call Jeffrey and Amanda," she said.

"Who are –?"

"Gavin's children from his first marriage," Margaret explained. "They both live in the Raleigh-Durham area."

She got up, walking away to the waiting room windows. She stared out into the gathering darkness as she placed her calls. Wyck caught snatches of conversation as she waited.

When Margaret came back, she said, "Thank you for being there with him. And for coming to find me."

"Of course," Wyck said.

"I keep thinking about how long he might have lain there alone, unable to get to a phone..." She swallowed hard. "I can take a cab back to my car. You don't have to stay with me –"

"I don't mind," Wyck assured her.

"They'll be moving him to a room and keeping him for a few days, the doctor said. I don't think Amanda and Jeffrey will be coming unless something changes. They were going to be here in a few weeks for Thanksgiving anyhow, so they may just wait." More to herself than to Wyck, she continued, "I was supposed to go to my mother in Richmond, but now... I don't know."

Just then, a nurse peered through a swinging door. "Mrs. Braithwaite? We're ready to transport your husband to his room."

"I'll wait here –" Wyck began, but "No," Margaret said. "Please come."

Together, they followed two of the nursing staff who were pushing a gurney and an IV pole, Gavin bundled up in blankets so that only his face was visible. Assisted by more nurses on the floor, they slid him into a bed as he yelled out in pain despite their attempts to be gentle. Getting him settled as comfortably as they could, they wheeled the gurney back to the ER as his new nurse took a fresh set of vitals.

"I'm Darlene," she said to Margaret and Wyck. "I'll be his nurse tonight. You're more than welcome to stay, but he's on morphine. He's going to be out. Dr. Walls wanted him kept as still as possible."

"Why don't I take you to get your car and get you some dinner?" Wyck suggested. "That way you can come and go whenever you need to."

Margaret nodded absently, looking as if she were incapable of making any decisions at the moment. She gave Gavin a kiss on the forehead and followed Wyck wordlessly back to the elevator and out to the parking lot.

Wyck didn't press for conversation as she drove back to campus. She dropped Margaret off at her car and followed her back to the house. She knew Mandy would be getting hungry, but had decided to cook something quickly for Margaret before going home.

Margaret led the way into the kitchen, dropping her purse and coat on a chair and just standing there, looking around blankly.

"Sit down," Wyck said gently. "Just give me directions to where things are. Coffee? Pans?"

Within a few minutes, she had fried up eggs and bacon and made toast. Placing a plate and cup of coffee in front of Margaret, she got a plate and cup for herself and sat opposite.

"So, Gavin was divorced?" Wyck asked, trying to generate conversation as she began eating.

"No," Margaret said, glancing up. "His wife died in a car accident. The kids were in high school."

"I'm sorry," Wyck said.

"He - they - were over the worst of it by the time we met," Margaret said, nibbling on a piece of bacon.

"And you two never wanted children of your own?" Wyck asked.

"It never really came up," Margaret mused. "I was busy with my career and Gavin already had a family. He didn't seem eager to start over. I think it worked out for the best; I get to be a grandmother to five great kids without having gone through the trials and tribulations of raising their parents," she said with a weak smile.

They ate in silence for a few minutes.

"You mentioned your mother," Wyck prompted.

"Yes," Margaret said. "My father died a few years ago, and my mother agreed to move to Richmond, to be closer. She said it was as far south as she would go," she said drolly.

Wyck tilted her head. "Where did you grow up?"

"Pittsburgh."

"Does your mother call you Margaret?"

"Why?" Margaret asked in surprise.

Wyck shrugged. "It just sounds so formal. I wondered if you were ever called anything else."

Margaret smiled again as she took a sip of her coffee. "I was Peggy to my family, but Gavin thought that was not dignified enough for his wife." She swirled her coffee, staring into it. "There was one person... She called me Meggie," she said, her face softening as she remembered. She stopped the motion of the coffee abruptly and her face looked worried and tired again. "But, no. Now I'm just Margaret."

When they were done eating, Wyck gathered up the dishes, putting them in the dishwasher.

She jotted her cell number on a business card. "Call me if you need anything, anytime," she said as they walked to the front door.

Margaret blinked rapidly as she stared at the card. "Thank you again," she said, her voice catching in her throat.

As she had in the waiting room, Wyck reacted instinctively, reaching her arms around Margaret. Margaret, instead of tolerating the contact stiffly as Wyck had expected, wrapped her arms even more tightly around Wyck, holding her closely. Surprised by the openness of the response, Wyck stayed there, holding her for long minutes before gently letting go.

"You're sure you'll be all right?" Wyck asked.

Margaret nodded. "I'll be fine," she said, meeting Wyck's eyes briefly as she stepped back.

Wyck stepped through the door, pausing on the stoop as Margaret pushed it shut. She couldn't be sure, but she thought she heard muffled crying from inside.

Late that night, Wyck lay awake on her cot, unable to quiet her mind. She could hear Mandy breathing deeply, occasionally whimpering as she chased something, kicking in her sleep. Reaching out, she laid a calming hand on Mandy's ribs, taking comfort in the dog's warmth and nearness. Margaret had needed calming, too. *She held on as if she were drowning,* Wyck thought as she lay there, trying not to wonder if Gavin ever held her like that, told her how beautiful she is... "Don't," she groaned, startling Mandy who raised her head to look around.

Wyck calmed her and Mandy settled again into a deep sleep, but sleep wouldn't come to Wyck. Seconds ticked into minutes and then into hours and still Wyck lay there, feeling agitated, uneasy, as if some warning were sounding, dimly, in her head - "no, not my head," she would realize much later. "It was my heart."

43

Chapter 6

"ARE YOU COMFORTABLE? CAN I get you anything?"

Margaret settled Gavin comfortably in his chair in the den as he grumbled, "I'm fine. Stop fussing!"

His hospital stay had dragged on for nearly two weeks, as the pain from his compression fractures had made it so painful to breathe and cough that he had developed pneumonia.

"You have to cough and use this to help you breathe deeply," the respiratory therapists told him time and again, handing him a plastic tube with a little ball that rose if he inhaled deeply enough.

Of course, the deep breaths triggered spasms of coughing which exacerbated his back pain so that he resisted their attempts to help him. Margaret thought she would scream at times as he became more and more unreasonable.

"Why can't I just go home?" he demanded.

"Because you still have pneumonia," she explained over and over. "You've got to be able to move more to help get yourself bathed and dressed." For the first time, she was forced to consider the very real possibility that she might not be able to care for him at home, at least not without help.

In the end, he improved enough to return home with a nursing aide coming to the house for four hours daily to help cover the hours Margaret was on campus.

Through all the hours spent sitting in Gavin's hospital room, and her time alone at home, and much of her time at work, she had kept Wyck's card in a pocket where she could touch it, hold it. Just knowing it was there made her feel better. She didn't want to analyze why.

She clung to the card and she clung to the memory of Wyck's embrace. Part of her knew she shouldn't....

"She's got to be twenty-some years younger than you," argued a pragmatic side of herself.

"You're twenty-seven years younger than Gavin," countered a more optimistic voice.

"That's different."

"What's different is how she makes you feel."

"You're married."

That reminder silenced everything.

Even in the safety and privacy of her thoughts, she couldn't let herself put words to the thought... the shameful, unforgiveable thought that she wouldn't be married forever. That realization floated around in the darker recesses of her mind like some half-forgotten dream that her conscious mind couldn't quite grasp. Every time it started to come to the forefront where solid thoughts took shape, she squeezed her eyes tightly shut and pushed it back where it belonged.

She hadn't seen Wyck again. She had told them that her time at the house would be curtailed through the holiday season. She was busy at the Biltmore House again, helping the staff get the estate ready for its spectacular Christmas display, and then she would be spending hours making wreaths and harvesting Christmas trees for those people who had placed orders.

Looking at a calendar, Margaret was dismayed to realize it was the week before Thanksgiving. She felt as if she were on a treadmill – *no, more like a hamster wheel, in a cage,* she thought – running madly but getting nowhere. "The last thing I feel like is having a house full of people to cook for," she grumbled resentfully, then immediately felt guilty as she remembered it was not likely that Gavin would have another Thanksgiving. Her plans had been to go to Richmond, as she usually did for Thanksgiving, while Jeffrey and Amanda and their families came to Asheville. All of that was up in the air now.

Gavin took care of some of that himself. "I don't want a bunch of people and noise in the house."

Margaret looked at him. "They'll want to see you," she pointed out. "Especially after the hospital."

"Yes, yes," he said irritably, waving his hand.

"Maybe they could come just overnight," she suggested placatingly. "I could see Mom for the day and come home Friday morning."

Gavin thought. "That would be all right," he conceded.

Margaret made the phone calls, and got everything arranged, including a last-minute take-out Thanksgiving dinner from a local restaurant. She was just hanging up when the telephone rang.

"Margaret?"

Margaret's heart leapt at the sound of Wyck's voice.

"How is everything?"

"We're doing okay," Margaret said. "Gavin is finally home. We were just making arrangements for Thanksgiving. The family is coming out Thursday to Friday and I will be going to Richmond for the same period. It's the only way I feel comfortable leaving him. What about you?" Margaret suddenly wondered. "What are you doing for Thanksgiving?"

"Oh," Wyck said, laughing a little, "I'll be volunteering at a church dinner that day."

"No family?" Margaret asked.

"No," said Wyck flatly. "Anyway, we never got to discuss again whether you wanted a tree or wreath or anything, so I was just calling to see...?"

Margaret pressed a hand to her eyes. Decorating the house for the holidays was another of those things that had been feeling too overwhelming even to contemplate.

Wyck, seeming to read her mind, said, "I'll help you get everything put up, all right? Would you like to pick out the tree and help cut it?"

"I've never done that," Margaret said.

"You said you're coming home on Friday?" Wyck asked. "How about Saturday? I'll pick you up at ten. We can have the whole house decorated, no stress. "

"That... that sounds really nice."

"And Margaret? You can't wear a suit."

On the other end of the line, Wyck hung up the phone. Her family had done as she predicted when her mother called a few days ago and put eight-year-old Michaela on the phone to beg her aunt to come home.

"I never get to see you," Michaela had pleaded.

Wyck's heart felt a tug – *as it was meant to* – but said, "It's too far away. I have to work. I'll try to get home soon."

"You always say that," Michaela said, and Wyck smiled, picturing her pout.

"What do you want for Christmas?"

"You," Michaela insisted stubbornly.

"She's more like you than your sister," Wyck's mother always said, and Wyck was beginning to believe it was true.

"Peggy? You haven't heard a word I've said."

Margaret's head snapped up. "I'm sorry, Mom. What were you saying?"

Muriel Collins looked at her only daughter and said, "Is it Gavin? Are you worried about him?"

Grateful to have an excuse for her listlessness, Margaret said, "Yes. He's only just home, and not doing terribly well."

"Well, he's my age," Muriel said philosophically, a fact Margaret's father had been most unhappy about.

The age difference between her and Gavin had continued to be a source of tension for several years before the Collinses had accepted the fact that their daughter had married someone old enough to be her father.

"Are you hungry? Ready for some leftovers?" Margaret asked. She and her mother had gone down earlier to the Thanksgiving buffet in her mother's assisted living facility. It was a nice place, with good staff, and it had eased Margaret's mind considerably to have her mother nearer than Pittsburgh.

As Margaret prepared plates for each of them, she said, "I'll have to leave in the morning."

"So soon?" Muriel said, sounding disappointed.

Guiltily, Margaret said, "I know it's a short visit, but I'll try to get back up here soon. I can't leave Gavin alone and the children are leaving tomorrow." To herself, she wondered, *they're almost as old as I am. Why do we still refer to them as 'the children'?*

Conversationally, she said, "Our new landscaper is going to take me out to cut our own Christmas tree this weekend." She frowned. "I may have to go shopping. I'm not sure I have anything to wear besides work clothes."

Muriel chuckled. "I used to wish I could get you out of blue jeans. Those patched, frayed, awful-looking things. You and that girl, what was her name? The one you met at Wellesley?"

Margaret swallowed, keeping her eyes on her plate. "Julia."

"That's it, Julia," Muriel nodded. Her sharp eyes peered at Margaret. "What ever happened to her?"

Margaret stopped chewing. "What happened was my life nearly ended," she almost blurted.

She and Julia had become inseparable, going home with one another during breaks from Wellesley, taking many of the same classes, rooming together. Innocently defiant in the face of the whispers - "I loved her and I didn't care who knew it," Margaret recalled - they had blithely assumed they would stay together always, planning their futures, going to grad school together, the brilliant careers they would both have, living a bohemian lifestyle, "living in sin," they had giggled, naked in bed together.

But it had all come crashing down at graduation when she and Julia tried to introduce their families to one another. Julia's insular Italian family had been polite but distant, while Frank Collins, somehow seeing what no one else did, had pulled his daughter aside.

"You will stop this... this -" he stammered incoherently, his face inches from hers, frightening, contorted with anger and revulsion, veins throbbing in his forehead. His hand twisted Peggy's arm painfully as he barely controlled himself. "If you ever see her again after today, I will cut you off," he threatened. "You'll never have another cent from me or your mother - not for school, not in our wills, nothing. We will never see you again. Do you understand me?" he snarled.

Margaret closed her eyes, trying to block out the memory of the look on Julia's face - the disbelief, the confusion, the utter disappointment - as Margaret, sobbing, had told her she couldn't see her again....

"Peggy?"

"I don't know what happened to her," Margaret said hoarsely. "We... didn't stay in touch."

"That's too bad," Muriel said innocently. "You were so close. I stayed in touch with my friends from school. You remember Hilda Brown..."

Her voice faded into the background as Margaret's brain was barraged by memories, things she hadn't thought of - "hadn't allowed myself to think of," she would have said - for nearly thirty years.

She hadn't spoken to her father for months, choosing St. Aloysius for grad school where she met Gavin, who quickly became a mentor and then more than a mentor. He'd been a handsome man, trim and fit even though he was in his late fifties. His attention had been flattering and, though she hadn't been aware of it at the time, she could see now that marrying Gavin had been, at least in part, a bit of revenge toward her father, a replacing of him with someone his age who could protect her. She had, privately, taken a savage pleasure in knowing that it ate at him. But he had no further means of threatening her and had had to learn to live with it. What she hadn't realized in her youth was that Gavin and the security he offered came with a price....

"You stay in the back seat," Wyck said to Mandy whose tail thumped a happy drumbeat against the seat as they arrived at the Braithwaite house.

Wyck rang the front doorbell and stepped back in surprise as Margaret opened the door dressed in khakis and winter boots with a plaid flannel shirt peeking out from under a down jacket.

"What?" Margaret asked self-consciously as Wyck smiled.

"Nothing," Wyck said quickly. "You look great. Like a poster for L.L. Bean."

Margaret frowned a little, not sure if Wyck was making fun of her. She turned back to the interior of the house. "Gavin, I'm leaving," she called. "I should be back –" she turned to Wyck with a questioning glance.

"Early afternoon," Wyck said.

"Early afternoon," Margaret repeated, pulling the door shut behind her.

"He'll be okay that long, won't he?" Wyck asked as they walked out to the truck.

"He should be fine," Margaret said. "He's getting around better now. I left him a turkey sandwich and a plate of leftovers for lunch."

She climbed into the passenger seat of the truck where Mandy obligingly placed her blond head in just the right spot for some petting as Wyck backed the truck around.

"So, where are we going?" Margaret asked. "To a tree farm?"

"Of sorts," Wyck smiled. "We're going to my place. Fifty-odd acres of woods, with several species of conifers. We should be able to find something you like."

"Why didn't you just have me meet you there?" Margaret asked.

Wyck glanced over. "This is easier than giving you directions." She adjusted the stereo volume and Margaret realized she had Christmas music playing.

"How was your Thanksgiving with your mother?" Wyck asked as she drove south out of Asheville.

"Oh, it was wonderful," Margaret said flatly.

Wyck gave her a questioning sidelong glance while keeping one eye on the road. Margaret shook her head apologetically. "It was fine, actually. Our conversation just dragged up some old memories, that's all."

"Unpleasant memories?"

Margaret turned away, looking out the window. "Memories best left where they were."

Mandy whined and gently nudged Margaret's arm with her nose.

"She can tell you're upset," Wyck said.

Margaret smiled and rubbed the dog's velvety ears. "Why Mandy?" she asked.

Wyck laughed, turning a little red. "Oh, I was in a bad place, wallowing a little - more than a little - when a client showed me this new litter of puppies. This one came to me, climbed into my lap and stayed there."

"But -?"

"Barry Manilow," Wyck admitted sheepishly. "The best broken heart music in the world."

Margaret smiled at this unexpected admission. "Except for 'Lola'."

Wyck laughed. "Except for 'Lola'. I must admit to being surprised that you know anything as mundane as popular music."

"I wasn't always a middle-aged academic snob," Margaret said ruefully.

"Well, I assumed you were once a younger academic snob," Wyck teased.

Margaret bit her lower lip. "Not always," she said softly, turning to look out the window again.

She took in the passing landscape as they left the outskirts of Asheville. A short while later, Wyck pulled off the paved road onto a gravel lane that wound its way through the woods, opening onto a grassy meadow with a large barn in a clearing. She stopped the truck and got out. Margaret followed slowly, Mandy bounding out behind her.

"Where's your house?" Margaret asked, looking past the barn for some other structure.

Amused, Wyck gestured toward the barn. "This is my house. At least it will be when I'm done."

"You're kidding," Margaret said dubiously, looking over the enormous building.

"Nope. Not kidding," Wyck said. She led the way to a side-by-side 4-wheeler already loaded with a chainsaw, handsaw, rope and twine. "Come on," she said, indicating the passenger seat. "We'll drive back to the trees and pick one out."

Margaret nervously belted herself into her seat and held onto the roll bars as Wyck steered the 4-wheeler onto a dirt track through the woods, occasional branches swiping at them as they rolled by. Mandy loped ahead of them as if she were their scout.

"Couldn't we just walk?" Margaret asked over the rumble of the engine.

"Sure we could," said Wyck, slowing to ease the 4-wheeler over a rooted segment of the trail, "if you feel like carrying the tree back."

"Oh."

Resigned, Margaret settled back into her seat and was actually starting to enjoy the ride through the invigoratingly cold air.

Wyck braked to a halt and said, "We should be able to find a very nice tree here. Do you want a spruce, or a pine, or a fir?"

Margaret, who disliked feeling ignorant on any topic, simply looked at Wyck, as she had not a clue as to the differences between various types of evergreens.

"Follow me," Wyck smiled. They wandered among the trees, Wyck showing her the various species and explaining the differences in their needles and branch patterns, crushing needles so Margaret could smell them.

"You're a very good teacher," Margaret commented.

"I know." Seeing the look that comment elicited from Margaret, Wyck hastily said, "I mean, I enjoyed teaching, and I think I was good at it, but..."

"Plants and animals are better," Margaret recalled.

Wyck grinned sheepishly. "Yeah." Getting back on topic, she said, "So, what kind of tree do you want? And how big?"

Within an hour, they were making their way back to the barn with an eight-foot Norway spruce trussed up and snugged onto the back of the ATV along with a few dozen feet of trimmed white pine branches.

Wyck transferred the tree to the bed of the pickup and secured it before hopping down and saying, "How about some lunch?"

Margaret agreed, curious to see how Wyck lived. She followed her inside where the aroma of something cooking made her mouth water. Wyck took her jacket from her, hanging it on a peg near the door.

"It's a work in progress," she said as Margaret stepped farther in, looking around.

"It's going to be beautiful," Margaret realized, peering up into the soaring spaces above, crisscrossed with beams and posts.

"It will be," Wyck agreed, "but it's a little rough right now."

Margaret noted the cot folded near the woodstove which was pleasantly warm, flames licking at the glass. Wyck went to check on the contents of the crockpot sitting on top of the stove.

"Um... can I do anything?" Margaret offered.

"Sure." Wyck pointed to a bag on the plywood counter. "There's a fresh loaf of bread. Would you mind slicing it while I dish this out?"

Margaret laid the sliced bread on a plate and brought it to the makeshift table as Wyck set down bowls of hot beef stew.

"This smells wonderful," Margaret said, sniffing the aromatic steam rising from her bowl as she perched a bit uncertainly on the stool Wyck indicated.

"Good food for warming you up after you've been out in the cold," Wyck grinned.

Margaret picked up her spoon and took a tentative bite. Her eyes widened in delight. "It's delicious." She buttered a slice of bread. "Gavin would never eat something like this if I made it."

Wyck raised an eyebrow. "Too plebian?"

Margaret laughed. "Yes, to be perfectly honest."

Wyck shrugged. "His loss."

There was a period of silence as they ate. Mandy settled into her dog bed where she could keep an eye on them.

Margaret glanced over at her and Mandy's tail thumped. "So, why were you drowning yourself in Barry Manilow?" she asked curiously.

Wyck blushed scarlet as she chuckled with embarrassment. "Oh, that. The typical tragedy of love lost," she joked.

"What happened?" Margaret asked, her interest piqued more than she would have cared to admit. To her surprise, Wyck's expression changed in an instant and Margaret could see the pain in her eyes – *she looks so... vulnerable*, Margaret realized and she felt a pang of regret for asking.

Wyck lowered her eyes, shielding them from Margaret's penetrating gaze. "That would be a topic for another time," she said softly. She blinked and looked up, her face once again wearing its more typical cheerful expression.

"Do Gavin's children come back out here for Christmas as well?" she asked, changing the subject.

"No," Margaret said. "They'll stay home with their families. It's usually just the two of us for Christmas. How about you? Do you go visit family?"

Like a chameleon, Wyck's expression changed yet again, becoming hard. "No," she said flatly. "I'll stay here."

"Alone?" Margaret asked, bothered by the thought. "But... you seem like you love the holidays so much. All the work you do helping people with trees and wreaths, working at the Biltmore... I don't understand."

"I do love the holidays," Wyck admitted. "But when being with family means strife and arguments, then... being with them over the holidays is not worth it. That is not how I want to spend my Christmas. I won't be alone, not all day. I volunteer again at the Christmas dinner and then go to a nursing home for Christmas carols after that. Mandy comes with me, wearing a Christmas bow. She loves all the attention. Then we get to come home where it's peaceful and we can fantasize about the perfect Christmas with our favorite movies."

When they were done eating, Margaret insisted on helping with the dishes, and then, not quite ready to go back, asked, "Would you show me the rest?"

Eagerly, Wyck led the way up the wide wooden stairs. "Had to have a working bathroom," she said, flipping on the light.

"You did all this?" Margaret asked, impressed. "The tile work, the plumbing?"

Wyck shrugged modestly. "Just about everything."

She showed Margaret the space that would become the second bedroom. "I'll lay hardwood floors and then put up eight-foot walls for privacy," she said. "But everything will be open to the roof timbers. I've put these large windows in each bedroom and I didn't want to lose all of this space and light."

In the master bedroom, Margaret stood before the bank of windows filling one wall, allowing a wonderful view of the mountains. "This will be spectacular at night," she said softly, and her head tilted back as she looked up.

"I think it will," Wyck agreed, fighting an inexplicable urge to reach out and caress the soft curve of Margaret's neck.

Margaret turned to look around and spied the guitar case in the corner. "You play as well?" She turned to look at Wyck. "Is there no end to the things you can do?"

Wyck blushed again. "Well, it's not like I'm good enough at any of these things to make a living at them," she said. "But, it serves for Mandy and me."

Margaret peered at her intently. "Will it always be just Mandy and you?"

Wyck looked at her for a few seconds, then blinked and turned. "We should probably get you home."

Chapter 7

MARGARET COULD HEAR GAVIN'S heavy footsteps coming into the den where she was draping an evergreen garland around the fireplace mantel.

He groaned as he settled breathlessly into his recliner and pushed back. "Aren't you going a little overboard?" he asked when his breathing slowed.

"I don't think so," she said brightly.

Wyck had stayed most of Saturday afternoon, helping put the tree up in the living room and stringing it with lights. She had woven the extra pine branches she had cut into garlands, and the wreath - "you made this?" Margaret had asked in amazement - now graced the front door, resplendent with brilliant red holly and nandina berries, along with dried pomegranates, lemons, apples and pinecones. The house hadn't looked this festive in years.

"Why are you doing this?" Gavin asked suddenly.

Margaret didn't answer immediately, continuing to work on the garland with her back to him.

"You think I'll have kicked the bucket by next year," he stated.

"No, Gavin, I –" she started to protest.

"You're probably right," he cut in matter-of-factly. "It's time to be realistic, Margaret."

Her shoulders slumped and she sank onto an ottoman.

"I don't think there will be any miracles this time," he said, his once-handsome face puffy from the steroids. "You heard them. We're out of options."

Margaret blinked hard, trying to stem the tears that threatened. Gavin hated displays of emotion – "maudlin," he called them, "honest," Margaret would have said.

More gently, he said, "The house looks lovely, my dear. I do appreciate the effort you're making."

There it is again, she thought. Back before she gave up golf to be home with Gavin more, the birdies would come just as she was getting frustrated enough to quit – always, they came just frequently enough to keep her coming back. It was like that with Gavin. Usually, time spent with him was driven by his overbearing, opinionated side – by far the most dominant aspect of his personality – but always, just when Margaret would be pushed to the point of wondering what she was doing in this marriage, a softer, gentler side of him would surface. A compliment, an acknowledgement of how he needed her – *and I'm always pulled back*, she thought now. *He always seems to know.*

But how could he know? How could he know that he wasn't the only one she was thinking of as she decorated the house and hummed Christmas carols? How could he know what it was she thought about at night – things she could only let herself think about in the dark, never in the light of day – so that she found herself looking forward to that time, to the hours at night when she could let her mind and heart go places they weren't normally allowed to go?

"Are you all right?"

Margaret's attention snapped back to the present. She nodded. "I'm fine." She stood. "I've got a bit more to do here, and then I'll get dinner ready."

"Thank God this semester is done."

Margaret turned to find Taylor beside her as she walked across campus.

"Are you through with exams?" he asked.

She walked on as if he hadn't spoken.

"Oh, come on," he said, reaching out for her arm. "You're not still angry about the gardener, are you?"

Margaret's icy silence was his response.

"I'm sorry, okay? Don't be angry," he wheedled. "You're my only friend."

"I can't imagine why," Margaret said coldly. "You may think you're funny, Taylor, but you go too far."

"I'm sorry," he said again in the closest approximation to sincerity Margaret had ever heard from him. "I shouldn't have teased you like that, but..." he pulled her to a halt, looking around to make sure they couldn't be overheard and continued in a low voice, "I have always thought – whether you would ever admit it or not – that you are secretly on our team."

He looked at her stunned face with a sympathetic expression and said, "If you ever want to talk about that, you know where to find me."

He gave her arm a squeeze and left her standing there.

"Dr. Braithwaite? Are you okay?" asked a passing student.

Margaret blinked. "I'm... I'm fine." She walked on to the classroom where she was giving her last exam.

She was barely aware of the students as they scratched away their responses. She had never said a word to Taylor – or anyone else – about Julia. How could he have guessed? Why had he teased her about Wyck in the first place? She gave herself a mental shake. Taylor was just being his malicious self. She began grading another set of papers as this two-hour block crawled along, feeling as if it would never end.

At long last, "Have a good break. It was a pleasure teaching you this semester." Her typical good-bye to them, sometimes true, more often lately, not.

When did that change? she wondered as she stuffed exam papers into her briefcase. *I used to love teaching.*

She walked across campus to her office, remembering Wyck's excitedly teaching her about trees and modestly admitting that she was a good teacher. *I would have said that about myself at one point,* she thought. In fact, she had said it once to Gavin, she recalled.

Flushed with the euphoria of having completed her PhD and the success of her first novel, Margaret had jumped enthusiastically into her first real teaching assignment. It had been a joy then. The students seemed eager to learn, and that, in turn, energized her.

"My dear," Gavin had chuckled patronizingly, "the material you are teaching could be taught by a chimp if it were trained properly. True scholarship comes from our own writing, our own research. Teaching is just a necessary evil that allows us to do our real work."

Margaret had refused to believe that, thinking Gavin old and jaded, though she never said so. *Now, I'm the one who's old and jaded,* she realized. Somehow, Gavin's attitude had seeped in, like a poison she had gradually absorbed until it became part of her. *When did that happen?*

That was one of the most appealing things about Wyck – she seemed so... content. Content to be her own boss, content to live in a barely habitable barn, content to have been a Rhodes scholar but not feel the need to tell anyone about it. It came from somewhere inside her, Margaret realized as she unlocked her door, without the need for validation or even acknowledgement from anyone or anything....

Margaret stood in her office in an inexplicably foul mood. She scowled at the papers waiting to be graded, and scowled at the thought of going home to Gavin. Seemingly of their own accord, her feet walked her out to her Audi, and she began driving south.

Wyck was bent over her workbench out in the outbuilding serving as her shop for now, painstakingly carving the edge of a hundred-year-old pine board, mirroring the contours of the huge hearthstone supporting her woodstove. She had scribed the rocky contours onto the wood, and was now using a combination of spokeshaves, drawknives and gouges, shaping it so that, once completed, it would fit seamlessly against the stone.

She loved work like this, work that engaged her eyes and hands, but left her mind free to drift, except that today, her mind was drifting to places it really shouldn't go, like how the sensuous curve of the wood reminded her of the curve of Margaret's neck as she'd looked around the bedroom....

Mandy barked and a moment later, Wyck saw the gleam of headlights coming through the leafless trees. No one ever came here, mostly because Wyck never invited anyone. She opened the shop door and followed Mandy out to where Margaret was getting out of her car.

"What's wrong?" Wyck asked. "Is Gavin okay?"

Margaret, who couldn't have explained - even to herself - why she had come here of all places, burst into tears.

Wyck led her inside, settling her in the armchair, and went to put a kettle on to boil. While the kettle heated, she came back and dragged over the apple crate. She sat on it, waiting while Margaret cried.

"I'm sorry," Margaret snuffled, taking her coat off and searching the pockets.

"Wait," Wyck said, and she ran upstairs, reappearing a moment later with a roll of toilet paper. "Sorry, I don't have any tissues." She sat back down on the crate. Mandy came over to sit, leaning against Wyck who draped an arm over her back.

Margaret accepted the roll with a watery smile, and tore off a few sheets, dabbing at her eyes and nose. "I don't normally do this, and I'm not sure why I came here."

Wyck smiled. "Well, I happen to think here is a pretty good place, and... you don't do what?"

"Cry," Margaret said, looking down at the crumpled toilet paper in her hands. "Public displays of emotion."

"I don't think Mandy and I count as 'public'," Wyck said. "Besides, crying is a good thing now and then. We promise not to tell anyone."

Margaret laughed a little, wiping her eyes again. "Thank you. I just didn't know where else to go."

Wyck and Mandy tilted their heads at the same time, in the same direction, so that Margaret had to laugh again.

The kettle whistled just as Wyck opened her mouth to speak. "Hold on," she said, holding her hands out. "I'll be right back."

She went into the kitchen, returning a couple of minutes later. "I hope you like Constant Comment," she said, handing a steaming mug to Margaret.

"I do, thank you," Margaret said gratefully, breathing in the orange and clove scent as Wyck resumed her seat on the apple crate. Mandy curled up at Wyck's feet.

They sat in a companionable silence for a long while, each sipping her tea as Wyck waited patiently.

"Is it Gavin?" she prompted gently when Margaret seemed unable to start talking.

"No... yes... it's everything," Margaret stumbled. "He's still struggling, a little worse nearly every day, and then Taylor -" She stopped, blushing deeply. She took another sip of her tea, and then reached to set it down on the upended half-barrel next to the chair.

"What -?" She picked up a copy of her novel lying there, and her eyes teared up again.

"Don't," Wyck said hastily. "I love it. It's beautifully written. You didn't tell me you had written a book."

"But it's over twenty-five years old," Margaret sniffed, "and I haven't been able to write anything worthwhile since."

Wyck felt off-balance, as if the earth were tipping on its axis, as Margaret permitted her to see yet more chinks in the impenetrable façade she presented to most of the world.

"Many of our greatest authors only had one truly good book in them," Wyck said helpfully. "The Brontë sisters, Harper Lee... Even if you never publish another book, you're in good company."

Margaret smiled and dabbed at her eyes again. "Part of the justification for my faculty position was based on the promise I showed as a young writer," she admitted, and gave a brittle laugh. "I am not living up to my potential, but Gavin is so powerful, they haven't dared do anything about that."

Wyck hesitantly asked, "So... what does that mean for you once Gavin is...?"

Margaret met her gaze. "I don't know." She sat back, heaving a deep sigh. "I suppose even if they let me go, I could live off Gavin's royalties, Gavin's life insurance, Gavin's investments..." Her expression darkened. "I'm fifty-two. Too old to start over, and too young to crawl into a hole. My career is in almost the exact same place it was twenty-five years ago."

"You've never written anything else?" Wyck asked.

Margaret glanced up at her. "I've started other books, but..."

"Would you like for me to read them?" Wyck asked. "I promise to be brutally honest, but gentle," she said with a crooked grin that made Margaret smile.

"I've never shown them to anyone," Margaret said reluctantly.

"Not even Gavin?"

"Especially not Gavin," Margaret said darkly. She looked at Wyck as if trying to make up her mind. "I... I would appreciate your insight." She looked around for the first time. "I'm sorry. You were probably working on something and I just dropped in on you like an atomic bomb."

Wyck stood. "Come on. I'll show you what I was doing."

She led the way through the kitchen and out the back door to the shop. There, the half-finished board sat clamped in a vise. "When I'm done, it should fit like the wood and stone are almost one substance."

"This will be beautiful," Margaret said in admiration. "You truly are an artist." For the first time, she began to really appreciate the vision Wyck had for the barn, the attention she was putting into the smallest details. "I can't imagine looking around and seeing your work in everything."

Wyck sighed. "It may never get done, but it does give a sense of pride to know you did it yourself."

Margaret ran her fingers lightly over the undulating contours of the carved edge of the board, and – just for an instant – Wyck wondered what it would feel like to have those hands touching her face that tenderly....

"Wyck, I know it's none of my business," Margaret said quietly, "but, I can't stop thinking about you, and Mandy, being by yourselves at Christmas. Won't you consider coming to spend it – Christmas Eve or Christmas Day – with Gavin and me?"

Wyck stood there open-mouthed for a long moment. "Thank you, Margaret, but... I don't think so." For a second, she seemed to be weighing whether or not to say something. "I'm just not very good company at Christmas. But thanks."

Margaret looked at her, obviously wanting to ask, but "I've taken enough of your time," she said abruptly. She went back to the barn where she donned her coat and gloves. "Thank you for letting me drop in on you like this."

"You're welcome here anytime, Meggie."

Wyck hadn't planned it. It just came out that way. Margaret's face softened into something "beautiful," Wyck almost said aloud.

"Good-bye," Margaret said, opening the door.

Wyck and Mandy followed her outside, waving her off as she drove down the lane.

Mandy sat leaning against Wyck's leg, looking up at her.

"Don't even say it," Wyck said, laying a gentle hand on the soft, warm head. "I am not going down that road again."

Chapter 8

MARGARET GOT UP AND stretched stiffly. *These have to be the most uncomfortable couches in the world,* she thought as she rubbed her sore back. She glanced over at where Gavin was sleeping in his hospital bed. Again.

Agitatedly, she began pacing, feeling like a prisoner here in this damn room and immediately feeling guilty about resenting it. Her frustration had been mirrored in Amanda's exasperated sigh last night when Margaret had called to tell her that her father was being re-admitted.

"Again? So soon?" Amanda had said in dismay. "Why?"

"It's his breathing again," Margaret explained. "The doctor said it's getting more difficult to get his fluid levels under control, because it has something to do with other things like heart rhythm and kidney function."

"So not his cancer."

"Not his cancer."

There was a strained silence on the other end.

At last, "I know tomorrow is Christmas Eve," Margaret said. "I'm not saying he's bad enough that you and Jeffrey need to come. I'm just calling to let you know what's going on. I will call you if things get worse."

"Okay," and Margaret could hear the relief in Amanda's voice.

She couldn't blame them. She lived right here with Gavin and was getting to hate this. It was harder for them, living hours away, with families. She understood, but these vigils were so lonely. It wasn't supposed to be like this.

"What are you going to do when he can't be at home anymore?" Amanda had asked the Friday after Thanksgiving.

Margaret had expected them to be gone by the time she got back, but they had put off leaving to talk with her. They pulled her into Gavin's office as soon as she got home, leaving their spouses and children in the den watching television. Gavin was upstairs sleeping.

"And what about the funeral?" Jeffrey interjected.

Margaret had stared at the pair of them. "Who says he won't be at home? I've always expected that we'll call hospice when... when he gets to that stage, and he'll die here."

"Not a hospital or nursing home?" Amanda asked.

"Not if it can be helped," Margaret said.

"That's a relief," Amanda said.

"Not to mention that an extended stay somewhere could eat up thousands," Jeffrey said.

Gavin stared out at them from photos all over the room – Gavin accepting yet another award, Gavin receiving yet another honorary degree, Gavin featured in yet another magazine or newspaper profile. It felt as if he was part of the conversation.

"Not to mention that he would prefer to be at home," Margaret had said coolly.

"Well, yes, that too," Jeffrey amended hastily.

"And what about the funeral?" Margaret asked, bringing them back to the other topic they had brought up.

"Has Dad made any arrangements?" Amanda asked.

"And what about the university?" Jeffrey asked.

"And where is he going to be buried?"

Margaret pinched the bridge of her nose, feeling a headache coming on. "You know your father. He has had the funeral arranged and paid for since he was first diagnosed. He and Jim Evans have some kind of memorial service worked out with the university. And he told me years ago that he had a plot next to your mother."

Amanda and Jeffrey exchanged a quick glance.

"That won't bother you?" Amanda asked awkwardly.

"No," said Margaret. "Why should it?"

"Well," Jeffrey said, expelling a relieved breath, "you know. Sometimes a second wife expects certain things..."

Margaret sighed. "Gavin had a special relationship with your mother. She was his connection to you. I'm not part of that. It's okay."

The relief on their faces had been so obvious it was almost comical, Margaret mused now as she stared out the window of the hospital room and realized a light snow was falling. She slipped her hand into her pants pocket and pressed her fingers against Wyck's card.

"Margaret, won't you come to our house this evening?" said Cindy Wilson, a colleague from Political Science. "We're just having a few people over for a little Christmas Eve get-together."

Margaret stood in the dairy section of the grocery store with a dozen eggs and some milk in a tote dangling from her hand.

"Thank you, Cindy," she said. "That's so kind of you, but no. I'll be going back to the hospital later, so... but wish Jerry a Merry Christmas for me."

"I will," Cindy said, giving Margaret a hug. "Give Gavin our best."

Margaret lingered, giving Cindy adequate time to check out so there would be no awkward conversation at the cash register. She knew Cindy's offer had been sincere, as had the others she'd received from various colleagues, but, after a dinner or an evening out – always by herself these days – they went home to spouses and children, to their lives, while she went home to… Sometimes, the contrast between their respective situations made it harder for her to go home at all.

"If you think it's hard now, just wait," she muttered to herself, looking around quickly to see if anyone had seen her talking to herself. *This is only a dress rehearsal,* she realized grimly as she added a carton of eggnog to her tote, refusing to look at the calories.

She paid for her groceries and made her way home. A flat December dusk had fallen under leaden skies that promised more snow to come. As she pulled into her driveway, her heart lightened at the unexpected sight of Wyck's truck parked there. Wyck stepped out from the front porch with a couple of grocery bags in her hands.

"Hi," she said as Margaret rolled down her window. "I didn't know how much time you'd had to get away for things like shopping, so I picked up a few staples for you."

"Why do you have to be so nice?" Margaret nearly blurted, but caught herself. "Won't you come in?" she said instead.

"No, I've got Mandy with me," Wyck demurred, swinging a grocery bag in the direction of the truck.

"She's invited, too," Margaret smiled.

"You're sure?"

"I'm sure."

Wyck went to the truck and opened the door. Mandy bounded out, gamboling around in the yard while Margaret opened the garage.

"Just enough snow to make Christmas white," Wyck said, following Margaret into the mudroom, wiping Mandy's snowy paws with a paper towel.

"The kids will love it," Margaret agreed.

"Um, the house was all dark," Wyck pointed out. "I didn't want to ring the bell. Is Gavin in bed already?"

"Gavin's back in the hospital," Margaret said. "Since yesterday."

"What's going on?"

"Same thing," Margaret sighed. "His heart and lungs."

"How are you doing?"

It wasn't that other people didn't ask that. It wasn't that people weren't solicitous of her. But something in the tone of Wyck's voice, the sincere expression on her face that said she was truly concerned with how Margaret was - she felt a sudden rush of emotion wash over her.

"I'm -"

Wyck went to her, laying a gentle hand on her shoulder. Margaret clutched the granite countertop to stop herself reaching up to grasp that hand.

"Since you now have two dozen eggs," Wyck was saying as she saw the contents of Margaret's bag, "how about I make you an omelette? A special Christmas Eve omelette?"

Margaret nodded. "This is becoming a ritual for us," she said, smiling weakly. "I'll make the coffee."

Wyck found some tomatoes, peppers and onions in the frig, and set about chopping them up while the olive oil in the pan heated.

Margaret got out plates and mugs while Wyck whisked the eggs.

"What do you normally do for Christmas Eve?" Wyck asked from the stove. "Church? Friends?"

Margaret stood looking out at the night, as if seeing something from long ago. "We used to go to the Episcopal church - but it's been years," she said.

"Why did you stop?" Wyck asked curiously.

Margaret frowned, trying to remember. "I think it was when Gavin was first diagnosed with lung cancer," she recalled. "He'd had surgery in October, and then was getting chemo and radiation, and just felt horrible. He didn't feel up to going that year, and we just never went back."

Stopped going to church. Stopped going out with friends. Stopped playing golf. Stopped living. It's as if we've been sealed up alive in a tomb - Gavin's tomb.

Presently, they were seated at the kitchen table, a single red taper lit - "for Christmas," Margaret said. Mandy ate a bit of scrambled egg and then curled up under the table.

"What about you?" Margaret asked. "Do you go to church?"

"No."

Margaret looked up at the edge to Wyck's voice. "Don't you believe in God?"

"Oh, I believe in God," Wyck said. "I just don't believe in people who claim to believe in God. I've met too few of those folks who live good examples of what they profess to believe."

Margaret tilted her head, seeing again that hurt, that anger in Wyck's face. "What happened?" she asked gently.

Wyck looked up, meeting eyes that were soft and gentle, reflecting the candlelight.

"I was teaching at a college in New Hampshire," she said. "My partner, Carla, was a high school special ed teacher."

Margaret held her breath, listening raptly.

"We'd been together for seven years... not really closeted, but not open, either, about our relationship. We were visiting her family for Thanksgiving." She paused, stabbing with her fork at a chunk of onion. "For some reason I have never figured out, her father chose that weekend to blow up in a rage over our relationship. He cornered me outside the house Thanksgiving morning. I'd gone out to get something from the car." Her jaw clenched a few times. "He shoved me up against the car and told me if I ever came back, he'd kill me."

Margaret's hand flew to her mouth, but Wyck went on.

"He locked me out of the house, while Carla's sisters corralled her inside to keep us from talking." Wyck stared at her plate. "All I had were my car keys. No phone, no wallet. I banged on the door and windows for a while, but no one would answer, so I went to the mall parking lot down the road and waited. I tried calling from a pay phone, but they wouldn't let me talk to her." There was a very long pause as Wyck swallowed painfully several times. "I waited for five hours before she came."

"Why?" Margaret asked, aghast.

Wyck looked up and her eyes were shining with angry tears. "Why did it take her five hours to come, or why was I stupid enough to sit there for five hours?" She wiped her napkin across her eyes. "She didn't want to ruin her mother's Thanksgiving and I... I kept thinking, just fifteen minutes more and I'll leave if she hasn't come. And when that fifteen minutes was up, I'd think, fifteen more."

"Oh, my God," Margaret breathed. "How could she do that?" but even as she said it, a vision flashed into her mind of the unspeakable hurt on Julia's face - hurt she had caused.

I was the coward in my story, she thought. *I was the one who let my father separate me from the person I loved. Am I any better, any different than Carla?*

"It wasn't just her," Wyck was saying. "It was her family - people I thought had accepted me as a sister, as her partner... It was a very long, very silent ride home."

"What happened after that?" Margaret asked, not really sure she wanted to hear.

"It was the beginning of the end," Wyck said. "She wouldn't talk about it, and, really, there was nothing more to say. It ate at me for weeks, until I went home alone that Christmas, and when..." Here, she had to pause again. "...when my family asked me where Carla was, I told them what had happened. My brother and sister-in-law, who belong to some born-again church, started ranting about this being God's way of saving me from my life of sin, a call to salvation." Her jaw clenched angrily. "And the rest of my family just sat there, looking uncomfortable, but not one of them spoke up to support me."

Her voice was bitter and hard as she finished, and Mandy, whining, sat up, resting her head in Wyck's lap.

"I'm so sorry," Margaret whispered.

Wyck shrugged. "I moved out not long after and, by August, I was down here at Virginia Tech, enrolled in the landscape architecture program. I haven't been back since."

"How long ago was that?"

"Three - no, this Christmas is four years," Wyck said. "Four peaceful, good years." She leaned over and kissed Mandy's furry head.

"You haven't seen your family for four years?" Margaret asked in astonishment.

Wyck shook her head. "Nope."

"So, this is why you prefer animals and plants?" Margaret asked, understanding at last.

Wyck nodded, holding Mandy's face in between her hands, Mandy's deep brown eyes gazing up at her. "She would give her life – literally – for me if I needed her. She will always be there for me, no matter what. And I would do the same for her." She blinked and looked up at Margaret. "I'm not naïve enough to think I'm immune to ever falling in love again, and I'm obviously stupidly loyal, but I hope I've learned something." Her eyes searched Margaret's, looking for something. "It would take... I don't even know what it would take for me to ever trust someone enough to take another chance on love."

Her eyes continued to probe, and Margaret found she could not meet that gaze. Lowering her eyes to her coffee cup, she said, "Jane Austen would argue that love is always worth taking another chance on."

"Yes, but," Wyck said, "Jane didn't live what she wrote, did she? She may have loved again after LeFroy, we don't really know, but she lived and died with her mother and sister, not with a lover or a husband."

She stood suddenly, gathering the plates and taking them to the sink. "Sorry. Didn't mean to burden you with all that. That wasn't what you needed right now."

"I asked," Margaret reminded her, but *why did I ask?* she wondered morosely, almost wishing she hadn't.

Wyck turned to her. "You said you would let me read some of the other things you've written."

Margaret blinked. "Are you sure?"

"I'm sure."

"I'll be right back," Margaret said.

Wyck had the dishes rinsed and placed in the dishwasher by the time Margaret returned with six smallish bundles of paper.

"The sum total of my work for the past twenty-five years," Margaret said ruefully.

Wyck reached out, but Margaret pulled back.

"Be gentle," Margaret said.

Wyck smiled reassuringly. "I will be."

A little while later, Wyck and Mandy were headed home. Mandy, rather than looking out the windshield as she normally did, sat facing Wyck from the passenger seat.

"What?" Wyck asked, glancing over.

When Mandy continued to watch her, she said, "I know, I know. I've never told anyone else but you about those things. Don't worry. It doesn't mean anything."

Chapter 9

WYCK GROANED A LITTLE, her neck and shoulders screaming from hours of overhead work with a nail gun, securing white beadboard to the ceilings upstairs. The electrical inspection had been completed just after Christmas, and she was now able to start getting walls and ceilings up. When she first bought the barn, she had intended to leave the ceilings open to the rafters, but her first winter there had convinced her that she needed insulation.

Mandy had dutifully followed her up and down the stairs for each load of insulation and then beadboard, carefully supervising Wyck's progress.

Shooting the last few nails into the boards, she climbed down off the scaffold and surveyed her work. She knew she could have saved time and money using beadboard panels, but she liked being able to stagger the seams of the individual boards so that it looked better to her critical eye as she fit them around the roof timbers.

"If I'm going to be lying in bed staring at this," she'd argued to Mandy, "I better like what I'm seeing or it'll drive me crazy."

Wincing as she bent over, she coiled the air hose and turned off the compressor. "Come on," she said. "Time for a break."

Together, she and Mandy descended to the main level where Wyck made herself a sandwich and gave Mandy a handful of baby carrots.

She sank tiredly into her armchair while Mandy happily crunched on her carrots. Chewing on her sandwich, Wyck picked up one of Margaret's manuscripts. She read a few pages as she ate and then, shaking her head in frustration, she set it aside and picked up another. She read another few pages and set it aside as well.

"Do you want to tell her?" she asked Mandy who cocked her head. "No?" She expelled a slow breath, her cheeks ballooning out. "This is going to be fun."

"Can I get you anything?" Margaret asked Gavin as he settled into an armchair and put his legs on the ottoman, legs that were still swollen and heavy, but not like before he was hospitalized.

"No, my dear," Gavin sighed. "I'm just going to read a while."

"All right, then," Margaret said, pulling a knitted throw over his lap. "Your book and glasses are there on the table and the coffee is brewing. I'll be back in a moment."

She went to the kitchen and stood staring out at the garden, trying not to think about how much she wished Wyck was out there. Gavin had been kept in the hospital until the twenty-sixth, nearly fifteen pounds lighter when all the excess fluid was gone, and breathing much easier.

So am I, Margaret thought.

She was startled by the ringing of the telephone. "I'll get it," she called. "Hello?"

"Margaret? It's Wyck."

Margaret closed her eyes and pressed her hand to her chest, trying to steady her heart. "Hello," she said, wondering if Wyck could possibly have known how much she wanted to talk to her.

"How's Gavin doing?"

"He's home, doing better, thank you."

Wyck cleared her throat. "I need to take a break from working on the barn and wondered if you were available to get together?"

"Yes," said Margaret. "What did you have in mind?"

"Well, I've read your manuscripts," Wyck said tentatively and Margaret could hear the hesitation in her voice.

"Why don't we meet at my office," Margaret suggested. "Campus should be nearly deserted now –"

"– so it will be safe to meet the gardener," Wyck finished for her.

"No," Margaret said, laughing. "I just have a feeling I need to hear whatever you've got to say in private."

"It's not that bad," Wyck reassured her. "I promised to be gentle, remember?"

"In an hour then?"

Margaret arrived first, leaving her door open, checking her e-mails as she nervously waited. Covertly checking her hair one more time in her office mirror, she spied Wyck approaching from across the campus and, watching from her office window, couldn't help smiling. Wyck's effortless gait, the swing of her one free arm, everything about her exuded a confidence Margaret couldn't ever remember feeling. Wyck looked up and, seeing Margaret, smiled and waved.

In a minute, Wyck was knocking on the door. Margaret stood to greet her, smoothing the khakis she'd chosen to wear instead of dress pants.

"So, Gavin is doing better?" Wyck asked as she sat, crossing her legs, her hands folded over top of Margaret's manuscripts.

Margaret came from behind the desk to close the office door, saying, "Yes, he seems to be much more comfortable. Tired, mostly."

She hesitated a moment before taking the other wooden chair next to Wyck rather than returning behind the desk.

"And you?" Wyck asked solicitously, her eyes searching Margaret's face.

Margaret could only meet that gaze for a moment before lowering it to look at her clasped hands. "I'm... I'm hanging on," she said.

"Hanging onto you," she longed to add, but didn't dare. "So," she said, pointing to the manuscripts on Wyck's lap. "Let's have it."

Taking a deep breath and speaking in as gentle a tone as she could, Wyck laid her hands on the loose pages and said, "These... these were written by Margaret Braithwaite. They're stiff, stilted, devoid of any kind of feeling or passion."

Her eyes focused on something over Margaret's shoulder and she suddenly leaned toward Margaret, so close Margaret could catch her scent as she reached to the bookshelf behind her, *so close, I thought she was going to kiss me*, Margaret realized with a pang of regret a half-second later.

"This," Wyck said, sitting back and holding up a copy of Margaret's published novel, "this is lyrical, beautiful. It speaks of passion and wildness. This was written by Meggie. A Meggie, I think, very deeply in love."

The slow flush creeping up Margaret's neck and cheeks told Wyck she was right. Margaret, unable to tear her eyes from Wyck's, longed to command her to stop, but couldn't.

Wyck set the unfinished manuscripts on the desk and shifted to face Margaret. "I don't know what happened to her," she said, "but Meggie is who you need to find if you want to write like this again."

She peered intently into Margaret's eyes and softly said, "I know she's still in there. I've seen her, when Margaret lets her guard down."

For long seconds, they stared at each other, and Wyck could see the softening, the yielding in Margaret's eyes – "I could see Meggie looking out at me," she would have said – when suddenly, a wall slammed down.

Margaret stood abruptly and went to her seat behind the desk. "Well, thank you for bringing these back to me," she said crisply, "and for your... critique." Her cheeks were more flushed now.

Wyck watched her staring at her computer screen for several seconds. "Margaret –"

"I'll just stay and get some work done while I'm here," Margaret said, tapping her keyboard.

"All right," Wyck said, honoring the dismissal. "Call me if you want to talk."

Margaret nodded tersely as Wyck let herself out. She waited until she heard the door at the end of the hall clatter shut before she buried her face in her hands.

"What is it, my dear?" Gavin asked. "You seem so restless."

Margaret turned from the kitchen windows where she had been staring out at the snow that had fallen overnight. "I guess I'm just anxious for classes to start next week," she said, though that was a stretch as she had gotten to the point where she dreaded the beginnings of new semesters.

She hadn't seen or spoken to Wyck in over a week – "not since you practically threw her out of your office," she reminded herself. She and Gavin had spent a quiet New Year's Eve and Day – no different from any other. "No beginning, no end, just days blending together into years as my life passes me by."

"I'm going out to get some air," she said, pulling on a pair of boots and donning a jacket, hat and gloves.

She stepped out onto the flagstones, covered in a couple of inches of dry, fluffy snow. Breathing deeply, she walked back toward the garden, a place she had never gravitated to before, when it was Gavin's space. But now, she felt Wyck out here, and she found herself wanting to be nearer. She wandered the paths, most of them sheltered from all but a dusting of snow, noticing things she had never seen before: benches placed in strategic spots for sitting and contemplating, plants chosen so that they provided color and contrast even now.

Far enough in to be out of view of the house, she stopped, standing with her arms wrapped around herself. She'd had another dream last night – Julia kissing her wildly, sliding her hand down, down to the wetness waiting for her touch, the frantic thrusting as fingers stroked, bringing her to an orgasm that woke her.

"I've had more orgasms in the last couple of months than in the past thirty years," she muttered to a cardinal sitting in a nearby shrub, cocking its little head at the sound of her voice.

Sex with Gavin had always been perfunctory – his clumsy hands pushing and prodding unfamiliar territory while most of his attention was focused on his primary objective. Fortunately, he had rarely wanted sex, seeming to prefer the intellectual companionship Margaret had provided and Margaret had been content to lead a mostly celibate life. A hysterectomy at age forty-seven had further inhibited any sexual desire. Until now.

Expelling a frustrated breath that hung in the air for a few seconds as a cloud of misty vapor, Margaret tried to turn off the words that had been playing over and over in her head....

"I don't know what happened to her, but Meggie is who you need to find if you want to write like this again."

How could Wyck in so short a period of time have seen through her to places no one else had seen – "no one else wanted to see," she corrected herself – in thirty years? She had reluctantly flipped back through her manuscripts and realized Wyck was right. Gavin could have written them. It wasn't her voice at all.

Do I even have a voice of my own anymore? she wondered as she walked.

That part of her, the part that had fallen wildly in love with Julia, had been buried for so long... buried to hide it – first from her father, then from Gavin – that she wasn't sure it still existed.

"It does," said a persistent voice in her head. "You know what it wants."

"I can't," she told herself sternly. "Even if I could, Wyck would never –"

"She must be lonely."

"She doesn't sound lonely. You heard her. She sounds angry and defensive –"

"– and hurt."

"Exactly. I ran away from Julia at the first threat from my father. What would possibly make her believe she could trust me?"

"She doesn't know about Julia."

"I know. But I would have to tell her."

Margaret stopped in her snowy tracks, listening to the sudden silence in her head. She shook her head and turned toward the house. "Go back inside to your husband," she told herself.

Chapter 10

"DAMN!"

Wyck stood up, looking at the nail protruding from the tongue of the cherry floorboard at her feet. It was her third misfire with the nailer as she laid this floor. Leaving the nailer sitting on the subfloor, she angrily swiped at the tears coursing down her cheeks.

She'd been crying for days. With no warning, no provocation, the tears would come and she seemed powerless to stop them.

Giving up before she completely ruined her hard work, she picked her guitar out of its case and sat cross-legged against the wall. Mandy curled up next to her, pressing close against her thigh, as Wyck's fingers played bits of melodies so well-known they did not require conscious thought.

Telling Margaret about that Thanksgiving and Christmas four years ago had been like waking a sleeping dragon. Thoughts of Carla, of those last months together, of the confrontation with her own family, kept pressing their way insistently into the forefront, refusing to stay tucked away in the forgotten recesses of her mind any longer. She'd been unable to sleep, finding herself instead endlessly reliving that interminable drive home, hands clenched tightly on the wheel, Carla crying silently in the passenger seat, not a word spoken between them for six long hours.

Then, still reeling from the feelings of betrayal from Carla and her sisters, Wyck felt, as acutely as if it had just happened, the shock and disbelief as her family sat by passively while her brother and sister-in-law harangued her.

"Was my love, my commitment to Carla so worthless that no one would defend it? No one would speak up and stand by me?"

Questions as unanswerable now as always.

And then, after that Christmas, had come the sinking realization that Carla had made a choice. Her family had pushed until she had to make one, and she had. It was for Wyck to decide whether she could live with it. Or not.

She remembered it was a cold, dreary day in February when she had quietly said, "I've found an apartment."

Carla had simply nodded, and Wyck realized she'd been expecting this – maybe even hoping for it.

"I can't afford to stay on this mortgage," Wyck had continued.

"My father will help me refinance and I'll pay you your half."

And just like that she had been neatly and quietly ushered from Carla's life. No begging her to change her mind, no saying things would be different if only she would stay, no... anything. Move on. Start over. There hadn't even been enough energy left in her to cry or strike out angrily.

But telling Margaret – *why did I do that?* – had been like some kind of catalyst, a trigger releasing a flood of emotions and memories and dreams.

The vibration of the guitar strings died away as tears ran unchecked down Wyck's face.

Margaret sat at a café in the River Arts District, sipping a chai while she read a new book on the impact Jane Austen had had on the development of the contemporary concept of the romantic novel. Sighing, she closed the book with a snap. No new insights there.

Glancing around the café to make sure no one she knew was there, she reached into her bag and pulled out a small notebook. She flipped it open and stared at the blank page staring back at her - taunting her, daring her to scribble something. She sat with pen poised, paralyzed, unable to think of anything to write.

Glancing up, she looked out the café's front window and saw Wyck walking by. She jumped up from her table and hurried to the door.

Wyck turned at the sound of her name. "Margaret," she said in surprise.

"Do you have a few minutes?" Margaret asked.

Wyck shrugged. "Sure." She followed Margaret back inside.

"What are you doing downtown?" Margaret asked.

"My office is on the next block," Wyck said, sitting opposite Margaret at her table.

"Do you want anything?"

"No, I'm good," Wyck said, observing the notebook, but saying nothing. "How have you been? I haven't seen you since -"

"- since the day I dismissed you from my office for telling me the truth?" Margaret finished for her, a wan smile tugging at one corner of her mouth.

Wyck tilted her head. "Yeah," she smiled. "Sorry about that. Am I forgiven?"

Margaret toyed with the lid of her chai and said, "You were right. It was just hard to hear."

"I know."

"It's just... I don't know if it's even possible to find that part of me again," Margaret murmured in a low voice. "It's been so long, and things are so different now. I'm so different now." She frowned. "But you're the only one who's ever been honest enough, insightful enough to -"

Wyck's eyes were suddenly moist and she had to blink and look away, her jaw clenched tightly.

"What is it? What's wrong?" Margaret asked quietly, reaching out without thinking to grasp Wyck's arm as it rested on the table.

Wyck didn't draw away, but it was several seconds before she could speak. "Talking to you about... everything that happened," she said through a painfully tight throat, "it all feels so fresh, so raw." She blinked and looked down at Margaret's hand, which was immediately withdrawn. "The last couple of weeks have been hard."

Margaret watched Wyck's face as she spoke. "Are you always this honest with your feelings?"

Wyck laughed a little and wiped a sleeve across her eyes. "This," she said, gesturing at herself, "is exactly what you get, good and bad." She sniffed. "Where I get into trouble is expecting other people to be as open."

Margaret squirmed uneasily.

Wyck glanced at her watch. "I have to go. I'm meeting a client. If the weather holds, I'll be out at your house later this week to resume some pruning."

"Okay," Margaret nodded. "I'll see you then."

Margaret pretended to busy herself with her books as Wyck exited the café, and then watched her through the window until she was out of sight.

Gavin made his way slowly down the hall. His fluid levels had remained under better control, which made walking and breathing easier, but with those problems now receding into the background, his back pain was becoming more pronounced. He didn't complain. He knew it was his cancer, and, as he had no intention of undergoing any further chemo or radiation, "what's the point in complaining?" he would have said.

As he passed Margaret's study, he heard the sound of her crying. He paused for a moment, listening, wondering if he should go in to her. She'd been crying a lot lately. He didn't know if it was his illness, or post-holiday depression, or... He went on to his bedroom –

the room Margaret no longer shared with him – and sat on the edge of the bed. A nap was what he needed. He glanced out the windows – the same view of the back yard shared by Margaret's study – and saw Wyck, high in an elm tree, sawing off some dead limbs.

Maybe she's going through menopause, he realized. Did women go through menopause after a hysterectomy? He supposed she was the right age. Linda had died in her thirties, so he had never been through this process with a wife. *You'd think one benefit of living to be an old man,* he mused, *would be a better understanding of women,* but he felt no closer to understanding them now than he had been when he first got married.

Gavin's eyes caught sight of an old man, bloated and sickly, staring at him, and it took a second for him to realize he was staring at his own reflection in the dresser mirror. A framed photo of himself – a younger, healthier self, taken on a nearby Civil War battlefield some fifteen years ago – sat in front of the mirror, taunting him.

His eyes suddenly narrowed as a thought occurred to him. He squinted at the wall as if he could see through it to Margaret standing at her window, crying, and then looked back out to where Wyck was lithely climbing higher in the tree.

"It must be menopause."

Wyck and Mandy came home from a run. Mandy's tongue lolled as she jogged easily beside Wyck whose cheeks were flushed a vivid scarlet, both from the bite of the January cold and from the exertion.

As they approached the barn, Wyck was surprised to see Margaret's Audi parked there next to the truck. She tried to ignore the not-so-vague realization of how pleased she was.

"Hi," Wyck gasped as Margaret climbed out of her car.

"I hoped you'd be home soon," Margaret smiled.

"To what do we owe the pleasure?" Wyck asked as Mandy danced in front of Margaret.

Margaret gave her an affectionate pat and said, "I shouldn't have come without calling..." as she followed Wyck inside, breathing in the outdoorsy smell emanating from her.

"Is Gavin okay?" Wyck asked as she pulled off her hat, gloves and windshirt.

"Yes," Margaret said, awkwardly trying to look anywhere but at Wyck's lean body, clad in tights and a close-fitting top. "I need to talk to you."

Wyck could see the troubled expression in her eyes as she stood, twisting her leather gloves in her hands. "Um... I'm rather pungent," she said with an apologetic grin. "Give me five minutes to shower, okay? You could make us some tea, if you don't mind. You know where everything is."

She flipped open a trunk Margaret had never noticed before, pulling out some clean clothes. "Sawdust protection," she said in response to Margaret's questioning glance.

Margaret turned to hang her coat on one of the pegs near the door and smiled as she heard Wyck say to Mandy, "Don't let her leave."

Within a few minutes, Wyck was back, wearing jeans and a fatigue sweater over a t-shirt, her damp hair mussed and her cheeks still pink. She tossed a couple of extra logs into the woodstove as Margaret brought steaming mugs of tea out to the living room.

Wyck accepted a mug, pulling her apple crate over to sit on as she had before, leaving the armchair for Margaret.

"What have you been working on?" Margaret asked, looking around.

"Upstairs mostly," Wyck replied, noticing Margaret's stall tactic. "Floors, walls, ceiling. The upper level is nearly done."

They both sipped their tea, Wyck enjoying the trail of warmth it traced down her gullet. As always after a cold run, she was now chilled.

"What is it, Margaret?" she asked when Margaret didn't seem able to start.

Margaret stared down at the cup cradled in her hands. "You've been so honest with me - about Carla and everything that happened, about my writing, about why you were so emotional the last time I saw you..."

Wyck could hear the tears in her voice before she saw the first one fall off the end of her long lashes.

"I haven't been as honest with you."

Wyck waited, puzzled.

Margaret took a deep, ratchety breath, and Wyck realized how nervous she was. "When I was at Wellesley, I... I was in love with another girl. Julia." She had done it. She'd said those words out loud to another person for the first time in her life. The universe was still in place and she was still alive and breathing. Gathering courage, she continued, "We were mad about each other. We naïvely thought we would stay together, but my father... he guessed somehow. Maybe others guessed as well – we were young and stupid, not very discreet – but... my father threatened to cut me off, completely, if I didn't end it with her."

The tears began to fall more freely and she had more difficulty speaking as she gasped, "I did it. I told her I couldn't be with her, couldn't see her again. The pain, the hurt in her eyes... I did to her what Carla did to you. I caved in to my father's demands. I never saw her again."

Wyck retrieved a box of tissues – she'd needed plenty of them recently – and sat back down while Margaret dried her eyes and blew her nose.

"I've never told anyone about that," Margaret whispered.

Wyck's heart was beating rather fast, and she knew it wasn't from her run, as she asked, "Why are you telling me?"

Margaret looked at her at last, her brown eyes glinting with the intensity of her feelings. "I had to tell you. You're the only one who sees me – the part of me that used to be Meggie," she said. "You were right. That's where my first book came from – it came from my love for Julia. It came from the passion we shared. I'd thought that part of me was gone – dead long ago. Nothing left but this dried-out shell that is Margaret Braithwaite, but... it isn't."

Her mouth was dry and she felt as if she might suffocate as she looked into Wyck's eyes. Without warning, her courage failed her and she quailed at the thought of saying any more.

"I have to go," she said, practically leaping to her feet.

Wyck jumped up and followed as Margaret rushed to the door where she grabbed her coat and wrenched the door open. Wyck reached around her, pushing the door shut as Margaret stood with her eyes closed, feeling Wyck's nearness.

Ever so gently, Wyck placed a hand on Margaret's cheek, willing her to turn and face her. Hesitantly, Margaret's eyes fluttered open and Wyck could see the terror there – all guards down, all defenses gone.

Wyck moved closer, her eyes sliding out of focus as she pressed her lips to Margaret's. Margaret, feeling as if time – and her heart – had stopped, resisted for a few seconds and then gave in to the emotions coursing through her, pressing her mouth more firmly to Wyck's, tasting her, feeling her, inhaling her. Everything had ceased to exist except this kiss – this blessed kiss, Wyck's lips and tongue so soft, and she yielded, wanting to yield everything....

She had no idea how long they were pressed together before they reluctantly pulled apart, breathless, aching. "I know I was a coward," Margaret murmured, "and I know that I'm married, but... I had to tell you."

This time, when she pulled the door open, Wyck let her go.

Why did you have to kiss her? Wyck asked herself for probably the hundredth time. She felt a soft nudge against her thigh from Mandy's nose and realized she'd been standing for who knows how long, halfway through getting Mandy's breakfast.

"I'm sorry," Wyck smiled as she scooped kibble into the dish, sprinkling some grated cheese over top. "Here you go."

Mandy took a couple of bites, then paused to look up at Wyck who was staring out the kitchen window again.

Though she had planned to resume some tree work at the Braithwaite place this week, she had avoided going over there, choosing instead to busy herself working on the barn. She had new floorboards laid nearly all the way through the upper level hallway and she was set to start the beadboard in the second bedroom. She worked until she was exhausted each night, but sleep still didn't come easily.

In her most honest moments as she spent sleepless hours tossing on her cot, she had to admit that Margaret's confession hadn't been a complete surprise – well, the part about turning her back on Julia was. Something in Margaret's novel had pulled at Wyck, and though the story hadn't involved a lesbian theme, the passages were so tantalizing in their description of feminine beauty that Wyck had wondered what was behind them. She also had to admit that she'd been feeling more and more strongly drawn to Margaret, despite her determination never to fall in love again – "with a married woman, no less," she could have added in disgust.

"I don't want this, damn it," she said aloud now, slamming her palm down on the plywood. Mandy, whining softly, left her breakfast to come over and sit, leaning against Wyck's thigh.

Taylor Foster sauntered out of his favorite men's clothing store downtown. They were ridiculously expensive, but carried unique and well-made items. With his purchases neatly folded in his shopping bag, he pulled on his deerskin gloves as he stepped out onto the sidewalk.

Looking up and down the busy street, he automatically scanned the men passing by. One never knew where the next hook-up might come from – a covert glance, a smile lingering just a second too long, and he knew he had a pending encounter. Sometimes they were gay, but more often, they pretended to be straight, though they knew a quick fuck with a man would be better than anything they got at home. And a quick fuck was all he was interested in.

Emerging from a neighboring office building was a figure that caught his eye. That cute butch gardener of Margaret's. What was the name? Ah, there it was on her truck – he smiled at the cliché.

"Ms. Fitzsimmons," he called, hurrying over to her. "Taylor Foster. We met in Margaret Braithwaite's office."

"I recall," Wyck said warily.

"I'm sorry we didn't get a chance to chat that day," Taylor said charmingly, but he could tell Wyck wasn't going to be as easily manipulated as most people.

"Yes, well, things have been busy through the holidays," Wyck said evasively, stepping closer to her truck.

"You know, I'm so glad Margaret has a new friend," he said smoothly.

With a neutral expression, Wyck said, "I really work more for Gavin than for Margaret." She glanced at her watch. "I'm sorry, Dr. Foster, but I've got to meet a client. Good day."

"Maybe we could meet for a drink sometime? You, Margaret and I?" he called as Wyck gave a curt nod before climbing into her truck.

Chuckling to himself, he watched her pull away from the curb. "Oh, yes, yes, yes," he said gleefully.

Margaret tarried in her office, busying herself with various unimportant tasks in preparation for spring semester, waiting until dusk fell before leaving campus, just as she had done nearly every day since her visit to Wyck - "that disastrous visit," she could have said.

"Why did you go out there?" she'd berated herself time and again. Even when she was alone, she blushed at the memory - not only of her acute embarrassment at everything she had revealed about herself, but of the way Wyck's kiss had reduced her to a quivering idiot. "You're behaving like you're sixteen and just had your first kiss."

Yet, no matter how many times she told herself she was being foolish, that the kiss had probably meant nothing to Wyck, she felt an almost overwhelming longing to see Wyck - to hold her, feel her, kiss her again....

Each evening, she'd been equal parts relieved and disappointed to find no pickup truck in the drive when she got home. Casually, she would query Gavin as to how his day had gone, hoping for some reference to Wyck, but there was none, whether because she hadn't been there or because he didn't think to mention it, Margaret didn't know and daren't ask.

"You confessed to treating Julia just as Carla treated her," she kept reminding herself. "Why would she trust you?"

Sighing, Margaret switched off her computer and turned to the coat tree next to her window, where she froze. Standing there on the quad, looking up at her was Wyck. With a tiny wave, Margaret invited her in.

Drawing the shade at her window, she turned slowly as she heard the door open behind her. She grasped the back of her chair to steady herself as Wyck stood there - the most beautiful thing she had ever seen.

Wyck pushed the door shut behind her, taking the precaution of flipping the lock. "We need to talk," she said.

Margaret nodded mutely, dropping into her desk chair as Wyck sat tensely on the edge of one of the wooden chairs facing the desk.

Taking a nervous breath, Wyck forced herself to begin what sounded like a rehearsed speech. "I didn't want to see you for the first time in front of Gavin," she said. "Or your friend, Taylor. I'm not that good an actor."

Margaret nodded. "I owe you an apology. I never should have barged in on you like that."

"And I... I shouldn't have..." Wyck stammered nervously.

"Are you sorry you did?" Margaret asked, praying that Wyck wasn't regretting the kiss - the one thing she'd been clinging to.

"No," Wyck blurted. "It's just... why did you tell me those things?" she asked, her eyes locked on Margaret's.

Margaret stared back like a deer caught in headlights, unable to look away. "I needed for you to know the truth... about me," she said at last.

"But why?" Wyck pushed, sounding a bit hesitant, as if she wasn't really sure she wanted to know.

Terrified, Margaret whispered words she never expected to utter again, "Because I love you."

Wyck pressed her hand to her eyes. "Don't. You can't," she groaned.

"I know," Margaret said in a barely audible voice. "But I do. You can't plan this. There is no logic, even when it's wrong..."

They sat in silence for long minutes, half the truth lying naked between them.

Swallowing hard, Margaret said, "I have to know. Am I alone in this?"

Wyck frowned down at her hands tightly clenched in her lap. "It doesn't matter."

Margaret nodded. "Gavin. I know. If I am alone in feeling this way, I'll find a way to deal with my emotions. I've done it for thirty years. I just have to know."

Unwillingly, Wyck raised tortured eyes to her. "No," she said softly. "You're not alone."

Margaret slumped back against her chair as if Wyck's admission had sapped the last of her strength. "What do we do now?" she asked miserably.

"Nothing," said Wyck, leaning her elbows on her knees as she stared at her feet. "Don't you see how impossible this is?" she asked angrily. "How we feel doesn't matter. None of this matters."

Without warning, she jumped up, yanked the door open and left, slamming the door shut behind her. Margaret sat for long seconds, her eyes welling with tears. "Wrong again," she whispered to the empty room. "Love always matters."

Chapter 11

MARGARET SAT IN HER study at home, writing rapidly with occasional glances out the window to where Wyck was transplanting some shrubs. Admitting her love for Wyck had unstoppered emotions that had been tightly bottled up for decades and suddenly, "I can write. I've found Meggie again," though the discovery was bittersweet.

"So much time gone," she lamented. "Half my life, and now I'm full to bursting with a love that can't be acknowledged."

"Be careful. Gavin is not stupid," warned a cautious voice inside her.

"Gavin has never noticed anything outside his own world: his garden, his work, his books."

Nevertheless, Margaret found that this new love made it easier to bear Gavin's grumpiness and his increasingly onerous demands. She knew his pain must have been worsening as he became surlier, and she was surprised at her own increased capacity for patience and tenderness with him. "How is it," she might have asked, "that loving her makes it easier to love him?"

She had also discovered that this increased capacity for patience and kindness extended to her students and colleagues as well. Even her undergrads seemed to respond to her renewed enthusiasm for teaching.

Taylor, of course, noticed immediately.

"'In the Spring a fuller crimson comes upon the robin's breast,'" he'd quoted conspiratorially just yesterday as he had let himself uninvited into her office, dropping into a vacant chair. Gesturing theatrically, he continued,

"'In the Spring the wanton lapwing gets himself a fuller crest;

In the Spring a livelier iris changes on the burnish'd dove;

In the Spring a young man's fancy lightly turns to thoughts of love.'"

Winking and grinning broadly, he said, "Or in this case, a young woman."

Margaret, her face reddening despite her efforts to keep her eyes on the paper she was reading on her computer screen, said, "Not so young, and quoting Tennyson does not make you a gentleman."

"I never claimed to be a gentleman," he returned, still grinning. "Whereas you, my lady, are not the virtuous wife you have claimed to be."

Her eyebrows raised imperiously. "Oh? In what way?"

He laughed. "Oh, come now. I can see the blush of new love on your cheeks, and I don't have to guess at its source."

She looked at him and calmly said, "I am as I ever was." She suddenly felt immensely grateful for Wyck's sense of honor, for she knew, if Wyck had come to her, she would not have been strong enough to resist. As it was, she had nothing with which to be reproached. *When did my life start sounding like a Jane Austen novel?*

Taylor's smile faltered at her calm countenance. "You and the gardener haven't –?"

Margaret stared at him disdainfully. Taylor's instincts might have been more accurate than she would have liked, but what he could never have fathomed was the possibility of an unconsummated love. *And that will save me,* she realized.

"Oh." He cleared his throat. "Well, I'm sorry, Margaret." He stood, but peered at her again, obviously having difficulty believing he was wrong. She met his gaze with clear, untroubled eyes. "I'll see you later," he said as he left.

She paused her pen now as she recalled that conversation, and, as she watched Wyck through the window of her study, her mind, of its own accord, picked up subsequent lines of the Tennyson poem,

> Well - 'tis well that I should bluster! -
> Hadst thou less worthy proved -
> Would to God - for I had loved thee more than ever wife was loved.
>
> Am I mad, that I should cherish that
> which bears but bitter fruit?
> I will pluck it from my bosom, tho' my
> heart be at the root.

"Am I mad, indeed?" she breathed.

Wyck had learned long ago that the best remedy for heartache was hard work, even when she was sorely tempted to wallow in her misery. If she'd thought she was working hard before she visited Margaret at her office, she was pushing herself even harder now - hours each evening at the barn, and non-stop during the day on various business projects. Unfortunately, much of the daytime work was at the Braithwaite home, a fact she frequently cursed.

Gavin had decided he wanted to transplant an entire bed of forsythia to a new location, and it had to be done before the weather warmed up enough for the bushes to bloom. This was proving to be daunting as it was still cold enough for the ground to be partially frozen. She exhausted herself using a pickaxe and a rototiller to break up the soil in the new planting bed, but she had to work much more carefully when it came time to dig up the forsythia. Mandy helped eagerly with the digging until a passing squirrel captured her attention.

"Some help you are," Wyck grumbled, allowing herself to steal a glance toward the house where she could see Margaret at work in her study. She quickly returned her attention to the job at hand. Gavin usually stayed near a window where he could supervise her progress and Wyck was determined that he have no reason to suspect anything.

I don't want this, she thought again and again as she dug tender roots loose.

She sat back on her heels. Love used to be something strong enough, powerful enough, to overcome any obstacle, but now... now, love felt like something that wasn't worth the risk - the risk of being left standing alone again; the risk of opening herself to someone who would know how to use her vulnerabilities against her. She was beyond denying that she was vulnerable. She was even beyond denying that she was in love with Margaret. But she was pissed about it. This did not in any way fit with her plans for her life.

"If you were going to fall in love again," she muttered angrily as she jammed a shovel into the rock-hard earth, "couldn't you at least have picked someone who wasn't married?"

And yet... lately, she found herself judging everything she did - here in the garden and at the barn - by a new standard. She wanted everything to be good enough, beautiful enough for Margaret. In this damnable set of circumstances, all she had to offer was the results of her labor. And despite her resentment at finding herself here, she had found a new, strange kind of happiness in dedicating her work to Margaret.

At night, she lay in her new bed in her newly completed bedroom, wondering if Margaret would ever share the spectacular view from the windows. She had finished the room with drapes and bedspread and pillows all chosen for Margaret, though she now doubted Margaret would ever see them. It seemed unlikely - and unwise - that Margaret would come back out to the barn with things as they stood currently.

Wyck paused now, braced against her shovel, staring up at the window of Margaret's study. *She might as well be Rapunzel in her tower.*

A few tiny yellow forsythia blooms were beginning to emerge as the transplanting was completed in late February.

Gavin came out on his scooter to inspect the results. "Good, good," he nodded in satisfaction.

"Have you decided what you want in the old forsythia bed?" Wyck asked.

"I was thinking about crepe myrtle," he said.

Wyck scowled a little as she looked around. "I don't think they'll do well here. Our winters get too cold –"

"I know all that," Gavin barked. "I've been gardening longer than you've been alive. I'm not an idiot."

"I didn't say you were," Wyck said tactfully.

"He doesn't mean it," he'd heard Margaret whisper to Wyck one day when he'd been particularly irascible. "His pain is worse, and it bothers him that I'm able to write now and he doesn't feel well enough to."

It had been the first time he'd heard them speak to one another in weeks. He knew they hadn't gotten off to a good start with one another – women were so catty that way. But they had seemed to have become friends until recently. He'd noticed how pointedly they seemed to avoid one another's company these past few weeks whenever they happened to be at the house at the same time. "They must have gotten into some kind of disagreement," he figured.

But Margaret's understanding only made him more irritable, especially because there was some truth to what she said. He had at least two more books in him – books he had been researching before his health started to decline last summer. He knew he was running out of time – "no more reprieves," his doctor had said – and it made him angry. As for Margaret's being able to write again, that was odd. For their entire marriage, she had struggled to produce a second book. Granted, her first had been too emotional and romantic for his taste, but it had been well received by those who like that sort of thing. This new book, though, had taken hold of her as nothing else had, and he found himself wondering why....

He glared up at Wyck. "I know crepe myrtle may fail here, but I still want to try them." He swept his arm around at the vast garden around them. "Do you think I created all of this by not taking the risk that some things would die? That some things would fail? If you let other people set the rules and tell you what your limits should be, how do you ever know what's possible?"

Chapter 12

MARCH GUSHED IN WITH day after day of steady rain that prevented any outdoor work being done. Wyck called Gavin to let him know she would return when the weather permitted.

Margaret was busy on campus giving and grading mid-term exams prior to their spring break.

"Hello, darling," said Taylor, peering around the edge of her door. "What are you working at so feverishly?"

Margaret kept her eyes on her computer screen, one finger running line by line down a spreadsheet lying on her desk. "It's the Friday before spring break," she reminded him, "and I am determined to get these grades in tonight. I don't want to have to come back in next week."

"They'll get mine when they get them," Taylor said airily, sitting and stretching his legs languidly.

Margaret spared him a brief glance. "If I were submitting myself for promotion, I'd be a little less cavalier about things like deadlines," she said pointedly.

He waved a perfectly manicured hand. "They can't deny me this time," he said smugly. "I was published twice last year."

Margaret, who knew from a couple of colleagues on the promotions committee that Taylor's promotion to associate professor was unlikely, said nothing further on the subject.

"So, what are your plans for break?" she asked instead.

He smiled toothily. "Oh, I'm off to D.C. Richer hunting grounds."

She paused to glance at him again. "You are being safe, aren't you?"

Taylor rolled his eyes. "Yes, of course," he said, but Margaret didn't believe him. "You know," he added, "there is such a thing as living too safely."

Margaret wasn't sure if he was talking about himself or about her.

"Have a good break, sweetie," he said, blowing her a kiss and leaving her to finish her grades.

It was fully dark by the time Margaret got home.

"Gavin?" she called as she let herself into the kitchen from the garage. "I've brought Chinese."

She heard his heavy footsteps on the second floor and then on the stairs.

"Chinese?" she heard him grumble. "You know I don't like Chinese."

"I know it's not your favorite," Margaret sighed as he entered the kitchen. "But I'm exhausted and it was on the way home."

She got two plates and set the takeout containers on the island. Despite his complaints, Gavin helped himself to large portions of each dish.

"I'm going to eat in the den," he said as he shuffled off in that direction.

Margaret stood looking at his retreating back for a few seconds, and then served herself with a shrug. He was so hard to figure out lately. She carried her plate and a glass of water upstairs to her study, eager to get back to her manuscript. As soon as she turned the desk light on, she frowned. Something was wrong.

Her manuscript pages – all written longhand – had been left in a specific arrangement, interspersed with pages on which she had made notes and jotted ideas and plot points. Things were not as she had left them. She could feel the heat rising in her face as she realized Gavin had been reading her work. It was the only explanation.

It had been an unspoken rule between them – neither would read the other's work in progress unless asked to comment on a section. "I would never have violated his privacy like this," she whispered, breathing hard.

There was nothing there to be ashamed of – just the opposite. She thought it was her best work yet, but she still felt violated. Her hands were trembling with anger as she considered what to do. Directly confronting Gavin was not always the wisest choice, as she had witnessed on numerous occasions over the years. She wondered suddenly if there had been more truth than she knew in the accusations that he had stolen work and ideas from his grad assistants. Those types of charges were not uncommon in academia, but Gavin's defense had always been so immediate and so ruthless that he invariably had come away the victor, usually at the expense of the other person's academic career.

Deciding she needed to think carefully about how to handle this, Margaret slid the manuscript into a desk drawer that she locked, pocketing the key.

The weather continued, wet and dreary, through the weekend. Not until Tuesday did weak sunshine break through to begin drying things out. Margaret, who had barely spoken to Gavin since Friday, left the house again, as she had been doing the past few days, to write at the café downtown.

Distracted by the thoughts running through her head, she paused her writing, staring out the window at nothing as she sipped her cappuccino. All weekend, she had been sorely tempted to go to Wyck to discuss Gavin's sneaking into her study to read her manuscript, but "it's no one else's business," she told herself. She wasn't even sure she could go to Wyck for a normal conversation, not after ... but she had also realized with a bit of a shock that she had no one beside Wyck in whom she could confide something so personal.

She knew hundreds of people on campus, had served on dozens of committees with them, but as she thought about it, she realized that conversations with colleagues never went beyond the university or inquiries after Gavin's health. Taylor, though he was her closest friend on campus, was completely untrustworthy. Margaret had learned long ago not to confide in him, as she had listened too often to his malicious gossip about others.

Sighing, she looked down at the pages in front of her and, giving up on getting any more writing done that day, packed up her things. When she got home, she couldn't help smiling when she saw Wyck's truck in the drive. From the garage, she went directly into the back yard. Following a wood-chipped path, she came upon Wyck, grunting as she wrestled a large shrub into a hole she had dug. Her jeans were coated with mud from the knees down, her face was sweaty with the effort of digging, but to Margaret, she'd never looked more beautiful. *How things have changed.* She smiled to herself.

"Hi," said Wyck in surprise, her face flushing at the sight of Margaret standing there.

For long seconds, they simply stared at each other.

"How are you?" Wyck asked at last.

A shadow passed over Margaret's features.

"What is it?" Wyck asked in concern.

"It's Gavin," Margaret replied. "No, not his health," she added quickly at the look on Wyck's face. "He read my manuscript. He went into my study and read my manuscript."

"Why?"

Margaret shook her head. "I honestly don't know, but..." she looked at Wyck, "I'm afraid he may suspect something about why I'm able to write again."

Wyck looked distressed. "But we haven't –"

"I know," Margaret said. "But... others have noticed there's something different about me, even if they don't know what. Taylor, of course, guesses and he guesses it's you. Gavin may not have much imagination, but he is not stupid."

Wyck frowned, staring at the ground while she twisted the heel of her boot into the mud. "What is the book about?"

Margaret laughed mirthlessly. "That's the ironic part. It isn't about us. It isn't even romantic in that way. It's about my father, my relationship with him. I just have a feeling Gavin has guessed where my inspiration is coming from."

Wyck stared at her helplessly.

Margaret gestured toward the house. "I should go in. I'm sure he heard the car."

Wyck nodded and returned to her work. Grabbing hold of the woody stems of the crepe myrtle, she glanced back to watch Margaret disappear around a turn in the path.

Inside, Gavin was at the kitchen table, chortling delightedly as Margaret entered the mudroom.

"What's so funny?" she asked.

"Your friend, the faggot," he said, grinning.

"What?"

He shook the paper and held it out for her to read. "He got himself arrested. Sex in a public restroom in Washington. Got caught with his pants down, being buggered by another man. Now, Jim will have the ammunition he needs to get rid of that fag once and for all."

"What do you mean?" Margaret asked, reading over Gavin's shoulder.

Taylor's mug shot was awful. He must have been roughed up. *That photo being published will upset him more than being arrested.*

"The university's morals clause," Gavin said with satisfaction. "This is exactly the kind of thing it covers."

Margaret bit her lip, inwardly cursing Taylor's stupidity. "It's the twenty-first century, Gavin," she said with more bravado than she felt. "What Taylor does on his time is his business. Surely, that morals clause can't touch this."

Gavin peered up at her, his eyes narrowed. "That morals clause is an agreement he made – we all made – to a privately-funded religious institution," he reminded her, using almost the exact same words she had used with Taylor himself only a few months ago. "I'll make sure he goes if it's the last thing I do," Gavin growled.

"Why?" Margaret asked in exasperation. "Why is this any of your business?"

"Because he offends me. His kind offend me," Gavin said.

Only later did it occur to Margaret that Gavin hadn't looked at her as he made that last comment.

Chapter 13

WYCK HELD HER BREATH as the man across the desk looked over her sketches and estimates.

"This looks good," he nodded. "Exactly what I had in mind."

"Wonderful, Mr. Mason," she said. "I'll get started the middle of April. I'll call you the week before to confirm a start date."

"Good." He stood to shake hands.

Wyck exhaled as he departed. Her third new job in the last two weeks. She looked at her calendar. Damn. She was getting almost more work than she could handle by herself as word of mouth spread and people saw the projects she had completed. It was getting to the point where she was either going to have to turn down work or create a waiting list. "Or hire help," she admitted reluctantly.

"My brother would be the perfect helper," Lorie Brooks had said just two days ago when she and Wyck were working in the tulip beds at Biltmore in preparation for the Festival of Flowers. Lorie was one of the full-time gardeners there and she and Wyck had become friends.

"Is he a landscaper?" Wyck had asked innocently.

"Nooo," said Lorie. "He... he hasn't worked in a while."

Wyck looked up from her weeding and mulching with a questioning glance.

Lorie looked around to make sure they were alone. "He's been in prison," she whispered.

Of all the potential reasons for his not working, this possibility had not even occurred to Wyck. "What for?" she whispered back.

Lorie looked uncomfortable. "Does it matter?"

"It does if you expect me to consider hiring him," Wyck said.

Lorie looked around again and leaned closer. "He was convicted as a sex offender."

Wyck's shock must have been reflected on her face because Lorie hastened to add, "He's not violent or anything. He... he fell in love with a minor."

Wyck's eyes narrowed. "How old?"

"Does it matter?" Lorie asked again.

"Yes! No," Wyck stammered, shaking her head. "Yes, it matters whether it was an eight-year-old or a sixteen-year-old, but no; I am not going to consider this. So no. It doesn't matter."

"Please think about it," Lorie pleaded. "He's been out of prison for almost six months and hasn't been able to find work anywhere. The... the minor was fifteen. He was one of my brother's students," she said miserably.

Wyck stared at her. "I... no. No," she said emphatically as she returned to her weeding.

"Everything is so black and white for you," Carla had said the one and only time they had almost discussed "the incident," as Wyck had come to think of it. "Everything is either right or wrong in your world, but it isn't like that for most of us. There are always other things, other people, to consider."

But Wyck, shrouded in her own pain and grief at the time, had not really heard her. Now, however, since her conversation with Lorie, she had been thinking a lot. About right and wrong, about black and white and how much leeway there could be for shades of gray.

Her initial reaction to Lorie's plea for her brother had been absolute – there could be no forgiveness for anyone who had committed such an act, but... "are there degrees of wrongness?" she had asked herself. A robbery was certainly wrong, but not as wrong as a robbery in which someone was shot and killed.

She had never known anyone who had been sexually abused as a child or teenager. She felt distinctly uncomfortable and unqualified to judge, but as she had considered, it had seemed to her that maybe there was a difference between an abduction or a violent encounter – no matter the age of the victim – versus falling in love with a teen who was a couple of years underage.

With some embarrassment, she recalled her own intense crush on Miss Stevens, her high school Latin teacher. She'd been fairly certain Miss Stevens was a lesbian, and looking back, Wyck thought how easily that relationship could have slipped past the boundary of propriety – "and legality," she realized now – as she had spent all those evenings at Miss Stevens' apartment, talking about everything sixteen-year-olds think and feel. *How in the world did she put with me?* It had never occurred to her before how her notes and flowers could have jeopardized Miss Stevens' career.

Groaning to herself as she looked at the Mason project, she pulled out her cell phone. "Lorie? It's Wyck. I know this is short notice, but could your brother meet me at my office today? Say in two hours? I'm not promising anything," she warned. "But, I'll interview him."

She busied herself with errands for a couple of hours, and returned to her office at eleven. She had no sooner taken her jacket off than there was a knock on the door.

"David?" she asked, turning to greet the tall man standing there. "I'm Wyck Fitzsimmons," she said, shaking his hand and inviting him to sit.

Hiding an embarrassed grin, she realized she'd expected a greasy, ill-kempt creep, not a clean-shaven, neatly dressed man in his mid-thirties.

David met her gaze frankly as he accepted the seat she offered. "Not what you expected?" he asked astutely. Wyck's blush was an immediate confirmation. "It's all right," he said with a wan smile. "It's not what I expected, either." He shifted in his chair. "Thank you for agreeing to see me. I know my sister pushed you into this."

"You understand that this is only an interview," Wyck said. Now that she was face to face with him, she was unsure about how to proceed. "David, I need to ask you some questions, not out of curiosity, but..."

"I understand," he said in his soft-spoken voice.

"I don't know anything about sex offenders beyond what I see in the news, but one of the things that seems to be a common theme is that they re-offend," she said, deciding to be honest with her concerns. "It would ruin me if I hired someone who..." She stopped, at a loss for the right words.

He nodded. "They – we often do," he admitted. "That's why part of my probation involves mandatory weekly group and individual therapy sessions. And polygraphs periodically as well. You have to know about those things up front because they would impact my hours." He frowned. "I can only assure you that I will do whatever it takes to make sure I don't go back to prison. Because if I violate my probation, I'm going back for life."

Wyck looked at him closely. She could see something haunted in his eyes, and she felt herself shiver involuntarily.

"What else would I need to know?" she asked.

"My probation officer would probably want to meet you and ask you about where I'm working," David explained. "I can't work alone at any location where there could be minors. I don't know if these restrictions will allow me to be of any use to you," he said matter-of-factly.

"We could probably work around those things," Wyck said. "Now... how much do you know about gardening and landscaping?"

An hour later, Wyck locked up her office and headed toward the stairs, having promised David that she would seriously consider his application. He was actually more knowledgeable than she had expected. Lorie had convinced him to take advantage of the prison's agriculture program. It had primarily involved growing produce for the prison's use, but the principles were sound.

"It's not like I could go back to teaching," he had said with a wry sense of humor. "It's kind of surprising how many places you can't work if you're not allowed contact with kids."

Wyck sighed as she descended the stairs. *What a waste*, she thought. She reached the lobby and stepped out into the marble-tiled foyer where she saw Gavin Braithwaite emerging from the law offices that occupied most of the main floor of the building. He didn't see her as he made his way out to the sidewalk with the aid of a cane.

Wyck followed him out, expecting to see Margaret waiting for him. To her surprise, Gavin got into the driver's seat of the black Lincoln that had always been parked in the garage, and she realized he must have come downtown alone.

Shrugging, she went two blocks to where her truck was parked. She was scheduled back out at the Biltmore for the next couple of days, but the remainder of this day was promised to Mandy for a hike out to the falls at DuPont State Forest.

"Oh, my God."

Margaret looked up in surprise as Taylor let himself into her office and quickly shut the door, leaning against it as if bracing for it to be bashed in.

"Oh, my God," he repeated, dropping limply into one of the chairs.

He looked terrible. She had never seen him so disheveled – his tie was loosely done, his shirt was wrinkled under his jacket, and there were dark circles under his eyes.

"I didn't think it would make the papers here," he whined.

Margaret sat back. "It's a small campus. Once they got word of it, of course it spread," she said, trying to be sympathetic.

He grabbed a folder off the desk and fanned himself. "My nerves are shot," he said. "Everyone is whispering and watching me."

"Well, what did you expect?" Margaret very nearly blurted, but bit it back. Aloud, she said, "It will pass," though she wasn't sure how long that might take. Taylor had made a lot of enemies on campus and they were delighted at the opportunity for some payback. "Have you... has anyone talked to you... officially?"

He stopped fanning and looked at her, blanching under his sun-bed tan. "What do you know?" he asked weakly.

Grimacing a little, Margaret said, "I've heard there will most likely be an inquiry," she said tactfully. "Do you have a lawyer?"

Taylor's eyes closed and he looked as if he might swoon. "Do I need one?"

When Margaret didn't say anything, he opened his eyes. "Gavin."

"I'm sorry," Margaret said softly.

"I'm ruined," he moaned. "I'm ruined." He fanned the folder agitatedly.

"Maybe not," Margaret said. "You might be able to negotiate something."

The folder paused. "Like what?"

"I don't know," Margaret said, throwing her hands up impatiently. "Maybe your resignation in return for a reference? I have no idea. Talk to a lawyer."

"Oh, God, I don't know how much more my nerves can take," Taylor whimpered, fanning himself again.

It's like talking to Mrs. Bennett, Margaret thought, shaking her head.

Lorie Brooks stopped on the path near the azaleas, listening. There, she caught the sound she was listening for – someone in the largest clump of azaleas was singing "Barbara Allen".

"Wyck!"

Lorie reached in, parting the branches. Wyck straightened up from the Biltmore azaleas where she'd been crouching, nearly swallowed by the bushes which were bursting with color.

Lorie's eyes shone with tears as she grasped Wyck's hand, pulling her out of the bush and said, "I can't thank you enough for hiring David. My whole family is so relieved."

Wyck smiled. "You don't have to thank me. So far, he's proving to be a fantastic employee. He gets to work early and works hard while he's there."

"And he's quiet," she nearly added.

One of Wyck's concerns about hiring David - anyone, actually - was that she would have to put up with a constant stream of idle chatter. Quiet and solitude were some of the aspects of her work that she most enjoyed.

"We'll work together on each new project until I'm sure you're comfortable," she'd told him, "and long enough to make sure who is going to be at the house."

David, once he knew what she wanted of him, was content to work in silence, speaking only when he had a question. Wyck was surprised at how comfortable he was to be around - "again, not what I expected," she would have said, and had started asking his opinion on various aspects of her designs.

"What do you mean?" he asked defensively the first time she asked him what he thought about her placement of a flowerbed.

"It's not a trick question," she assured him. "I want to know what you think."

Hesitant at first, David was demonstrating a good eye for detail, and soon was anticipating Wyck's needs, retrieving the needed equipment from the truck before she could ask. Their first project together at the Braithwaite house was to rebuild one of the crumbling stone walls. They carefully disassembled the existing wall to reuse the rock, and began digging for better drainage so that the wall could settle on a more solid bed.

"I've been putting this off," Wyck panted as they shuffled the heavy stones, keeping an eye out for any snakes emerging to begin warming themselves in the welcome April sun. "Two people will make this so much easier."

David paused, looking around admiringly. "This place is really something," he said.

"Yes it is."

They were both startled by Gavin's voice behind them as he rolled silently along on his scooter.

"Who are you?" Gavin asked gruffly.

Wyck stepped forward. "Dr. Gavin Braithwaite, my new assistant, David Brooks," she said.

David stepped forward to shake Gavin's hand. "Sir," he said politely.

"I've gotten busy enough that I needed an extra set of hands," Wyck explained.

Gavin's narrowed eyes studied David intently. "You look familiar," he said.

"That's probably because I was one of your students at St. Aloysius," David said.

Gavin nodded. "Ah, yes. Brooks. Now I remember. History major."

"Yes, sir," David said, looking pleasantly surprised at Gavin's memory.

"I thought you were going to be a teacher," Gavin said.

The expression on David's face shifted as Wyck quickly said, "He's not the first to decide that teaching is more hassle than it's worth."

"Hmmph," Gavin grumped. "True enough." He turned his attention to their work.

"We'll lay a perforated drain line to divert the water coming down this hill," Wyck explained. "And the new wall should stay put for a hundred years."

"Is this a garden party I wasn't invited to?" Margaret asked, appearing out of nowhere.

Wyck cursed herself as she felt her face grow hot at the light in Margaret's eyes. She began the introductions again. "Dr. Margaret Braithwaite, this is David Brooks, my new assistant."

"Dr. Braithwaite," David said, stepping forward to shake Margaret's hand. "I'll just get back to work," he mumbled, turning back to the ditch they were digging.

Wyck talked to Gavin a few minutes more, outlining the plans for the next few weeks as Margaret hung back, watching.

"Oh, and I've got tickets to Biltmore's spring flower show," she said. "I'd be honored to take you. It really is spectacular."

Gavin grimaced and declined, but "I'd like to see it," Margaret said, as Wyck had hoped she would. They made plans for the following week and then Gavin and Margaret returned to the house.

Wyck waited until she was sure they were out of earshot before saying, "I didn't realize there was a connection here. Are you all right?"

David nodded. "I didn't know whose house it was." He shrugged. "I wouldn't have thought he'd remember me, anyway."

"But he did. Do you think he remembers anything else?"

He shrugged again. "It was in all the local papers. Who knows?"

Wyck looked back toward the house. "I think his memory is longer than we know."

"You were right," Margaret said, taking in the abundance of color as she and Wyck toured the Biltmore's spring gardens. "These gardens are magnificent at this time of year."

She bent to look more closely at an orange tulip. "Such an underrated flower," she said. "So simple compared to something like a rose, but look at the perfection."

Wyck, who was having a hard time looking at anything but Margaret, squatted down next to her, reaching out for the same flower, cradling Margaret's hand as she did so.

"We don't have any of these, do we?" Margaret asked softly, letting the contact linger.

"No." Wyck stood abruptly and walked a short distance away.

"What is it?" Margaret asked, following her.

Wyck focused on the vines climbing the ornate lattice-work partition and said, "Sometimes... I want you so much, it hurts."

"I know," Margaret murmured. She sighed. "Let's walk."

As Wyck led her around other sections of the gardens, Margaret filled her in on Taylor's situation.

"Gavin is determined to have the university use this to get rid of him. Taylor will probably just resign without a hearing."

Wyck frowned. "How can they do that? This had nothing to do with his teaching."

Margaret paused to admire a bed of alyssum and dianthus - all new words to her as she learned the vocabulary of flowers. "We all sign a morals clause when we're hired. It's rarely enforced - I mean, there have been affairs and divorces and all the typical goings on, but Gavin has made it a personal vendetta to get rid of Taylor." She bit her lip. "He keeps saying Taylor's kind offends him."

Wyck turned to look at her. "What do you think he means by that?"

Margaret's face reflected her worry. "He's been acting so strangely - reading my manuscript, calling me all hours to see where I am, things he never did before. It's as if he has guessed... about us."

"But we haven't done anything," Wyck protested.

"I don't know that that would matter to Gavin," Margaret said. "He's not emotional or romantic, but he is possessive of what's his, and he's very good at reading people." She looked at Wyck, allowing her love to show without reservation or guard. "I don't want to hurt him, but I don't know how well I've been able to hide my feelings."

Wyck's hand twitched as she started to reach for Margaret's hand, and stopped herself.

"You know," Margaret murmured, "Taylor would say if we're going to be accused, we should at least enjoy what we're being accused of."

Wyck gave her a sardonic smile. "Under the circumstances, Taylor is probably the last person we should be taking advice from."

Gavin sat at his computer in his office at home, jotting notes as he peered intently at the computer screen. "I knew I remembered him," he muttered to himself as he wrote. He pulled his Rolodex near and flipped through the cards inside. Finding the one he sought, he tugged it loose.

He reached for the telephone and punched the numbers on the card. "Terry? Gavin Braithwaite... Fine, fine. Listen, I've got something for you... What? No, this isn't about a new book. It's something else entirely. You remember that child molester about ten years ago? The schoolteacher who molested a fifteen-year-old boy? Well, he's out of prison and back in Asheville now... What? Well, maybe he's legally allowed to be out, but isn't the public legally entitled to know where he is and what he's up to?" He sat breathing heavily for several seconds as he listened. "I know exactly where you can find him. Be here tomorrow morning."

Chapter 14

MARGARET WALKED ACROSS THE quad, noticing for the first time how beautiful the campus's landscaping was. Beds of flowers were scattered everywhere; white and pink dogwoods were in full bloom, as were the cherry and crabapple trees. And redbud. She'd discovered that redbuds were one of her favorites. She smiled as she contemplated how her world had changed since Wyck's arrival in it.

She climbed the stairs of Braithwaite Hall to her second floor office and saw Wyck holding a piece of paper against the frosted glass of her door, writing a note.

"What is it?" Margaret asked as she pushed through the stairwell doors.

Wyck whipped around at the sound of her voice. "He... I can't believe... What is wrong with him?" Wyck stammered, incoherent in her anger.

Alarmed, Margaret unlocked her door and ushered Wyck inside, closing and locking the door behind them. "Sit," she said, taking the neighboring chair and Wyck's hand. "Tell me what has you so upset?"

Wyck's jaw worked back and forth a few times. "David, my new employee, he's... he's recently out of prison... for molesting a minor." She saw the look of revulsion on Margaret's face. "I know, that was my reaction at first, too. I work with his sister at the Biltmore, and she told me more about it. He was a high school history teacher, and got involved with a fifteen-year-old. A boy. It was stupid, and it was illegal, but it wasn't rape." She closed her eyes. "I'm not making excuses for what he did, nor is he, but he's now a registered sex offender, and will be labeled that way for the rest of his life."

Trying to set aside her own distaste over the story, Margaret asked, "But what has upset you so?"

Wyck's nostrils flared. "Last week, when I introduced you both to him, Gavin remembered him as being a student of his from St. Aloysius. Apparently, Gavin remembered a bit more than that, because this morning, as we were working, a reporter and a photographer showed up at your house while we were working, asking questions."

Margaret's hand flew to her mouth. "Gavin called them?"

"It seems so."

"What did you do?" Margaret asked, aghast.

"Stand your ground and don't say anything," Wyck had said in an undertone to David as she stepped forward.

The reporter was firing questions, "Why did you return to Asheville? How do the neighbors around –" he consulted his notes, reading off David's address – "feel about having a child molester in the neighborhood? Why are you doing this kind of menial labor?"

David had refused to respond, turning his back on the two men and continuing to stack rock. Wyck had stepped in between them. Ignoring the photographer, whose camera was clicking madly, she'd said to the reporter, "Mr. Brooks is abiding by every term and condition of his probation. That's all we have to say."

Turning on her instead, the reporter had persisted, "Why did you hire a known child molester?"

"I thought he deserved a second chance," Wyck had responded. "Now, if you'll excuse us, we have work to do."

"They finally left when they realized we weren't going to say anything further," Wyck said angrily. "They just stood there watching us stack rock for about fifteen minutes and eventually got bored when nothing more exciting happened."

"How did they know where he lives?" Margaret asked in puzzlement.

"He has to register," Wyck said. "It's on the Internet."

Margaret stared down at Wyck's hand still holding tightly to her own. "Was Gavin there?" she asked quietly.

Wyck nodded. "Inside, watching from the kitchen. I saw him once they left." She shook her head. "Why would he do that?"

Margaret shook her head. "I don't know, except to say that, for Gavin, things are black and white."

Wyck was reminded of her own initial reaction to David's story. "That part I can understand. Gavin could have told me he's not welcome to work at your house. But to actively try and sabotage the guy's effort to rebuild his life... I can't understand that," she said. She looked up at Margaret. "This was beyond black and white, Margaret. This was... an attack. It was vindictive. I don't know if I can continue to work for someone as homophobic as Gavin," she said in a strained voice.

Stricken, Margaret squeezed Wyck's hand and, "Please, please don't say that. If I didn't have you to look forward to - even though it's only now and then - I don't know how I would manage." Her voice cracked and her eyes filled with tears.

She placed a hand on Wyck's cheek and, tentatively, drew her near. Tenderly, they kissed, long and deep, soft mouths sending shockwaves of desire coursing through both of them. Resting their foreheads against each other, Wyck said weakly, "I'll stay, for you."

"I'm sorry, Wyck," said Mr. Mason. "But my wife and I agree; we don't want someone like that working anywhere near our home and our kids."

Wyck nodded wordlessly and turned to go. This was the third such conversation she'd had with her clients since David's story, complete with photos of him and Wyck, had come out in the paper last week – largely sensationalized, with extensive portions of it drawn from the speculation of supposed experts in the field of treating sexual predators. Wyck guessed that was the only way the reporter could get enough material for his story as neither she nor David had spoken to him, but it didn't seem to matter. The first two times clients cancelled with her, she'd tried to argue that he'd served his ten years, that he wasn't the same person, that he deserved a second chance, but to no avail. In this latest case, she'd considered pointing out to the Masons that their "kids" were hardly at risk as they were in college and rarely home, but she decided she would be wasting her breath.

Clenching her jaw, she slammed her truck door and sat, stewing. She still had enough work to support herself, but losing these jobs meant she didn't really have the overload for which she'd hired David in the first place, only "that's the least of my worries," she would have said.

Her voice mail at the office had been filled with vitriolic messages, mostly from people who had no connection to her, some of them hateful, calling her horrible names and saying she deserved to burn in hell for hiring a child molester. It had been even worse for David, as his address had been published. After two bricks through windows, his landlord had told him he couldn't put up with this anymore, and, though he had no legal right to break the lease, had asked David to look for another place to live. Various vehicles had been seen cruising slowly by his place; his car had been vandalized with neon orange paint spelling out "pervert" and "cock-sucker" across the body. The neighbors had presented David with a petition with over a hundred signatures, demanding that he leave the neighborhood.

Pulling out her cell phone, Wyck called him. "Don't bother coming to the Masons'," she said when he answered.

"You lost that one, too?" he asked quietly.

"They told me when I got here this morning."

"Wyck, you have to let me quit before you lose all your business."

"No," she said stubbornly. "I'm the one who decides who works for me, not narrow-minded, bigoted –"

"Wyck," he cut in, "we're not talking about simple prejudice because we're gay," – one of the few personal conversations they'd had – "If we were, I would agree with you, we shouldn't give in, but this... this is harder than that. I did something people find unforgiveable. You're making business decisions based on your emotions, and that is not good business."

She knew he was right, and it galled her all the more that she might very well have to let him go just to keep the business afloat. But not today.

"How are you with carpentry?" she asked.

"Why?" he asked with a short laugh.

"I could use an extra pair of hands putting up my kitchen cabinets," she said. "I had the next three days set aside for the Mason job, so... seems like a good time to get some other things done." She gave him directions and headed home.

Pulling out of the Masons' driveway, she saw a black pickup pass her. The occupants of the pickup – two white guys in their twenties – craned their heads around to stare at her as they passed. As she drove away, she noticed the black truck had turned around and was behind her. They continued to follow her as she left the outskirts of Asheville. Without warning, she pulled into a gas station and watched them as they drove by, still turning to stare at her.

When she pulled out a few minutes later, she saw no sign of the pickup and continued on her way home. Mandy welcomed her when she got out.

"No, it's not a holiday," Wyck smiled as she rubbed the soft coat. "We're just going to work here today."

Mandy's ears pricked up and she turned to look at the drive. A few minutes later, David's old Ford Taurus pulled into view, the orange spray paint covered over with patches of black spray paint.

"Nice paint job," she said sarcastically. "Going for North Carolina redneck?"

He shrugged as he got out. "Until I can afford to have it repainted, this will have to do." He looked around. "All this is yours?"

"Ours," she corrected, patting Mandy. "This is my partner, Mandy."

"Your partner?" he chuckled, rubbing Mandy's head.

"The best kind," Wyck smiled. "We never fight. She's always in a good mood. It works well. Come in."

He followed her inside, nodding his approval at what he saw. "This is really something," he said admiringly.

"Thanks," she said. "I've been putting the kitchen off only because I can't handle the cabinets by myself, so... if you're willing?"

"Sure," he said, rolling up his sleeves. "Just tell me what to do."

For the next couple of days they worked, getting all the upper cabinets hung in place first.

"Have you found a place to live yet?" Wyck asked as she screwed a cabinet to the stud behind it.

"No," said David, holding the cabinet steady for her. "No one will rent to me right now. My parents live outside Asheville, so we've talked and I think I'll move in with them for a few months, until things die down. People will forget."

Wyck glanced down at him. "You think?"

"I hope."

They finished the uppers late that afternoon. "I'll put crown moulding along the tops to finish them off," she pointed out. "Tomorrow, we'll tackle the lowers. They'll take longer. The floor isn't level," she explained, "so we'll have to shim the bases to keep everything square."

She and Mandy walked him out. "Let's get started at eight –"

She broke off as Mandy raced down the lane, barking. Wyck tore after her, yelling. Mandy was standing at the end of the lane, still barking with her hackles up as Wyck heard the sound of tires driving away down the road.

David ran up to them. "What was it?"

Wyck shook her head. "Not sure. She never acts like this. Some-one drove away."

They walked back to the barn where David got into his car.

"Be careful driving home," Wyck said.

"I will."

Chapter 15

GAVIN WAS SITTING IN the kitchen when he heard Wyck's truck pull up. Curious, he watched out the window as she and Mandy made their way with a wheelbarrow and tools back toward the wall they'd been working on.

"Hmmph," he snorted. Heaving himself to his feet, he lumbered out to the garage and got on his scooter.

"Where's your helper?" he asked a few minutes later as he wheeled down the path to where she was on her knees, resuming the interrupted stacking of the rock for the retaining wall.

She kept working, her back to him. "He's working another job," she said curtly.

Gavin's bushy eyebrows furrowed. "You haven't fired him?"

He thought perhaps she hadn't heard him as several seconds passed without a reply, but then Wyck stood and turned to him.

"No, Gavin," she said coldly. "I haven't fired him. Unlike you, I figure if the legal system has punished him and laid out his probation requirements, it is not my job to continue punishing him. Why can't you let this go?"

Gavin's face became livid, with splotchy patches of red rising in each cheek. He looked quite deranged as he shouted, "Some things can never be forgiven!" His jowls quivered as he trembled in his fury.

Alarmed at his reaction, Wyck stared at him. "If you have anything to say in regard to the garden, fine. Otherwise..." and, deliberately, she turned her back on him again, and went back to her work.

"You're fired!" he barked.

She wiggled a rock into place in the wall and then slowly, she got to her feet and turned to face him once more. "Do you mean that?" she asked quietly.

"Yes, I do!"

"Fine." She bent to load her shovels and trowels and rakes back into her wheelbarrow. Holding her sledgehammer with trembling hands, she resisted the urge to use it on the wall, wanting to smash the rock to bits. Instead, she placed it also in the wheelbarrow and marched past Gavin, calling Mandy to her. She threw everything into the bed of her truck, fighting the angry tears stinging her eyes. This was her biggest contract, the one she counted on to keep everything else afloat.

"You're being stupid," hissed a voice inside her head. "This is not smart."

"I don't care," she shot back. "I will not work for that bastard any longer."

She opened the truck door for Mandy, and slammed it as she climbed in. Putting the truck in gear, she squealed her tires as she pulled out, snorting with satisfaction as she looked in the rear-view mirror and saw the black tire marks she'd left in the driveway.

Margaret glanced out her office window and saw that it had started to rain. "Brilliant timing, as always," she muttered, pulling her purse and an umbrella off her coat rack. The late April weather had warmed enough that she hadn't worn a coat to work that morning. Trotting through the parking lot, her pants legs were soaking wet by the time she got into her car. She shook the umbrella and laid it on the floor on the passenger side.

She drove home through the spring downpour, grateful for automatic garage doors as she turned into the driveway. No sooner had she entered the mudroom than the front doorbell rang. Grumbling, she went to answer it, wondering where Gavin was. To her surprise, a police officer was standing there wearing a neon yellow rain slicker over his uniform, water dripping from the visor of his cap.

Consulting a notebook in his hand, he said, "I'm looking for Margaret Braithwaite."

"I'm Dr. Margaret Braithwaite," said Margaret, startled.

"Dr. Braithwaite, do you know a landscaper named Mary Fitzsimmons?" asked the officer.

Margaret's heart stopped. "Yes," she gasped. "I'm sorry, please come in." She stepped back to let him in. "What's happened? What's wrong?"

Gavin emerged from the den wearing crumpled khakis and his old maroon cardigan. He looked as if he had been sleeping. "What is it?"

Impatiently, Margaret shushed him.

"Did you receive any messages from her today?" the officer asked.

"I... I don't know," she said. "I was teaching all day. I haven't even checked my phone. Why?"

"Your number was the last number called from her cell phone," he said, jotting notes as he spoke. "Are you a friend or relation?"

"I'm a friend," said Margaret. "She doesn't have any family nearby. Please, what's happened?" She squeezed her eyes shut, praying it wasn't that Wyck had been killed in a car accident.

"Could we check your phone, please?" he asked politely, but firmly. Clearly, he wasn't going to tell her what had happened until he got more answers.

"What is going on?" Gavin asked as they walked past him to the kitchen where Margaret dug her phone from her purse.

She saw that there was indeed a voicemail from Wyck.

"Could you put it on speaker, please?" the officer asked.

With another fervent prayer that there was nothing incriminating in Wyck's message, Margaret pushed the buttons. In a moment, Wyck's voice came over the speaker, saying, "Margaret, Gavin and I had a little confrontation about David this morning. He fired me and I walked off the job, so..." She sounded angry. "... I don't know when I'll see you again. Please call me when you get this message. I – never mind. Please call me."

Margaret looked up in shock at Gavin who had followed them into the kitchen. "Gavin, what did you do?"

"What was this confrontation about, sir?" the officer asked seriously.

Gavin sat heavily. Margaret pulled out a chair for the police officer and took another herself.

"Sir?" the officer prompted.

Looking disgruntled, Gavin said, "It was about the man she hired to help her. David Brooks. He's a –"

"He's a registered sex offender," the officer said. "What was the argument?"

"I didn't think she should have hired him," Gavin said defensively.

Risking Gavin's wrath, Margaret said, "My husband leaked a story to the newspaper that he was working for Wyck – Ms. Fitzsimmons."

"I know about the newspaper story," the officer said. "According to our files, there have been multiple reports recently of vandalism and threats to both of them since it came out."

"What?" Margaret gasped.

"I didn't know anything about that," Gavin said, frowning.

"Where were both of you this afternoon about two?" he asked.

"I was on campus, teaching. I have a two o'clock lecture," Margaret said.

"I was here all day," Gavin blustered impatiently. "Now what is this about?"

"They were assaulted, Fitzsimmons and Brooks, this afternoon, in a field where they were working," the officer said. Margaret's hand flew to her mouth in horror. "It appears they were beaten by more than one assailant, probably with baseball bats. They're alive, but in critical condition."

Margaret's eyes filled with tears and even Gavin looked abashed.

The police officer consulted his notes. "And there was a dog... a golden retriever. She was beaten as well."

"Is she alive?" Margaret breathed, begging for the right answer.

He nodded. "She's at an animal hospital... Blue Ridge. The number was on her tags. Do you know who she belongs to?"

"She's Wyck's," Margaret said.

"You say she doesn't have any family in the area?" the officer asked.

Margaret shook her head. "They're all up in New Hampshire somewhere. What hospital are they in?"

"Mission."

"Would they – can I see her?" Margaret asked.

"I don't know, ma'am," he said sympathetically. "Since you're not family... but tell them you were the last one she called and that we've been to speak to you. Maybe that will help." He stood. "If we think of any other questions, we may be back in touch."

"Of course," Margaret said, walking him back toward the front door.

As soon as he left, Margaret returned to the kitchen where Gavin still sat at the table.

"Where are you going?" he asked as she put her raincoat on, tugging her purse onto her shoulder.

"Where do you think I'm going?" Margaret replied icily. She turned to him and said, "I don't know if you've ever prayed, Gavin, but you'd better pray now."

Margaret sat next to the hospital bed, holding Wyck's hand, practically the only part of her that wasn't broken, though her knuckles were scraped and bruised. Her face was swollen and discolored, her eyes mere slits in the middle of the puffy flesh where she'd been hit, one eyebrow cut badly enough that it required stitches; her lips were split, with dried blood in the cracks; more dried blood caked her hair where the ER staff had done a cursory cleaning to check her scalp for any other cuts or injuries. Her left thigh was broken and was strapped in a brace to immobilize it. Several ribs were also broken and had punctured a lung, requiring a chest tube to suction out the blood and excess fluid from her chest cavity. Nearly every inch of her was bruised and battered.

Her eyes dry now, Margaret sat for hours, praying as she had never prayed before, whispering to Wyck, "Please, please don't leave me."

The critical care supervisor had allowed Margaret in when she heard her story, but couldn't give her any information on David's condition. "Privacy regulations," she said apologetically.

"She looks worse than she is," the nurse had said when Margaret gasped in horror upon first seeing Wyck. "She's sedated to keep her still, but she can probably hear you. Talk to her, let her know you're here."

Margaret nodded off sometime during the night, her head dropping to her chest. She startled awake as Wyck stirred with a moan. Margaret sat up, groaning as she grabbed her cramped neck.

"Margaret?" Wyck mumbled through lips that couldn't move.

"I'm here," Margaret said, standing to lean over the bed. Tenderly, she placed a hand on Wyck's cheek. "I'm here."

Wyck's eyes could only open the tiniest bit as she looked around to see where she was. "David?" she asked.

"I don't know," Margaret said. "He's here in the critical care unit also, but they won't tell me anything about him."

Wyck gave a sharp intake of breath as she remembered. "Mandy?"

"The police said she's alive and at an animal hospital. I'll call and check on her when they open," Margaret said soothingly.

"What time is it?" Wyck asked.

Margaret looked at her watch. "It's two a.m.," she said with surprise. "So, everything happened about twelve hours ago. What did happen? Do you remember?"

Wyck thought for several seconds. "We were planting trees on a farm... they came out of nowhere... three of them with bats... we used our shovels, but..." Tears leaked out of the corners of her eyes.

"Shhh," Margaret said, reaching for a tissue to wipe the tears away. "It's all right now."

Wyck tried to move, and cried out in pain.

"Please stay still," Margaret said. "I'll get your nurse," but the nurse came into the room just then.

"Would you mind waiting outside for a moment?" she asked.

Margaret nodded and stepped out. There, in the corridor, were three people, a man and woman who appeared to be in their seventies and a stocky thirty-something brunette. The younger woman came over to Margaret.

"I'm David's sister, Lorie," she said. "I work with Wyck at the Biltmore. How is she?"

"I'm Margaret Braithwaite, a friend of Wyck's." She shook her head. "I don't really know. Broken leg, broken ribs, punctured lung... How about David?"

Lorie's eyes filled with tears. "His arm was broken so badly it was poking through his skin in the field... the doctors are worried about infection. His face, the eye and cheek bones are broken and he has internal bleeding..."

"I'm sorry," Margaret said, horrified.

"I guess they're lucky to be alive," Lorie murmured, dabbing at her eyes with a tissue.

"Yes," Margaret realized with a shudder. "They both are."

"Why?"

That question reverberated – through Gavin's mind and in Margaret's anguished voice when she finally got home around six a.m. to find Gavin sitting in the den in a darkened house.

"There must be a reason," Margaret said with a deadly calm to her voice as she sat on the ottoman facing him.

"...this is our secret... if you ever tell anyone, something horrible will happen..."

Margaret started to reach for a lamp, but "No!" Gavin said. "Leave it off."

Patiently, then, she waited in the dark, and he knew she would keep waiting.

She could hear his breathing, fast and shallow, and wondered what on earth could be so difficult.

"When I was a boy," he began at last, "I was sent to a boys' school. Sixth grade through twelfth. When I was thirteen, some of the older boys started teasing me, calling me 'pretty' and 'girly' and... one day, three of them came into my room, and they..."

"The more you fight, the harder this will be," says one while the other two pin his shoulders and head down against the bed, mashing his face against the sheets. Gavin struggles to breathe while the third grabs the waist of his pants and yanks them down around his knees. "...this is our secret," they hiss in his ear while behind him, the third boy thrusts and pants. When Gavin cries out in pain, they stuff part of the sheet into his mouth, gagging him as the boy behind him gasps with his release. He pulls away and they switch places, keeping Gavin pinned to the bed until they all have a turn...

At this point, Gavin's breathing was so ragged Margaret was afraid he might faint, but in a hoarse whisper he continued. "I couldn't stop them... I wasn't strong enough to... I'm not... I'm not..." He sobbed into his hands, the first time Margaret had seen him cry in all their years of marriage, and she knew, without being told, that he was speaking this secret aloud to another person for the first time in his life.

She leaned forward from the ottoman, and wrapped her arms around his shoulders as he shook with the force of his sobs. She held him until he began to quiet and then sat back.

"I'm glad you told me," she said, understanding at last. "It explains a lot."

He wiped his eyes with a handkerchief. "Is Wyck badly hurt?"

"Yes, she is," Margaret said. "And David is even worse. Both of them could have been killed."

He shook his head. "That's not what I wanted."

"I know," she said. "But you are partially responsible."

He nodded. "Tell Wyck, when she's better, tell her that I'd like her to come back." His jaw worked back and forth a couple of times before he added, "Brooks, too."

Margaret reached for his hand. "I think it would mean more if you told them."

He nodded again and then said, in the most humble tone Margaret had ever heard him use, "There is one other thing I need to know... I know I'm not an easy man to live with, and you're still so young, so beautiful, but... are you... have you...?"

"I have never been unfaithful to you, Gavin," Margaret said quietly.

Chapter 16

WHEN MANDY WAS READY to be released from the animal hospital, Gavin suggested they bring her to their home so they could keep an eye on her – "something I would have done anyway," Margaret was prepared to argue, but it hadn't been necessary. Though Gavin had shown no sign of wanting to speak again about what had happened to him as a youngster, he had been showing a gentler, more humble side of himself – a side that prompted him to insist the new dog bed be placed in the den near his chair.

Mandy's beautiful coat was marred by several shaved areas where lacerations had had to be stitched, and one of her rear legs was in a cast, but she was her usual sweet-tempered self, even when the stitched places had to be gently cleansed. She gave Margaret's hand a small lick as the wounds were dabbed with an antiseptic pad and a gooey ointment, and then settled back with a sigh into her bed.

"She's fine," Margaret said soothingly to Wyck who had been frantic about what would happen to Mandy.

She was almost as frantic about calling her clients. "I can't just not show up for jobs," she insisted. Margaret, in the end, had agreed to bring Wyck's day planner in which were the telephone numbers she needed. Nearly all of her clients, when she called them, had already heard about what had happened, and reassured her the work would be waiting when she was healthy again. "I'll call you as soon as I know a date," she told them.

Gavin accompanied Margaret to the hospital when Wyck was moved out of the critical care unit nearly a week after the attack. When Margaret wheeled him into the hospital room, his face had turned ashen at the sight of Wyck's injuries, including the chest tube that was still siphoning blood out of her chest cavity.

"When you're ready," he said in a conciliatory tone, "I would very much like for you to return to work at our house. Brooks, too."

Wyck had stared at him through eyes still blackened and puffy. "David is still in critical care with an arm so badly infected, there is a chance he may lose it."

Gavin sat there, stricken. Margaret laid a hand on his shoulder, and Wyck averted her eyes from this new closeness they seemed to share.

"Won't you come home with us for a while?" Margaret pleaded another week later when Wyck was finally ready to be released from the hospital, her fractured femur now stabilized by surgical hardware. The chest tube had been removed, though her broken ribs were still excruciatingly painful as she hopped on crutches.

"No," said Wyck flatly, a dark expression shadowing her face, which still bore scars and bruises from the beating she had taken.

"Wyck," Margaret said, "Gavin is sincerely sorry about everything."

"Why are you making excuses for him?" Wyck asked accusingly.

"I'm not!" Margaret protested in shock. "Nothing excuses what he did, but... there is a reason. Please. Let us help you."

"Thank you, Margaret," Wyck said stiffly. "But I don't believe I could accept help from Gavin under any circumstances."

"What about accepting help from me?" Margaret asked.

Wyck looked away and didn't answer that.

"I would appreciate a ride to get my truck," she said. "I think it's still at the police lot."

Margaret insisted on following Wyck home. "Mandy can't jump into the truck and you can't lift her," she pointed out reasonably. Wyck had no choice but to agree.

When Margaret came to pick Wyck up from the hospital, Mandy was in the back seat. Wyck couldn't speak for long minutes as she dropped her crutches and awkwardly tried to get her injured leg into the back seat and get close enough to get her arms around the dog whose tail thumped happily as Wyck squeezed her.

Margaret drove her to the police impound lot where Wyck was able to claim her truck. When they got to the barn, Wyck slid down from the truck, grimacing a little when her left leg impacted the ground. She pulled her crutches out and limped to the door, followed by Margaret and Mandy, also limping along on her casted leg.

"Oh, Wyck," Margaret breathed, looking around as she entered the barn. "Everything you've done..."

New furniture filled the main level, creating cozy seating around the woodstove. The floorboards, pine on this level, were laid. The old board Wyck had carved to fit against the hearthstone lay snugged seamlessly against the contours of the stone. Wyck turned on a stained-glass lamp that cast a warm glow over everything, including a new cherry dining table.

"Did you make this, too?" Margaret asked in astonishment, running her hands over the smooth wood.

Wyck nodded modestly. "Not the chairs. And the kitchen's not done yet," she shrugged, "but everything else is pretty much finished."

"May I?" Margaret asked, pointing upstairs.

Wyck nodded, helping Mandy get comfortable in her bed.

Margaret gasped as she entered the master bedroom. Her hands clasped over her chest, she took in everything, all the details – "all the love," she whispered – recognizing that it was for her. Though they had never dared talk about the possibility of living together, she knew Wyck had prepared a place where they could live and love and make a life together. She stood for a long time before she went downstairs where Wyck was easing back into an armchair, trying to hide the pain in her ribs.

"It's beautiful," Margaret said softly.

Wyck looked at her without saying a word, but her eyes spoke volumes.

Margaret squatted next to the chair, taking Wyck's hand. "I know what you want, but I can't... I can't leave him, and I can't hurt him... not now."

Wyck nodded, pulling her hand free. "Thank you for taking care of Mandy," she said matter-of-factly. "I think I need to rest now."

Margaret got to her feet, wishing there were something she could say to make this better. "I'll call you tomorrow?"

"Sure."

Wyck remained seated as Margaret reluctantly let herself out the door. Mandy struggled to her feet and limped over to sit beside the chair as Wyck buried her face in Mandy's neck and wept.

Margaret walked across campus accompanied by glorious May weather – brilliant sunshine and temperatures in the upper sixties. Students lounged about in the grass, some playing Frisbee or football, others cramming in some last-minute studying before final exams as they celebrated the end of the academic year – but for Margaret, a pall hung over everything.

"Do you need help?" she asked, stopping by Taylor's office.

"With what?" he asked icily as he pulled books off shelves, placing them in a waiting box on his desk. "Putting my life back together? Finding a new job? Or did you mean just carrying boxes?"

"Taylor, I'm sorry," Margaret said sincerely. "I truly am sorry this happened. Where will you go?"

He paused his packing and glanced at her. "I've sent CVs out to various universities who had openings posted, but none has called about an interview," he said morosely.

He looked at her more closely as she sat. "How is she?"

Margaret's eyes were suddenly bright with tears. "I don't really know. I call her daily and she says she's fine, but... she doesn't want to see me."

Somehow, in the aftermath of the assault, all pretense between Margaret and Taylor had been dropped. Taylor seemed, finally, to have developed a sense of discretion – "or at least an appreciation of his former complete lack of it," Margaret would have said – as a result of his having to stand in the crucible of scrutiny resulting from his police charge. He was more solicitous of her, which surprised her, given that his troubles would normally have triggered every selfish impulse he possessed. She had found herself pouring out to him how much she loved Wyck – loved both Gavin and Wyck, which Taylor listened to sympathetically – up to a point.

"You do realize how much damage that sanctimonious bastard has caused," Taylor pointed out, unable to hide his bitterness toward Gavin. "And yet you defend him, say you love him."

"You don't understand him," Margaret protested, wishing she could have explained, to Taylor and to Wyck, what it was that had driven Gavin to do what he did, but she knew he would have died of shame if anyone else – especially Taylor – knew his secret.

"No, I don't," Taylor said coldly. "And I'm sure Wyck doesn't, either."

And that, Margaret knew, was the key. Wyck could not bring herself to forgive Gavin for what he had done and, by extension, some of that blame, that culpability, was hers as well.

"Go to her," Taylor said sagely as he and Margaret each carried a box of books out to his car. "No matter what she says, go to her."

Wyck limped to the front door as Mandy let out a couple of half-hearted woofs, her tail thumping while she stayed lying comfortably in her bed. Wyck peered through the window before unlocking the door to find Margaret standing there with a few bags of groceries.

"Hi," Wyck said, standing back to let her in, tucking something into her back pocket.

"What did you do to your truck?" Margaret asked as Wyck closed the door, securing the two new deadbolts.

"What?"

"Your business name is gone," Margaret said. "You haven't given up the business, have you?"

"No," said Wyck. "But having my name plastered all over the doors was like having a bullseye painted on after Gavin made sure everyone knew I was the employer of the pervert child molester."

Choosing not to respond to that, Margaret said, "I thought you might need a few things. I owe you from when you did this for me, so..." She set the bags down on the floor and bent to pet Mandy for a minute.

Wyck gasped a little in pain as she picked up two of the bags and carried them into the kitchen.

"Let me do that. Where are your crutches?" Margaret asked, following her with the remaining bags.

Wyck shrugged. "I'm trying to go without them most of the time, now." She stood with her back to Margaret, pulling items out of the bags. "So, what brings you out this way?"

"I didn't know how much energy you have for cooking and thought you might like a hot meal," Margaret said brightly. "I have a great recipe for pork chops. You sit down and let me get to work."

Wyck sat at the table while Margaret moved around the kitchen, still laid out with plywood counters. The granite order had been put on hold until Wyck knew the extent of her hospital bills.

"How's David?" Margaret asked as she laid the pork chops in a pan.

"Lorie called yesterday," Wyck said. "He has to have another surgery to try and clean up another pocket of infection in his arm. He's on heavy-duty IV antibiotics, and she says he'll probably have to go home with them for about six weeks."

"Will he be able to come back to work for you, do you think?" Margaret asked from the stove.

Wyck shrugged again. "I don't know yet how much use he'll have of that arm. And... I've been thinking, I may want to keep the business small, take only the jobs I can handle."

Margaret turned to look at her, but she was frowning down at the table, tracing the wood grain of the tabletop with a finger.

"That might be smart, at least for a while," Margaret said. "You'll probably need time to build your endurance back up as well. The police still haven't made any arrests?"

Wyck shook her head. "I think they have some suspects based on our descriptions, but... nothing yet."

Margaret scrubbed a couple of sweet potatoes, poked the skins with a fork and put them in the microwave. "How are you feeling?"

"Better," Wyck said. "Mandy should get her cast off tomorrow, and we can start going for walks."

"That will be good for both of you," Margaret said. "Where are your plates?"

"I'll get them," Wyck said, standing up.

"What is that?" Margaret demanded, spotting the bulge in the small of Wyck's back as her sweatshirt hitched up a little.

Wyck immediately tugged her shirt back down over the 9 mm pistol snugged into a holster on her belt.

Margaret slid the pan to a cool burner and went to her, saying, "Wyck, a gun? The extra locks? Taking your name off your truck?"

Wyck's eyes blazed. "When was the last time your life was threatened because you were a lesbian, Margaret? Oh, that's right. It would never happen to you because you'll never acknowledge the truth of who you are, right? You'll lie and deny and get married so no one will know." Wyck's nostrils flared as she breathed hard, her face contorted by an ugly combination of fear and anger and self-loathing.

Margaret felt as if she had been slapped.

Wyck's eyes filled with angry tears. "I'm tired, Margaret. Tired of loving someone who won't or can't love me back the same way. I did it with Carla and now I'm doing the same thing with you. I'm tired of having my heart broken. Tired of looking over my shoulder to see if I'm being followed by people who might hurt me and Mandy. I'm tired of being afraid." Her tears spilled over.

"Wyck -" Margaret came to her, tried to reach out to her.

"Don't," Wyck said, putting a hand up and sidling away from Margaret. She turned from her, her arms folded defensively, refusing to meet her eyes. "Don't. This is too hard."

"Please," Margaret said. "Don't push me away. I love you -"

"And Gavin," Wyck cut in. "You love me and Gavin. But you're with Gavin," she said bitterly. She held up a hand before Margaret could speak, "I know why; I understand why, but don't you see? Can't you see how impossible this is? How much this hurts?"

Cussing under her breath, Wyck used her sleeve to wipe the tears from her face.

"Please go," she said.

Margaret looked at her helplessly. "Wyck -"

"Please."

Chapter 17

SWEAT WAS POURING DOWN Wyck's face as she jammed a post-hole digger into the earth in preparation for the pergola she was building, but the sweat wasn't from the heat. The pain in her thigh and ribs was nearly enough to drop her to her knees, except she was afraid if she went down, she'd never get up. Her doctor had been angry at her plans to go back to work so soon, but "No work, no money," she reminded him. She'd lost so many jobs right before the attack that her cash stream had almost completely dried up. She thanked her New England frugality that had prompted her to set aside a certain amount in savings so that she had a cushion to carry her through this dry spell, but it was rapidly being depleted, and she didn't have the luxury of staying at home any longer.

Trying to pace herself now, she dug the last hole to the needed depth and turned to the bag of concrete mix lying nearby. She wanted this job to be perfect – the Masons had agreed to re-hire her after the assault made the news, and she didn't want to disappoint them.

She'd been able to complete a few smaller jobs - mostly getting loads of mulch down before the weeds got too out of control, but had avoided taking on anything really heavy like laying flagstone. She hated to turn down jobs, but she knew there was no way she could physically handle anything that strenuous yet - "if I'll ever be able to again."

The ribs she knew would heal in time, but she still had a limp she couldn't seem to lose, and kneeling and squatting were very difficult. "What kind of gardener can't squat?" she asked herself in frustration, resorting at last to a kind of rolling cart that she could sit on.

Mandy was bouncing back more quickly than she, now that her cast was off. She had hopped about on three legs for a while out of habit, but was now trotting along smartly after the squirrels, though she didn't jump at them the way she used to. Long walks were the best they could manage together - no runs, and she kept Mandy on a leash to make sure she wasn't tempted by a passing deer or rabbit.

Her cell phone rang as she was shoveling concrete into the last hole. She let it ring. Job offers and requests for designs and estimates were starting to roll in again. One person she hadn't heard from was Margaret. Not that she'd expected to. *Not after what I said to her,* she thought glumly.

Wyck closed her eyes against the memory of what she'd blurted. It had been honest, but cruel, and part of her regretted it bitterly - "but only part." The other part was glad of the reprieve from the pain of having to see Margaret and watch her interact with Gavin. She tried to ignore the guilt she felt when she thought about how attentive - how loving - Margaret had been during her time in the hospital.

"No," she muttered aloud to herself. "It's better this way."

Margaret lay in bed and, as she had done every night since her visit to Wyck, heard those accusing words reverberate in her head. Those horrible, true words. Everything Wyck had said was true - Margaret had always lied and hidden who she really was, and marrying Gavin had removed any future possibilities that someone might suspect she was a lesbian. She'd never faced the kind of confrontations Wyck had - only the one time with her father, and she had capitulated completely.

"You know you aren't worthy of her," a shamed voice said inside her head. "You've known it since you met her."

Hot tears leaked out of the corners of her eyes and slid back into her hair. Restlessly, she turned onto her side, punching her pillow into the crook of her neck.

From down the hall, she heard the sound of something crashing and falling. Throwing off the covers, she raced down to Gavin's room to find the bed empty. She hurried into the bathroom where Gavin lay moaning on the floor next to the vanity, several pill bottles scattered about, a water glass lying shattered with shards scattered everywhere. Turning on the light, she gasped at the blood covering the side of his head, already pooling on the floor.

"Gavin!" she cried, grabbing a towel and gently dabbing his scalp to see a jagged gash where his head had hit the edge of the marble vanity. "Don't move."

She grabbed the phone from the bedside table and dialed 911.

What was fifteen minutes felt like fifty as she waited for the ambulance.

"No," she said when the EMTs at last had him loaded onto a gurney and asked if she wanted to ride with him. "I'll be there shortly."

She looked blankly at the blood congealing on the floor as they wheeled him away. *I'll never get this cleaned up if I don't do it now.* Forcing herself to focus on this one task, she went downstairs to gather a roll of paper towels and some disinfectant. Sweeping all the glass together with a wad of paper towels, tears began to fall, blurring her vision as she cleaned and scrubbed the pool of blood.

"Ouch!"

She looked down, blinking to clear the tears from her eyes and saw a piece of glass sticking out of her thumb with her own blood dripping onto the floor – *my clean floor*. The tears gave way to sobs as she knelt on the cold marble floor, rocking back and forth.

"How is he?" Amanda asked breathlessly as she and Jeffrey rushed into the hospital lobby to find Margaret waiting for them. They had left immediately when she called.

"He's not good," Margaret said. "He says he fell because of a new pain in his back, and when they did a scan, they found a new compression fracture in his spine... and his liver now has even more cancer. They're holding a bed in the ICU, but... we need to talk first."

She ushered them to a quiet corner where there were a few chairs. Jeffrey and Amanda exchanged puzzled glances as Margaret said, "They can only move him to the ICU if we're going to pursue more aggressive means of stabilizing and prolonging his life." She paused, waiting for the impact of her words to settle. "Your father has always been adamant that he didn't want any machines or resuscitation, but... this gets into a gray area."

"How so?" Jeffrey asked with a frown.

"There is no more chemo or any other treatment for his cancer at this stage, but his potassium levels have dropped so low that his heart will be affected if they don't give him potassium and aggressively regulate his fluid levels," Margaret explained. "But the potassium isn't indicated if we decide on palliative care."

"So, he's either going to die of heart failure or his cancer," Amanda said.

Margaret nodded. "Basically, yes."

"What does Dad say?" Jeffrey asked.

"He's on some very heavy pain medication, so he's only lucid for brief moments," Margaret said with a shake of her head. "And, his medical directive doesn't really deal with this. That's why I waited until you got here."

"I don't think we can just let him die by denying him care," Amanda said.

"He is dying, Amanda," Jeffrey said, more harshly than he meant. "No matter what we do."

"They said they can keep him comfortable," Margaret said.

Amanda blinked away tears. "What do you think we should do?"

Margaret took a deep breath. "I think your father would not want to have his days prolonged if it means being confined to a hospital bed," she said gently. "If we're voting, I'm voting for keeping him comfortable and letting him go."

"Are you sure you're not just tired of taking care of him?" Amanda asked in a shrill voice.

"Amanda!" Jeffrey said sharply. He glanced at Margaret. "She didn't mean that."

But the expression on Amanda's face looked as if she did mean it.

"I think you'll be shocked at how frail he is," she said to them, trying to keep her voice level. "Maybe you should go in to see him before you make a decision."

Is she wrong? Margaret asked herself as they left her. She felt torn and she knew she couldn't deny that part of her would feel relieved at having this death vigil at an end, not that she would rush Gavin there, but....

She stepped outside through the automatic doors. Expelling a deep breath, she walked down the sidewalk, shaded by an avenue of trees. She felt dizzy with exhaustion and stopped to lean against one of the trees, pressing a hand to her eyes.

"Margaret? What's wrong?"

She looked up to find Wyck standing there. "What are you doing here?" she asked, wondering how Wyck could have heard about Gavin already.

Wyck gestured toward the hospital. "David's back in. I was just coming by to visit."

She and Margaret stared at each other, each drinking in the details of the other's countenance. Margaret could see that, over the past few weeks, Wyck's cut eyebrow was growing back in white. The scar gave her a roguish appearance, but to Margaret, she was more beautiful than ever.

"Is it Gavin?" Wyck asked.

Margaret's chin trembled as she struggled not to burst into tears again. "His cancer and his heart... he's terminal, they say."

Wyck's hand twitched, but she quickly stuffed her hands into her pockets. "I'm sorry. Is there anything I can do?"

Margaret blinked rapidly and shook her head. "Thank you, but there really isn't." She glanced back toward the hospital. "I should be getting back inside."

Wyck nodded and walked with her silently, still with a slight limp.

"I'm this way," Margaret said, pointing down the corridor that led to the ER.

"Call me if you need anything," Wyck said lamely, knowing Margaret would not call.

Jeffrey was snoring lightly as he half-lay against the arm of the sofa in Gavin's room while Amanda and Margaret sat on either side of the bed in chairs. Gavin had had a restless night despite the pain medication he was receiving.

"I don't understand how he could be so bad all of a sudden," Amanda had said the evening before when the doctor came in on his rounds. "Why is he so yellow?"

"The body can maintain a precarious balance for quite a while," the doctor explained, "then when something happens to throw the balance off, things cascade – much like dominos. His liver is shutting down; that's why he's so jaundiced."

Margaret stood now, stretching painfully, grateful this had waited until exams were over. She wasn't sure how she could have coped with work and all of this.

"I need to move," she whispered. "Be back in a bit."

Out in the hall, east-facing windows offered a view of pink-tinged clouds as the sun came up. Rubbing the back of her stiff neck, Margaret walked down the corridor toward the elevators and stopped suddenly.

Wyck was sitting in one of the chairs gathered there. Margaret felt a rush of warmth inside at the sight of her – as if she had taken a strong drink. Wyck stood when she saw her.

Without words, Margaret moved into her waiting arms, allowing Wyck's strength to enfold her and comfort her – "I'm so tired," she would realize later. "Tired of being strong for everyone else." She felt she could have stayed in Wyck's embrace forever. They stood like that for long minutes, until the elevator dinged on their floor.

Pulling apart, they sat as two people in white coats got off the elevator.

"Have you been here all night?" Margaret asked, holding tightly to Wyck's hand.

Wyck shook her head. "I went home to take care of Mandy and came back," she glanced at her watch, "about an hour ago." She looked at Margaret's tired face. "How is he?"

Margaret shrugged. "No major changes. We're just waiting. They don't expect him to go home this time," she said quietly. She nodded in the direction of Gavin's room. "Amanda and Jeffrey are here. I think both their families will arrive later today..."

"...to say good-bye," went unspoken.

"Is there anything that needs doing at the house?" Wyck asked. "Cleaning? Groceries?"

Margaret searched Wyck's face – "this most beloved face," she could have said, but instead, she said, "Why are you always so good to me?"

Wyck looked down at Margaret's hand still clasped in her own. "Not always," she mumbled, her brow furrowed. "I'm so sorry... the things I said to you..."

"What did you say that wasn't true?" Margaret asked. "You were right. I've never risked anything... never stood up to anyone..." She shook her head as the elevator opened again. "That's Gavin's doctor," she said as she saw the man getting out. "I'd better go." She stood, and turned to look back. "Will you be here later?"

"I've got to go to work, but I'll be back," Wyck promised.

Margaret nodded and followed the doctor down the hall, pausing once to look back and make sure Wyck was really there.

Chapter 18

WYCK PULLED INTO THE parking lot of the funeral home, watching other cars arrive, the occupants – mostly middle-aged and older, conservatively dressed in suits, though one man arrived in full Confederate regalia – making their way in through the open doors to join the queue shuffling past Gavin's family to his casket. With a sigh, Wyck got out to join them.

The vigil at the hospital had gone for three more days. Margaret, Amanda and Jeffrey had finally started staying with Gavin in shifts so that they could get some much-needed rest. Wyck had stopped by the hospital as frequently as she could before or after work, often in the middle of the night – not to see Gavin, only to offer support to Margaret during the lonely hours.

They had found a quiet sitting area out of the flow of traffic where they could sit for brief bits of time – "precious bits," Margaret murmured – before she resumed her vigil. Mostly, Margaret was resigned and dry-eyed and just needed to talk, but occasionally, she felt overwhelmed by everything. At those times, she seemed to crave the feel of Wyck's arms around her, and *I could hold her forever*, Wyck thought, until "What is this?"

Margaret jumped to her feet at the sound of Amanda's voice. "This is my friend," she said bravely, though her face was red. "And our landscaper. Wyck Fitzsimmons, this is Gavin's daughter, Amanda."

Wyck nodded but didn't bother trying to shake hands, as Amanda looked livid.

"I certainly don't hug my friends like that," she said waspishly. "How long has this been going on?"

"How long has what been going on?" Margaret returned sharply.

Amanda looked Wyck up and down. "You know exactly what I mean," she said, breathing hard.

"Don't be ridiculous," Margaret snapped. She turned to Wyck. "I'll see you later." She walked away, leaving Amanda no choice but to follow after one last dirty look at Wyck.

After that, Wyck called before coming up to make sure Margaret was alone. "Are they giving you a hard time?" she asked anxiously.

Margaret sighed. "I don't think Amanda knows what to think," she said. "She's angry with me, anyhow."

"Why?"

"She thinks I decided to withhold medical care so Gavin would die more quickly," Margaret said, her voice tight.

"That's ludicrous," Wyck said. "You've taken care of him for years."

Margaret shrugged. "Stress does strange things to people, and this is stressful, even if we all knew it was coming."

Margaret waited until one night when she knew no one else would be there. "Won't you come in and see him? Please?" Margaret pleaded. "I've told him you were here."

Reluctantly, Wyck agreed, entering Gavin's room with some trepidation. Despite having been told, she was not prepared for how skeletal his face had become, how wasted his body was under the covers. She stepped up to the bed with Margaret who leaned forward, gently calling Gavin's name.

His eyes blinked open and recognition dawned on his face. "How's my garden?" he asked in a raspy voice. His yellowed eyes moved back and forth between Wyck's face and Margaret's. "Our garden."

Wyck felt Margaret's fingers brush against hers. She leaned forward and said, "It's a mess. You let the weeds get completely out of control. It will take me weeks to get it back in order."

Gavin's mouth twitched in an approximation of a smile, and he kept looking back and forth between the two women. "Forgive me," he croaked.

Margaret glanced at Wyck, who blinked rapidly, her jaw working back and forth as she struggled with her emotions. At last, she nodded and Gavin's eyes closed as he drifted into the half-conscious state that had become his norm.

Forgive me.

Such a simple thing to ask, Wyck thought now as she stood in the receiving line, watching Margaret shake hands and hug people who were filing past. She glanced over at Gavin's open casket – not a good idea in her opinion. *Simple to ask and so terribly hard to do.*

She knew she would be forever scarred – physically and emotionally – by the events Gavin had set in motion. Out in the truck was her handgun, tucked securely next to her seat. When she walked out of the funeral home this evening, she would be scanning the surrounding area first for signs of anyone acting suspiciously. She would do the same, gun in hand, when she pulled up to the barn later tonight. She would barricade herself behind her securely locked doors and call Mandy near for comfort. Precautions she knew many people lived with all the time, but which felt to her as if they had shuttered her life. When she and Mandy went for walks now, she couldn't relax, enjoying nature, laughing at the antics of Mandy pouncing after the small animals they encountered; she was constantly on guard, vigilantly scanning every tree and bush and shadow for danger, listening for footsteps, her hand occasionally reaching back to make sure she could quickly get to the holster snugged against her back if need be... and she hated herself for being so afraid. She had nodded to Gavin – a concession to a dying man – but truly forgiving him was not something she'd been able to do yet. He'd stolen something from her she didn't think she could ever get back, and it made her angry.

Then, "You don't have to come today. He's gone," Margaret had called to say a few days ago.

Wyck didn't know what to say. "Are you all right?"

She could hear Margaret sniffle. "Yes," she said thickly. "It was peaceful. Everybody was here. We're going to go back to the house and get some rest."

Wyck hadn't had a chance to talk to her since except for one brief call from Margaret to tell her what the funeral arrangements were. Watching Margaret's face as the queue shuffled along, Wyck could see dark circles under her eyes and knew she probably hadn't been sleeping. At last, she reached the family. Amanda, eyes shooting daggers as she recognized her, turned away. Jeffrey, apparently ignorant as to who she was, gave Wyck a handshake and thanked her for coming. Margaret, her eyes betraying her for a few seconds, gave Wyck a perfunctory hug and whispered, "Please stay."

Wyck went to sit in a corner of the viewing room where Margaret could glance over and see her. She felt movement behind her, and realized someone had seated himself in the next row back. She looked around in surprise as Taylor Foster leaned forward. "The king is dead," he said in a low voice so that only Wyck could hear. "Long live the queen."

Wyck snorted a little. She still didn't like Taylor, but he was viciously funny in a totally inappropriate way.

He came around into her row of seats, and sat back, crossing his legs, smoothing the razor crease in his trousers as he said, "Well, this must feel like a weight lifted from your shoulders, both of you."

Wyck frowned a little. "What do you mean?"

He smiled. "Margaret has told me everything," he said conspiratorially. "I know how you feel about each other. I still don't understand the whole 'no sex' rule you apparently had..."

"I'm sure you don't," Wyck wanted so badly to retort, but held her tongue.

"...but now, you're free," he said glibly.

156

She peered at him to see if he was serious. He was. "Um, I don't expect it will be that simple," she said.

The expression on his face was one of complete incredulity. "Of course it is. Gavin's dead. There's nothing in your way now."

Margaret glanced across the room, holding Wyck's gaze for a few seconds. Wyck bit her lip. *If only it were that simple.*

"So, it's arranged," Jim Evans said. "We'll have a memorial service on campus in August when everyone is back."

"That sounds good," Jeffrey said, taking his glasses off and cleaning them with his tie. "By then, we'll have the rest of his affairs in order. We meet with the lawyer later today."

Margaret's jaw tightened. Jeffrey's behavior, always somewhat pompous, had become even more so since his father's death. It was as if he were establishing himself as the new patriarch of the family. Thus far, Margaret had kept quiet, not wishing to start a row when emotions were running high anyhow. It was easier to let Jeffrey assume command - for now.

Jeffrey and Amanda had stayed for the meeting with the attorney to read Gavin's will so that the spouses and grandchildren could get home. Somewhat nervously, Margaret dressed for their appointment. "It seems so exaggerated to wear black," she murmured as she sorted through her clothes, "but color will send the wrong signal." In the end, she decided on a charcoal gray suit. They drove together in Gavin's Lincoln. As they entered the building where the law office was, Margaret noticed with some surprise the sign in the lobby listing Fitzsimmons Landscaping on the third floor. Glancing skyward, she wondered if Wyck was up there. They entered the hushed space of the law offices on the main floor and were ushered into a small conference room.

After just a few minutes, two men entered, one of them carrying a folio. They introduced themselves - names Margaret immediately forgot - and shook hands all round before inviting everyone to sit.

"Well," began one of the men, "things are fairly straightforward. There is a sum of money to each of you," he nodded toward Amanda and Jeffrey, "and to each of the grandchildren, though they cannot have the money until they reach age twenty-five. The remainder goes to Margaret who is also the beneficiary of his copyrights, with the request that she name you her beneficiaries in turn." He peered through his half-glasses at the documents in the folio. "I doubt any of that comes as a surprise. The most significant change was one Gavin made in regard to the house just a couple of months ago."

Margaret held her breath at these words. A couple of months ago?

The lawyer continued, "The house is to be donated to St. Aloysius University –"

"What?" Jeffrey and Amanda demanded at the same time while Margaret sat in stunned silence.

The attorney held up a calming hand, "The property is to be donated to the university, but the contents, including all the art, belong to Margaret with the proviso that it will remain Margaret's home rent-free for as long as she lives or wishes to remain there..." Here, he paused, frowning at the wording of the document, "...in accordance with all terms and conditions of her employment at the university." He looked up and smiled. "Not sure what that has to do with anything, but... there you are."

Margaret impatiently waited for Amanda and Jeffrey to get packed and leave.

"I thought we were going to have lunch downtown?" Amanda had asked in confusion when Margaret went straight to the car after leaving the law offices.

"No... I'd rather not," Margaret had said. "Please, let's go home."

Jeffrey and Amanda exchanged worried glances but acquiesced. "It's not so bad," Jeffrey said as he navigated the Lincoln through downtown traffic. "I mean, none of us expected him to give the property to the university - that's a bit of a blow - but, still, you can stay as long as you want to."

Margaret had nodded absently, but said nothing. "*...in accordance with all terms and conditions of her employment at the university.*" Only she had understood exactly what Gavin meant.

"He knew."

"How could he?"

"I don't know, but he did. That's why he changed the will. And he knew I would understand why."

She was beyond caring if she was rude in making it clear she wished for Amanda and Jeffrey to leave that afternoon - she needed time alone.

When at last she was by herself, she stood listening to the silence - absorbing for the first time the reality that never again would she hear Gavin's heavy footsteps thumping through the house, would never hear him coughing or clearing his throat the way he used to, would not hear him complaining about not being able to get out to his garden. Standing there, the house empty and quiet for the first time in nearly two weeks and she alone for the first time since Gavin's death, Margaret tried to embrace her new situation... the freedom of being away as long as she pleased without having to worry about whether Gavin had eaten or if he had taken his medicine, and the utter loneliness of coming home after every outing to a dark, empty house, knowing her companion of nearly thirty years would not be waiting for her. She didn't feel like crying. In fact, she wasn't sure she felt anything at the moment. It was as if her entire being had been injected with an anesthetic.

She considered calling Wyck or going to see her, but if she did, she would have to explain about the will, about the house, and she didn't want to have to think about that right now. She didn't want to think at all. She went upstairs to the master bedroom, still full of Gavin's clothes and shoes and combs and watches and cuff links and all the myriad trappings of a life. Amanda hadn't been able to face emptying the room of her father's things, though Jeffrey had suggested they get it done while they were there to help. Jeffrey and his wife, Cecilia, had stayed in here, the only signs of them now the rumpled sheets on the unmade bed.

I don't know when I'll get this done now, Margaret thought vaguely, opening a dresser drawer and wondering if she would ever feel like using this room again.

She walked into the bathroom, cleaned and straightened up now, with no sign of Gavin's last fall - no broken glass, no blood, no mess except for the used towels drying on the rack.

It felt strange somehow, that a life gone left behind so many little things that needed to be cleaned up or given away or thrown away and she suddenly understood why her mother had had such a hard time getting rid of her father's things.

"They're just things," she had said to her mother after the funeral. "There's no reason to hang onto them."

"I'll do it when I'm ready," Muriel had insisted, her eyes filling with tears as she stroked one of her husband's sweaters, pulling it to her and smelling his cologne.

Once the things were gone, what was left?

At least Gavin had left behind children and a volume of work that people will continue to read, she realized as she looked around. *What will you leave behind? One book, a few students who might remember you and... what?*

She pulled the bedroom door shut and went down the hall to her own study. There, she opened the drawer with her unfinished manuscripts - *no need to lock them up any longer,* she thought vaguely as she closed the drawer again.

Pulling her desk chair closer, she opened another drawer and pulled out the current manuscript, the one about her father that she hadn't touched in weeks, and began to write.

Chapter 19

FOR A WEEK AFTER the funeral, Wyck kept herself busy with other jobs, hesitant to call or go by the Braithwaite place.

"How soon is too soon?" she asked herself, and she knew she wasn't asking merely about calling or seeing Margaret. For months, Gavin's living presence had stood between them, and now, his specter remained. She had no idea when, or even if, Margaret would feel that she could act on the feelings they shared. And so she waited.

At last, the telephone rang and it was Margaret.

"Can you come to the house for dinner?" she asked.

That evening, Wyck and Mandy rang the bell and waited on the front porch. When Margaret opened the door, she and Wyck just stood, staring at one another.

"Hi," said Wyck uncertainly.

"Hi."

Mandy broke the tension by sidling in for some attention, her tail wagging furiously. Margaret smiled as she bent to pet her and stepped back to allow them in. Mandy trotted into the den and dove into her bed, sighing contentedly.

Wyck, letting Margaret set the rules, did not initiate a hug, but walked on through to the kitchen, where Margaret had things cooking in a couple of pans on the stove.

"I hope you like stir-fry," Margaret said. "I guess I should have asked."

"I do," Wyck said as she opened the bottle of Biltmore wine she had brought. She poured for both of them while Margaret finished the dinner preparations.

They sat at the kitchen table, already laid with place settings and glasses of water.

"How are you?" Wyck asked as they began to eat, noting how thin Margaret's face looked.

Margaret frowned at her plate. "I thought - I would have expected that I would have been better prepared for this, after all the years of dealing with his illness, knowing when it came back last summer that it was going to be terminal at some point, but..."

Wyck reached out and took Margaret's hand in hers as Margaret blinked tears away.

"You've been so patient," Margaret murmured, looking at up at Wyck.

Wyck shook her head. "I've just been worried about you," she said. "I didn't want to bother you with phone calls or visits if you needed time."

Margaret nodded, squeezing Wyck's hand. "I did... I do. Everything for so long has revolved around Gavin - his needs, his appointments, his schedule, his everything. I need some time to figure out what I need." She smiled. "Besides you."

Wyck felt she could breathe again. She released Margaret's hand and resumed eating. "I had wondered about coming out to clean up the garden. I'm sure it needs a lot of work."

"We can go take a look after dinner if you'd like," Margaret said, glancing out the window.

When they were done eating, they wandered outside into long

shadows cast by the late evening sunlight, Mandy eagerly sniffing and exploring. Wyck steered them back to the wall she'd been working on when she and Gavin had quarreled. It was exactly as she'd left it – half-built, rocks strewn about, waiting to be laid in place. Wyck squatted down with a grunt and placed one, wiggling it into position.

"Would you mind if I started back up?" she asked, looking up at Margaret. "I mean, that is if you want me to continue here. I didn't mean to assume –"

"Yes, I want you to continue," Margaret smiled. "I don't think I could let anyone else touch this garden."

Wyck stood and they resumed their walk along the path. Shyly, Margaret reached for Wyck's hand, holding it as they walked. In a small clearing bordered by azaleas and peonies, Margaret pulled them to a halt.

"I know I'm not being fair to you," she said softly. "We've waited so long –"

"Shhh," Wyck said, stepping closer. "I would wait forever for you. You'll know when the time feels right. Just... let me be with you."

Margaret smiled, laying a gentle hand on Wyck's cheek. "I don't deserve you," she said. She leaned nearer for a kiss, gentle and sweet, which Wyck returned hesitantly. After a moment, they parted and resumed their walk, just enjoying being together as Wyck pointed out various features and made mental notes on all that needed to be done.

When they returned to the house, Margaret walked Wyck and Mandy to the foyer.

"I'll see you tomorrow," Wyck said with one more soft kiss.

Margaret opened the front door, quickly looking up and down the street before stepping out to stand on the porch as Wyck and Mandy got into the truck and drove away. Turning back to the house, she scanned the street one last time before closing the door.

As May slipped quietly into June, the garden gradually began to live up to its potential again. Weeded, mulched, pruned, the plants thrived, growing a little wildly.

"It looks different," Margaret commented, coming outside to wander around with Wyck. "I never really paid attention before, but something is different."

Wyck smiled. "It's less formal," she said. "I'm letting the plants do what they want. Gavin, I think, kept everything much more structured."

Not just the plants, Margaret thought, looking down at the jeans and loose-fitting linen shirt she wore – the first such clothes she'd owned in nearly thirty years. Touring the garden now, she realized the plants weren't the only things starting to break free of Gavin's restraints.

"I feel like I can breathe again," she'd tried to explain to Wyck.

New clothes were only the beginning. Inside the house, too, she'd started changing things. Slowly, she'd been boxing up Gavin's belongings from the bedroom, putting the boxes in the attic. "Amanda and Jeffrey can go through these when they feel like it," she said to herself as she carried box after box up the attic steps. She still hadn't moved back into the master bedroom, preferring her room for now.

She'd re-decorated the den, painting the walls a fresh cream color. She took down the heavy drapes and moved Gavin's old, heavy leather club chair and ottoman to his study, replacing them with lighter pieces of furniture and gauzy drapes, giving an airy feel to the room which had always felt somewhat like a dungeon to her. Gavin's study, she'd left as it was, simply pulling the door shut.

"Ready for some lunch?" she asked now.

Wyck and Mandy accompanied her back inside. Wyck had been working there two to three days a week, around and in between other jobs, and she and Margaret had fallen into a comfortable routine of eating lunch and dinner together on those days.

"How's David doing?" Margaret asked as she got out bread for sandwiches.

"The infection seems to finally be under control," Wyck replied as she poured water for herself and sweet tea for Margaret, "but the healing of the fracture is not going well. Lorie said they're hoping it will speed up now that he's off the antibiotics."

Mandy lay under the table as they sat. "How's the book coming?" Wyck asked.

Margaret wiped a bit of mayonnaise from the corner of her mouth before saying, "It's going really well. I think I'm about half-way through this first draft." She glanced up at Wyck. "Would you read it when it's ready?"

Wyck's eyes lit up. "I'd love to." She took a bite of her sandwich. "I was wondering if you would like to go for a walk through the neighborhood later, after I'm done? Get some air, move?"

"Oh," Margaret said hesitantly. "I don't think so. I've got things to do here. Maybe through the garden?"

Wyck watched her for a few seconds before nodding. "Okay."

Up in her study again after lunch, Margaret sat at her desk, the pages of her manuscript ruffling gently in the breeze coming through the open window. Out in the garden, she could hear Wyck singing as she so often did, without even realizing she was doing it. Margaret paused her pen, smiling as she listened. A vague memory stirred in her mind, something she'd read long ago. She got up and pulled a worn volume of Wordsworth from her bookshelf. Flipping through the pages for several minutes, she found at last the poem she sought.

> Behold her, single in the field,
> Yon solitary Highland Lass!
> Reaping and singing by herself;
> Stop here, or gently pass!
> Alone she cuts and binds the grain,
> And sings a melancholy strain;
> O listen! for the Vale profound
> Is overflowing with the sound.
>
> Will no one tell me what she sings? -
> Perhaps the plaintive numbers flow

For old, unhappy, far-off things,
And battles long ago;
Or is it some more humble lay,
Familiar matter of today?
Some natural sorrow, loss, or pain,
That has been, and may be again?

Whate'er the theme, the Maiden sang
As if her song could have no ending;
I saw her singing at her work,
And o'er the sickle bending –
I listened, motionless and still;
And, as I mounted up the hill,
The music in my heart I bore,
Long after it was heard no more.

Margaret lowered her book, closing her eyes as she listened to the clear tones of Wyck's voice. "'The music in my heart I bore,'" she murmured.

Chapter 20

WYCK'S EYES OPENED IN the darkness as she tried to figure out what had awakened her. She turned and saw that Mandy's head was up also, listening as she lay in her bed next to Wyck's. Sliding her hand under her pillow, Wyck pulled out her pistol, listening hard. She heard a thudding sound as if someone had knocked one of the trashcans over.

Her heart in her throat, she slid out of bed as soundlessly as possible, giving Mandy a hand signal to stay. Holding the gun in front of her, aimed skyward, she crept toward the stairs, grateful she had used extra-thick subflooring with plenty of screws so that nothing creaked. Praying her injured leg would hold her steady, she descended the stairs as quietly as she could, stopping half-way down to scan the dark main level. The overcast skies outside offered no illumination as she continued down the stairs.

Pausing at the bottom to listen, she heard again the scuffing sounds that had awakened her. It sounded as if they were coming from the back porch. Breathing shallowly through her open mouth, her heart beating a million times a minute, Wyck tiptoed into the kitchen, watching the windows for any signs of movement or shadows. Suddenly, the dim outline of Mandy's dog door - locked now at night - was obscured by the shadow of someone moving on the other side. Wyck aimed the gun, trying to control the trembling of her hands as her finger started to squeeze the trigger and - heard the scratching of little claws on the dog door.

Rushing to the back door, she fumbled the key into the two deadbolts and flung the door open in time to see a mama raccoon and three babies scurrying away. They had knocked the lids off all of the trashcans and tipped one on its side.

Wyck closed the kitchen door, and sank to the floor, her heart still pounding so fast she thought she might pass out. She set the gun down and pressed her trembling hands to her face as Mandy, knowing she wasn't supposed to have come down, slunk over to Wyck and lay with her head resting on Wyck's thigh.

"You cannot keep living like this," Wyck whispered through clenched jaws.

She got shakily to her feet and stood braced against the island, bits of quartz and mica in the new granite twinkling like tiny stars in the dim light. Placing the pistol on the countertop, she turned to the back door. She slid her feet into the mud shoes kept sitting next to the door, and stepped out onto the back porch, accompanied by Mandy. Her fists tightly clenched, Wyck strode off into the night, past the ruins of the farmhouse, through the neighboring pasture to a trail that she and Mandy had walked hundreds of times as it meandered through the woods. Forcing herself to move without pausing to listen and scan for what danger might be out there, Wyck walked and walked, breathing in the night air, hearing owls hoot and bats squeak and little things scurry about in the undergrowth. Mandy, instead of trotting about haphazardly to sniff as she would normally have done, stayed protectively near Wyck's side. Coming to a field where she had planted hundreds of evergreen seedlings - pines and spruces and firs - Wyck stopped at last.

She realized she felt weak and nauseous now that the adrenaline had left her body. She fell to her knees, her hands braced on the ground, her head hanging, and she began to cry. She cried for David and she cried for Mandy and how scared she had been for both of them after the attack; she cried for herself - for the physical pain she was still dealing with, for the hatred she felt toward the men who had attacked them, for how much she wanted to hurt them in return, for all the things they had taken from her.

Wyck clawed her fingers into the earth as she cried, feeling the soil and bits of grass and sticks and small stones. She could feel a worm wriggle away from her grasping fingers. She lifted handfuls of dirt, inhaling the damp, earthy smell and it calmed her. This was real, this was "wick," she whispered. "And I am wick, though I haven't been living like I am."

Mandy whined and pawed at her. Wrapping an arm around Mandy's warm body and pulling her close, she looked up at the sky, at the clouds scudding across a sliver of a moon, and felt at peace for the first time in a very long time. It was a feeling she remembered vaguely, like a wisp of a dream that danced on the edge of her consciousness. She stayed very still, letting the feeling settle into her, giving it time to take root.

She didn't know how long she stayed there, but she gradually became aware that her thigh was screaming in pain. Getting awkwardly to her feet, she and Mandy limped back home.

"You know," Wyck said casually the following week, "I haven't been out to a restaurant or anywhere else since... since I was in the hospital."

The catharsis of the raccoon episode had stayed with her - "mostly," she would have clarified. There were still moments of, not panic exactly, but times when she stopped suddenly, taking in her surroundings, listening for suspicious sounds. "Well, some of that is common sense," Margaret said when Wyck told her what had happened and tried to explain the effect it had had on her. "I am glad you're leaving the gun at home now."

Wyck looked down at the pruning shears in her hand. "And you've stayed here at the house for weeks. I don't think you've left except to get groceries. Don't you think it's time we went somewhere, did something together?"

Margaret simply stared at her. It hadn't occurred to her that Wyck might want to go anywhere but, in the back of her mind, she'd known this was inevitable. It wouldn't occur to her until much later how significant it truly was that Wyck was suggesting this. *Why didn't I realize what it meant for her to want to be out in public?* she would wonder. She was a bit surprised herself at how content she had been to stay at the house, where before she had chafed to get away. *Maybe it wasn't the house I wanted to get away from,* she realized. The other issue - one that she hadn't acknowledged to herself, much less to Wyck - was whether she was ready to be seen in public with her. She remembered very clearly her own initial reaction to Wyck's androgynous appearance. It was unavoidable that she would start running into colleagues and friends. They would naturally be curious about whom she was spending time with now that Gavin was gone... *and they'll know,* she thought, knowing it was a cowardly thing to worry about, but worried just the same.

"Margaret?" Wyck prompted, her eyes watching Margaret's face as she waited for a response.

So they had agreed to meet for lunch at a restaurant near Wyck's office downtown. Margaret arrived early, casually dressed in khakis and a gauzy tunic top. She perused the menu as she waited.

"Margaret! What a nice surprise to see you here."

She looked up to see Jim Evans standing next to her table. "Jim," she said, standing to hug him, but internally cursing the decision to meet Wyck at this restaurant.

"Please, sit down," she said to Jim now, indicating the vacant chair at her table.

"Are you sure?" he asked, looking around. "Aren't you meeting someone?"

"Just a friend who said she might be available," Margaret shrugged. "So how are things on campus?"

"Oh," he sighed. "It won't be the same without Gavin around, bothering me all the time." He reached for her hand, holding it between both of his. "How are you doing? I should have come by long ago to check on you, but –"

"I'm fine, Jim," Margaret interrupted. "Really. Have you found a new faculty member for the history department?"

"I think so," he said, releasing her hand and sitting back. "We've made an offer, just waiting for him to accept." He peered at her closely and as his eyes wandered up and down, she suddenly felt self-conscious about her casual attire, so unlike the things she had worn when Gavin was alive. "You look good, Margaret. It's kind of fortunate I ran into you, as we haven't had a chance to discuss Gavin's bequest to the university. That was a bit of a surprise, eh?"

Just then, Wyck entered the restaurant. Margaret saw her over Jim's shoulder, sparing her the barest half-glance before returning her attention to Jim. "Yes, it was," she agreed as she saw Wyck hesitate and then take a seat by herself at a separate table.

Jim glanced at his watch. "Are you being stood up?" he asked, looking around. "I'd be happy to buy you lunch."

Margaret hesitated for a moment and then forced a smile onto her face. "That would be lovely."

Her heart sank as Jim signaled a server. Wyck got up and left the restaurant.

The axe swung through the air with unerring accuracy, and the log split neatly in two. Reaching for the stack of whole logs, Wyck placed another one on the splitting block and tossed the split pieces onto a growing pile. Sweat poured off the end of her nose and dripped from her chin, and her damp t-shirt clung to her. She heard a car pull up at the front of the barn, as Mandy barked and trotted around to greet the visitor.

Wyck didn't look up as Margaret appeared around the corner, accompanied by Mandy. Without acknowledging her arrival, Wyck swung the axe, missing the center of the log so that only a chip of wood flew off as the axe glanced off the edge. Grinding her teeth, Wyck swung again, this time hitting the middle with a dry crack from the wood as it split.

"Wyck, I'm sorry," Margaret said as Wyck tossed the split chunks to the side.

Wyck ignored her, placing another log on the block. Margaret stood, waiting while another three logs were split before saying, "Please, can we talk?"

Wyck paused her work, letting the axe rest on the ground with her hands braced on the handle as she breathed heavily, sweat dripping in a steady stream from her face. Her blue eyes were fierce as she raised them at last to Margaret.

"I'm feeling a little like Jesus with Peter, here," she said quietly. "This was twice. I'm asking myself if there will be a third denial?"

Margaret pressed a hand to her eyes. "You don't understand. That was the president of the university."

Wyck's eyebrow raised just a tick as she stared wordlessly.

Expelling an exasperated breath, Margaret said again, "You don't understand." She flung both hands in the air. "Gavin gave them the house."

"What?" Wyck wiped her dripping chin on her sleeve.

"In his will. Gavin left the house to the university." Margaret closed her eyes. "I should have told you."

"What are you talking about? I was there. He said the house would be yours," Wyck said, perplexed.

Margaret looked at her with an anguished face. "He changed his will."

Wyck's mouth opened, but no sound came out.

"Can we talk?" Margaret pleaded.

Wyck led the way through the door into the kitchen, pausing at the sink to rinse her face. She toweled off as Margaret followed her inside, looking around.

"You've finished it," she said in awe, running a hand over the granite. She turned and looked at Wyck with shining eyes.

"I did it for you." Wyck didn't say it aloud, but Margaret saw it in her face, the unspoken words flung angrily into the tense air between them.

Walking into the great room, Margaret sat on the sofa while Wyck placed a towel on the floor and sat with her arms wrapped around her knees, waiting.

"When we went for the reading of Gavin's will," Margaret began, her hands tightly clenched in her lap, "the lawyer said that Gavin had come in a couple of months ago to make a change."

Wyck suddenly recalled the morning she had seen Gavin coming out of the law offices in her building. Her eyes narrowed as she listened.

"He left the house to St. Aloysius," Margaret continued, "but with the condition that I can stay there rent-free for as long as I live or want to be there..." Here, her voice took on a bitter tone as she quoted, "... 'in accordance with all terms and conditions of my employment at the university.'" She stared hard at Wyck. "Do you understand what that means?" she asked almost accusingly, as if it were Wyck's fault. Without waiting for a response, she said, "It means he knew. He knew about us. He set things up so that if anyone finds out about us, if we live openly, the university can use the same morals clause they used against Taylor, and I lose my house and my job."

Long seconds passed as Wyck stared at her hands, pulling at a splinter in her palm. Weighing her words carefully, she said, "I can understand how hard this must be for you. I agree; it seems Gavin knew about us and he set things up for you to have to make some difficult choices, but... you've already lost the house, Margaret." Trying to keep her voice neutral, trying not to betray the turmoil she was feeling, she added softly, "What you have to decide is how much more you're ready to lose."

Chapter 21

"BUT PEGGY, I DON'T understand," Muriel Collins said, upset. "This is so sudden."

Margaret focused for a moment as she adjusted the settings on the laptop on the dining table. "I'm setting up an e-mail account for you, Mom, so we can talk every day. At least when I first get there. We'll talk more than we do now."

"But why? Why are you doing this all of a sudden?"

Margaret sat back, struggling to keep her emotions in check, something that had been nearly impossible over the past couple of weeks. "I need some time away. It's too hard to be on campus with Gavin gone," she lied. "It's just a sabbatical to England for one semester. I'll be back by Christmas."

"But you'll miss the university's memorial for Gavin."

"Another good reason to be out of the country," but Margaret didn't say it.

Muriel looked at her daughter who wouldn't meet her eyes. She knew the stubborn set of that jaw, the same expression Peggy used to have as a little girl when there was something she didn't want to talk about. Always, she'd been introspective, unwilling to talk about things that bothered her, not like other little girls who blathered away, chattering endlessly about meaningless things.

"Margaret Ann Collins," she said, and she saw Margaret's mouth twitch. "I know you better than that." She reached for her daughter's hand. "What is it, really?"

Margaret's eyes filled with sudden, unwanted tears.

"You're being completely unreasonable!" she had blurted to Wyck that day at the barn. "Why can't we be together quietly, without shouting it out to the world?"

Wyck had looked at her with an inscrutable expression. "Margaret, you can't have lunch with me in a restaurant," she said pointedly. "We're a long way from shouting anything. You haven't even reached the point where you'll be seen with me in public."

"But what if people say we... we started while Gavin was still alive?" Margaret asked, thinking of Amanda's reaction in the hospital.

"We did," Wyck reminded her. "We started loving one another while Gavin was alive. And we haven't done any more since he died than we did while he was alive, but there are some people won't believe that." She watched Margaret warily.

"How do we even know it could work between us?" Margaret had asked, getting up from the couch and pacing agitatedly. "If it didn't, and I'd already lost the house, what then? I know I don't own the house, but it's my home. Can't you see how much I stand to lose?"

"Can't you see how much you stand to gain?" Wyck didn't say it, but the words hung between them, as clearly as if they had been shouted. A shadow fell over Wyck's features. "I do see. I really do."

The steadiness of her voice was harder for Margaret to hear than if Wyck had yelled and raged.

"I think," Wyck said, choosing her words carefully, "it would be good for you to take some time. You obviously have a lot to think about and... I think some time would be a good idea."

"What is it?" Muriel prompted now. "Is there someone else and you feel guilty about it?" she guessed shrewdly.

Margaret stared at her mother through her tears.

"What did you and your father argue about? When you graduated from college?"

Margaret's mouth fell open. "You knew about that?"

Muriel chuckled. "How could I not know?" she asked. "Both of you stomping around the house like angry bears, not talking to one another. He would never tell me." She watched her daughter with inquisitive dark eyes – and Margaret suddenly remembered thinking when she was a girl that her mother had eyes like a bird, sharp and bright. The same eyes she had inherited.

Margaret lowered her gaze. "It... it was about Julia," she said in a small voice, feeling like a little girl.

"You loved her?"

Margaret looked up in astonishment. "You knew that, too?"

Muriel shrugged. "I thought it was just an infatuation, and then you married Gavin and I thought maybe everything was settled, but... you never seemed happy with Gavin. Not like you were before. It was like a light had gone out."

Margaret reached for a tissue and blew her nose. "There is someone else," she admitted.

"A woman?" Muriel asked.

Margaret nodded, her eyes tearing up again.

"Gavin's gone, Peggy. I know you were faithful to him because that's the kind of person you are," Muriel said. "But you're young. Why shouldn't you love again? And nowadays, who cares if it's a woman?"

"Since when did you become so liberal?" Margaret asked through a watery smile.

"Since I got old enough to realize that love is too precious to let pass you by," Muriel said with a sad smile. "One of my closest friends here, Iris, just lost her partner last month. They were together for over forty years, but never told anyone. Our generation didn't talk about these things. Jan's family just swooped in and took her away when she died. Iris never got to have a funeral or a service; she has no support from people here because no one except me and a few others had any idea what they were to each other."

"How sad," Margaret murmured, her eyes filling with fresh tears.

Muriel peered at her daughter with her probing gaze. "So, why are you running away?"

"I'm not –" Margaret began, but stopped short at the look on her mother's face. "It's not that simple." She explained about Gavin's will and the house and the university's hold over her. "This relationship could cost me my home and my job," she finished.

"Or it could give you a reason to live," Muriel observed. "Something you haven't done for a long, long time, Peggy. Remember, love isn't always easy."

Wyck sat in her office, staring out at the rain slashing at the window, her heart feeling as leaden as the skies.

"I didn't want to tell you in a letter," Margaret had said over the telephone a few minutes ago as she explained about her sabbatical. "You're right, I do need some time to figure some things out, and I need some distance... from here, from you. While I'm in England, I can do some research and I can write."

There had been a long, tense silence as Wyck sat with her elbows braced on the desk, her forehead pressed to her fingers.

"I know I shouldn't ask," Margaret said, "but I was hoping you would agree to continue looking after the house and the gardens. My accountant will be paying the bills for me while I'm away, so he can continue to pay you for your work."

"Sure." Wyck's voice was clipped, short and she knew Margaret heard it.

"Wyck, I love –"

"Don't!" Wyck said still more sharply. "Don't."

She could hear the tremor in Margaret's voice as she forced herself to say, "I know I'm taking the chance... I can't expect you to wait for me."

"That's good of you," Wyck said, grimacing at the bitterness she heard in her own voice, but she couldn't help it. "Because I fall in love so easily. It only took me four years to allow myself to fall in love with you," but she didn't say that part.

"When do you leave?" Wyck asked instead.

"Saturday," Margaret said. "It's last minute, but Jim Evans worked with me to make it happen. I'm at the office now, getting a few books I'll need. And there are still several things I need to take care of at the house." She hesitated and then said, "Could I see you before I go?"

"Why, Margaret? So we can torture each other?" Wyck asked, unable to mask the anguish in her voice.

Long silent seconds passed as they both sat on the phone.

"If you change your mind," Margaret said at last, "come by anytime."

Wyck didn't know how long she sat staring out at the rain before she stirred. Locking the office, she exited the building without a rain jacket or umbrella. It was a warm summer rain, and she didn't bother hurrying to her truck. Pulling out from her parking space, she wiped the wetness from her eyes, not all of it rain, as she drove aimlessly.

It was such a helpless feeling, having to sit and wait for Margaret to decide if she, Wyck, was worth everything she stood to lose. Because Wyck truly did understand the enormity of what Margaret was risking. Gavin had played his cards well, using the security he offered as a way of holding Margaret to him, even after he was gone. Part of her wanted to argue, to persuade, but... "I can't." This couldn't be something Margaret agreed to because she was talked into it. "If I did and she wasn't ready, she would come to hate me for it. She has to decide it's worth the risk. All I can do is wait," she argued with herself as she drove.

Without realizing how she came to be there, Wyck found herself driving through Margaret's neighborhood. She pulled over and parked, turning the ignition off. For a long time, she sat as the rain pounded the hood and blurred the windshield. Several times, her hand reached for the door handle. "Don't be stupid," she muttered aloud, but "since when have I ever done what's smart?" she could have added.

Getting out of the truck, she walked past a few houses to the Braithwaite place. Lights were on already as the storm clouds had brought an early twilight. Rain streamed down her neck into the collar of her polo shirt and her feet were wet in her sodden deck shoes as she walked around the back of the house. There, she could see the kitchen, lit up but empty. Backing away, she looked up to the second floor and saw the light on in Margaret's study. Squinting as she raised a hand to shield her eyes from the raindrops beating down, she could see Margaret standing at her desk. Wyck stood for long minutes, squinting up through the pelting raindrops, knowing she should leave, but wanting so desperately for Margaret to see her....

Margaret glanced up in time to see a blur of movement through the rain. Pressing her face to the window, she couldn't be sure what was down there. Dashing down the stairs and through the house to the front door, she flung it open to see Wyck nearly at the end of the driveway.

"Wait!" she called. Wyck didn't hear her, or if she did, she kept walking. Margaret ran out into the rain. "Wyck!"

Wyck paused, turning to see Margaret running through the rain to her. They stood in the downpour, Margaret's eyes blinking the wetness away as rivulets of rain ran down her face. She stepped closer.

"Don't go," she said, reaching up to hold Wyck's face in her hands and kissing her hard. Wyck's arms wrapped around Margaret's shoulders, pulling her close and kissing her back as they stood, partially obscured by the curtain of rain.

Margaret pulled away at last and, taking Wyck by the hand, led her to the house. Inside, she pushed the front door closed, and pressed Wyck wordlessly against it, kissing her again, desperately, hungrily, as she slipped one thigh between Wyck's, moaning breathlessly as she increased the pressure of her pelvis against Wyck's. Her hands found Wyck's breasts, felt the hard nipples pressing through her wet shirt and bra. Forcing herself to stop, Margaret took Wyck's hand again and led her upstairs to her room.

"Was this –?"

"He was never in here," Margaret whispered, anticipating Wyck's reservation.

Reassured, Wyck took the initiative, unbuttoning Margaret's drenched blouse and pushing it from her shoulders, brushing her fingertips lightly over her collarbones and down her chest to the lacy edge of her bra, causing goosebumps to erupt all over Margaret's skin as she shivered in anticipation, forgetting all her prior worries about what Wyck would think of her body. Wyck unfastened Margaret's bra, tossing it aside as she bent to take one firm nipple in her mouth. Gasping, Margaret's hands flew to Wyck's wet hair and pulled her mouth more firmly against her breast as Wyck's hands ran down her back, pressing Margaret's hips into her. She paused as Margaret grabbed the hem of her polo shirt, pulling it over her head and undoing her bra.

She paused for a moment, her eyes shining as she took in Wyck's body. "You are so beautiful –"

"Shhh," Wyck interrupted, stepping closer and pressing her fingers to Margaret's lips. "No words. Just be with me..." she whispered, pressing her mouth to Margaret's again as they backed up to the bed.

They lay together under tangled covers, listening to the continuing rain outside as the gray afternoon light faded into true twilight, neither of them wanting to disturb the moment. They lay on their sides, facing each other, Margaret's fingers lightly tracing the outline of Wyck's delicate features while Wyck's hand caressed Margaret's side, following the sensuous curves of her waist and hip.

Margaret ran her hand through Wyck's hair, dry now, but mussed as usual, smiling as she recalled her initial indignation at Wyck's careless appearance.

Reluctantly, Wyck said, "I have to get home to Mandy. And you have to pack."

"Maybe I could –"

"You know you have to go," Wyck said, closing her eyes. "I know you have to go."

She felt Margaret's lips, feather-light, on her eyelids. They fluttered open.

"I do love you," Margaret murmured.

"And I love you," Wyck said for the first time, her face softening. "But we both know that may not be enough. You have to be sure. And I need to know you're sure. Any doubts, for either of us, will be a constant thorn, pricking at us, never allowing us to truly trust each other. That's not the life we want."

"No," Margaret admitted reluctantly.

Margaret watched as Wyck slid out of bed, searching for her discarded clothing and dressing quickly. She stood over the bed for a moment, looking down into Margaret's dark eyes, feeling as if she could drown in them. Leaning over, she kissed her slowly, lingering as long as she dared, and then forced herself to go.

Chapter 22

"HOW DOES THE ARM feel?" Wyck asked David as she handed him a soda.

He pulled up the sleeve of his t-shirt to reveal a series of scars over the outer part of his arm. His elbow remained bent slightly, unable to straighten completely after spending months immobilized in casts and splints. "It hurts," he shrugged, "but at least I can use it some now."

He sat back and looked around as he took a drink. "This place looks really nice. You did a great job."

"Thanks," Wyck said, glancing around also. "But I kind of wish now I'd taken my time, left myself more to do," she sighed.

"Why?"

"Nothing." Wyck shook her head. "How was it for you today? Being down at the police station? Seeing them?"

David's face took on the vacant, haunted look she had seen when he talked about being in prison. "It was weird. I want them to be punished, but I didn't really want to have to see their faces again.

You know... things happen in prison. The guards can't stop everything; sometimes they don't want to. You expect it in there, but... it's not supposed to happen out here. And not to you."

Wyck looked down at the drink in her hand. "It wasn't your fault."

He watched her closely. "You seem better than you did for a while afterwards."

She nodded. "I am. It was hard. I jumped at every sound, every shadow." She laughed sheepishly. "I carried a gun with me everywhere I went."

"How'd you get past that?"

She expelled a breath, dropping her head back on the chair, staring up at the timbers above. "I don't really know. There was a raccoon rattling around on the porch one night. Scared the shit out of me. I almost shot her without even knowing what I was shooting at. That scared me more than being scared." She picked her head up and looked at him. "I had shut myself up, boarded my life up, trying to keep Mandy and me safe, but... it was like those bastards were standing over me all the time, stealing my life. Something snapped that night, and I just decided I couldn't let them do that anymore. The gun is tucked away in a drawer and Mandy and I are living again."

He nodded. "Then, why –? You seem sad."

Wyck swallowed hard. "I am," she said honestly. "I love someone who... It's complicated. She stands to lose a lot if our relationship becomes public knowledge, and she's got to decide whether it's worth it."

"Margaret Braithwaite?" David guessed.

Wyck stared at him. "How did you –?"

He gave a small shrug. "Just something in the way she looked at you, and the way you wouldn't look at her," he said with a grin. "I don't think anyone else would have guessed."

"Well, Gavin did," Wyck said, a trace of bitterness in her voice. She explained the terms of the will.

"So, where's Margaret now?"

184

"In England until Christmas," Wyck said.

"And you're stuck here, waiting?" he asked. "That sucks."

Wyck let out a bark of laughter. "Yes. It does suck. And it's only been a few weeks." She blinked hard to clear the wetness from her eyes. "How about you? Are you seeing anyone? You are allowed to, aren't you?"

"Oh, yeah," he said sarcastically. "I'm allowed as long as I disclose to them at the beginning that I'm a convicted sex offender and that anything that happens will be discussed in my therapy sessions with other sex offenders and will be part of the record of my next polygraph. Guys are just lining up to be with me under those conditions."

"Whoa," Wyck said.

"Yeah. That's why I've got to get back to work. I really need to stay busy," he said, immediately holding up a hand. "Not with you. I didn't mean that. Even if you were willing after everything that happened, I can't do that kind of work, at least, not right now. I need an office job. Dealing with all my hospital bills, I kind of got interested in medical billing. If I could get a job doing that, I'd be in the basement of a medical practice somewhere. It could work."

Wyck nodded. "I'll be glad to give you a good reference. Just let me know."

"Thanks," David said gratefully. "And I hope things work out for you and Margaret."

Margaret climbed a small knoll that afforded her a breathtaking view of a broad valley below, the shimmering waters of a narrow lake filling the valley floor, and breathed in air that could only have belonged to the English countryside after a summer rain.

She had spent the last few weeks at Chawton, reacquainting herself with the place where Austen did most of her writing, and researching the library's collection of women writers of the period – most of them obscure compared to Austen, Shelley and the Brontës.

When Margaret was younger, when she had regularly come on her Austen pilgrimages, first as an undergrad with Julia, and then later by herself as Gavin had spent all of his time visiting the gardens at the great houses, she had visited Austen's grave at Winchester, the rectory at Steventon – all the typical stops along the trail with all the other Austenphiles paying homage to their heroine.

But in the years since her last visit, at least ten – she couldn't really recall anymore – something had shifted in her view. *I'm now older than she was when she died,* Margaret had realized as she wandered the grounds of Chawton House, perhaps retracing the same paths Jane had walked when visiting her brother there, *and I've done less with my life, despite my advantages.*

"But unlike Jane," said a contrary voice in her head as she paused to look around, "you have a real love waiting for you, more real even than Julia was – let's face it, how many twenty-two-year-olds could have stayed together their whole lives? – if you are just brave enough to be with her despite what people say."

"Ah, there's the rub. What would Jane make of me?" Margaret responded.

Margaret had tried unsuccessfully to silence this other voice in her head ever since she had left Asheville. It kept popping up at unexpected moments, taunting her and challenging her, reminding her of what she had left behind. *As if I need reminding,* Margaret thought ruefully, as the mere memory of that wet afternoon with Wyck could reduce her to a quivering mess, often at the most inconvenient times.

"Is something funny, miss?" the sales girl had asked in bewilderment in the Chawton gift shop as Margaret stood in line to purchase yet another copy of *Persuasion*.

The bemused smile slid from Margaret's face as she blushed furiously. "No, nothing."

Now, as Margaret breathed deeply and looked about at the hilly countryside surrounding her, an old man hobbled toward her, one very crooked leg causing him to limp. A black and white Border collie trotted beside him.

"Will there be anything else, Mrs. Braithwaite?"

Margaret turned to him. "No, Mr. Hopson, thank you so much."

"Well, your things is all in the cottage and there's food in the kitchen." He doffed his frayed lad's cap, twisting it in his gnarled hands. "Me and the missus are sorry to hear about your loss."

"How did you –?" Margaret began, but stopped, realizing that, of course, the friend of a friend from London who helped find this cottage would naturally have mentioned that she was a new widow. She didn't mind. It would forestall prying questions about why she wanted solitude if people assumed she was in mourning. *You should be in mourning*, she reminded herself, but didn't want to think too hard about that.

He turned to point back down the dirt lane to another small house about a half mile away. "Me and the missus are just there, if you need anythin'."

"Thank you," she smiled.

He peered at her curiously. "A poet, are you?" he guessed.

Her eyebrows raised in surprise. "Why would you say that?"

He smiled, revealing a few gaps in his teeth. "Why else would a young woman come all the way up here by herself to rent a bit of a cottage in Wordsworth country?"

She smiled in greater surprise. "Do you know Wordsworth, then?"

He cackled. "Good gracious, miss. How could we not when all the tour buses is runnin' about, carrying tourists all over the Lakes?"

"Well, that's why your cottage suits me so well," she said, pointing to the tiny stone house, roses clinging to its walls, looking every bit the quintessential English cottage. "Three miles from Coniston, on a road too little for the buses, and the agent promised me peace and quiet."

"And you'll have it, miss," Mr. Hopson said, rubbing a hand over his bald head. "Me and the missus will see to that. No one and nothin' gets by but that we see it. Most like, the only ones you'll see will be me and Wisp here runnin' the sheep."

"Thank you again."

He donned his cap, tweaking the brim. "Well, I'll just leave you then. Up with you, Wisp," he said, opening the car door so the dog could jump in. "You come get us anytime if you need anythin'," he repeated, climbing in after Wisp. The aged car started with a bang. Mr. Hopson waved his cap one last time as, with a loud grinding of the gears, he drove back down the lane.

Margaret entered the cottage, softly lit by the sunlight coming in through the leaded casement windows. The cozy sitting room was furnished with a pair of comfy, overstuffed chintz armchairs near the fireplace and a round dining table with an oil lamp sitting in the center. Off the sitting room was a tiny bathroom, clearly added long after the cottage was built, and a bedroom, also with an oil lamp on the dresser. Peering apprehensively into the kitchen, she breathed a sigh of relief as she saw a mini two-burner electric cooker and a small icebox.

"At least the kitchen has electricity," she mumbled to herself, feeling very gratified that she had sent as many e-mails as she had while she had Internet access. It hadn't even occurred to her that the cottage might not have power. Ruefully, she set her laptop bag down on a dining chair. "Guess I'll be buying more paper and stamps."

Wyck looked up to make sure Mandy wasn't wandering too far off and then turned her attention back to the last few stones waiting to be set in another wall of Gavin's that had needed to be rebuilt. This one bordered a flagstoned terrace, so Wyck carefully chose flat capstones so that the wall could also serve as seating. She was grateful to be working in the shade, but even so was soon sweating as she knelt in the oppressive July heat.

"This is way better than the one Gavin built," she said with satisfaction as she surveyed her work.

She knew it made no sense to feel that she was in competition with him – with his memory – but she couldn't help it. Margaret had been gone a month, though it felt much longer to Wyck.

"I'll try to e-mail," Margaret had said the morning she left.

"No promises," Wyck said. "You don't know what kind of Internet access you're going to have, and I don't -"

"You're right," Margaret said. "It's not fair to leave you like this and keep you hanging on, waiting for me to send messages."

A car horn beeped.

"That's the shuttle."

"I could drive you to the airport, you know," Wyck said.

Margaret stepped closer, taking Wyck's face in her hands. "This is hard enough here." She kissed Wyck, a soft, lingering kiss that neither wanted to break, but the horn sounded again, more impatiently this time. "Goodbye," Margaret murmured.

There had been just two e-mails since, messages that Wyck had printed off and read until she had them memorized.

Now, Wyck sat back, mopping her sweaty forehead with her t-shirt sleeve. With a small groan, she pushed heavily to her feet, her left leg still weaker than the right. Calling Mandy, she wandered the paths, looking the landscape over with a critical eye. There was the site she had proposed for a new pergola and flagstone seating area, and over there, she and Gavin had talked about building a wooden fence and planting a hedge of raspberries and blackberries, but she wasn't willing to take on any of those projects now.

"Not after what you did," she muttered as she walked. Knowing the house would be going to the university, that it was in essence only on loan to Margaret, had removed any excitement Wyck had felt at creating anything new here. "I'll fix and maintain, but that's all," Wyck had cautioned Margaret.

Making a mental list of what needed to be done, she made a wide loop through the property, angling back toward the house. Gathering up her tools, she called Mandy who was busily sniffing a burrow dug under the roots of an oak tree, and headed back to the truck.

She drove to her next job, a new project for a guy named Branche. He wanted a paver patio to replace a broken concrete pool surround. It was a big job, but she had priced it to make it worth her while, and he had agreed. She was pleased to see the dumpster already in place in the driveway and that the pallets of pavers had been delivered along with a large pile of decomposed granite. Nothing felt more frustrating than being ready to start a job and running into delays because materials hadn't been delivered. "Well, almost nothing," she could have said, trying to keep her mind off Margaret.

She got Mandy situated in the shade with a bowl of water while she began breaking up the concrete with a sledgehammer. Her t-shirt and jeans were soon drenched with sweat, and both she and Mandy looked longingly at the pool.

"Don't even think about it," she said as Mandy gathered, ready to leap into the water.

Loading the chunks of concrete into a wheelbarrow, she walked them out to the dumpster, load after load, methodically working her way around the pool.

She was about a third of the way done when a Lexus convertible pulled into the driveway, past the dumpster and into the garage. Without looking up, Wyck continued tossing the concrete pieces into the dumpster as a woman emerged from the garage.

She simply stood there until Wyck paused and glanced at her. She had a Prada bag hanging from one shoulder, and Wyck suspected it wasn't a knock-off. She wore a visor over her blond hair and a sleeveless Lacoste tennis dress that fit her lean body very closely, showing off tanned arms and legs as she lifted her expensive-looking sunglasses up to get a better look at Wyck.

Wyck used the hem of her t-shirt to wipe the sweat from her eyes, the woman's eyes immediately taking in her lean mid-section.

"You're the landscaper my husband hired?" she asked in surprise.

Wyck nodded. "I am Fitzsimmons Landscaping," she said. "Sorry if the driveway is a little cluttered now. I should be done in about three weeks."

One finely arched eyebrow raised as she looked Wyck up and down, saying in a silky voice, "Oh, there's no hurry."

Chapter 23

THE VALLEY STRETCHED OUT below her as Margaret paused to catch her breath. Fields dotted with grazing cattle and sheep were demarcated into a checkerboard pattern by rock walls and hedges, and in the distance she could see a couple of tour buses rattling along one of the paved roads. Stooping to pick up her totes, she resumed the three-mile walk back to the cottage. The Hopsons had very kindly stocked her little kitchen for her arrival, but this morning, she had decided to walk into Coniston to pick up some additional groceries, and to mail two letters - one to her mother and one to Wyck.

"Here, dear, there's no need for that," Mrs. Hopson had declared as she spied Margaret ambling by their house on her way to town. "I'll get Archie to drive you."

"No, thank you, Mrs. Hopson," Margaret had smiled. "It's a beautiful morning. I'll enjoy the walk."

"All right, dear," said Mrs. Hopson, sounding unconvinced as she wrung her hands in her apron.

Halfway back to the cottage, Margaret was ruing her enthusiasm for walking, as the totes filled with her shopping weighed more and more heavily on her arms.

Mrs. Hopson was keeping an eye out for her return and snagged her as she approached their house. "Now, I insist you come in for a rest while the kettle boils," she said, taking Margaret's bags from her. "We'll keep these chilled," she said as she put the tote with milk and eggs in the refrigerator.

She settled Margaret at the spotless kitchen table as she made tea for both of them. "Archie and Wisp's out movin' the sheep," she said as she bustled about.

Margaret got up and went to the open back door. "Mrs. Hopson, this is beautiful," she said in wonder as she stepped outside into a garden awash in color.

"Do you like gardens, dear?" Mrs. Hopson asked, following Margaret outside as she took everything in.

"I... I don't know much about them myself, but I have a very dear friend who loves to garden," Margaret said. *Funny, I thought only of Wyck, not Gavin,* she realized later.

"Archie always says 'them's can make things grow outta nothin' has a special gift'," Mrs. Hopson said proudly.

Margaret smiled at her. "Well, I think he's right. You do have a gift."

"Oh, tut," Mrs. Hopson said, waving her hand at Margaret, but she looked pleased.

By the time Margaret got back to her cottage, a soft rain had begun to fall. She made herself a quick lunch and then pulled out of the second tote a packet of paper along with a bottle of ink and an old-fashioned nibbed pen. The oil lamps had inspired a desire to write as Jane would have. *If only the talent came with it,* she thought wryly as she dipped the pen in the inkbottle and immediately created a large inky blotch as she touched pen to paper. "I wonder if this is how Rorschach got started?" she grumbled as she blotted the ink.

With practice, she learned how deeply to dip the pen and found herself immersed in the literal flow of the words onto the page. Picking up where she had left off in her manuscript, she spent the remainder of the afternoon writing, helped by a few glasses of wine. When at last she stopped, laying her reading glasses aside and rubbing her eyes tiredly, she felt an enormous sense of accomplishment at seeing the stack of pages lying there, filled with line after line of inky squiggles. "My words, my thoughts," she said aloud to the empty cottage. "Never again will I have to be nothing more than someone else's research assistant."

She got up from the table and went to her open door with a fresh glass of wine. It still mystified her that the concept of screens had never caught on in Britain as flies buzzed freely in and out of the windows and doors. The rain had stopped and the late afternoon sun, with its slanting rays, was illuminating the world with a golden light that shimmered on the raindrops covering everything.

She sighed as she looked about, trying to forget how upset Gavin made her lately. Each time she'd thought of him the last couple of weeks, it had been with anger and resentment. It felt disloyal, somehow, to be so resentful of her dead husband, but when she remembered how Gavin had belittled her writing - "not that I was writing anything to praise," she had to admit, "but it wasn't just my writing. It was me, everything about me - the way I dressed, the way I taught, the way I talked - he wanted everything about me to be in his image." Guiltily, she had to admit that what she felt more than anything was relief that that part of her life was over - more than grief, more than loneliness, more than love. She knew it wouldn't always be so. Someday, there would be forgiveness....

The wine glass dropped from her hand and shattered on the limestone stoop as she leaned heavily against the jamb.

"Forgive me."

It hadn't been Wyck he'd been asking for forgiveness - at least not for calling the reporter and setting in motion the events that had led to the attack. It was she, she and Wyck together, that he'd wanted to forgive him - for the things he had already done and couldn't undo. In a flash, she understood everything - the insecurity that had dogged him as he saw his wife falling in love with someone else, a someone who was a woman, a someone he hadn't a clue how to compete with so that the only way he had left to fight for her, to keep her loyal to him, was to control the things he could leave her....

Sandra Branche stretched languidly on a floating raft drifting across the pool as Wyck laid pavers in a herringbone pattern, stealing occasional glances at the taut, tanned, bikini-clad body so obviously being displayed for her benefit. Wyck hoped the dark sunglasses she was wearing against the glare of the water and the light-colored pavers were enough to hide her glances. She tried to focus on what she was doing, but was admittedly distracted.

"Damn," she muttered, seeing that she had messed up the pattern. She had to pull out three pavers and redo them.

"Why don't you take a break and jump in," Sandra invited, as she had done nearly every day over the past two weeks.

"No, thank you," Wyck said, as she had declined every prior invitation. "Why don't you go play tennis or whatever it is you do?" she wanted to say, but Sandra seemed to have suddenly felt the need to be home every day. *How many of these women are there in this town?* Wyck wondered. *And do their husbands know their wives are into women?* She didn't want to think about how much that thought might titillate them, and she had no intention of becoming Sandra's latest conquest. Even Mandy hadn't liked her, refusing to come when Sandra tried to call her, and for Wyck, that confirmed her suspicions that this was a woman to stay away from.

Sandra slid off her raft and swam to the edge of the pool, climbing the stairs out of the water with a feline slinkiness. She returned a few minutes later with two icy glasses of tea. "You look hot," she said with such a straight face that Wyck couldn't tell if she had intended the double-entendre or not.

"Thank you," Wyck said, accepting one of the glasses and trying not to watch as Sandra tilted her head back and ran her glass down her chest in between breasts barely contained by her bikini top.

Wyck choked on her tea, coughing and gagging. "I'm fine," she gasped as Sandra took the opportunity to step closer and wrap an arm around her shoulders.

"Why don't we go inside? You could use a breather," Sandra purred. "You've been working so hard."

Wyck slid away from her. "I'm fine," she repeated. "Got a lot more to get done. Thanks for the tea," she said, gulping down the last of it and handing the glass back.

Her cheeks puffed out as she expelled a slow, calming breath and went to the pallet of pavers to grab another armful of stones and get back to work.

Wyck was not about to have a fling with a client's wife, but, "Damn, she's beautiful," she said to Mandy when she got home later that afternoon. Mandy whuffed in such a clear attitude of dislike that Wyck had to laugh. "But not as beautiful as you," she said, ruffling Mandy's velvety ears.

Wyck peeled off her sweaty clothing and stood for a long time under a cool shower, letting the water cascade over her head and face as her body gradually cooled. When she was dried off and dressed, she went downstairs.

"Your turn," she said, taking out a brush. Mandy stood with her eyes half-closed as Wyck brushed her. "You are so easy," Wyck grinned as Mandy leaned into the brush strokes, panting with obvious pleasure.

"Ready for our dinner date?" she said when she was done. She retrieved a bottle of wine from the frig and then she and Mandy got into the truck.

A short while later, Wyck was driving slowly down a road she had never been on, a few miles outside of Asheville, scanning mailboxes. "I think this is it," she said, turning in and parking next to David's repainted Taurus.

"You found it!" David smiled as he answered her knock on the front door.

Wyck and Mandy entered the little house. "This is nice," Wyck said.

"It's not bad," David shrugged.

"Any trouble so far?" she asked.

He shook his head. "I had to register, of course, but I don't think anyone recognizes this road, since there's no real neighborhood. No neighbors, either," he said, sounding relieved.

Another car pulled into the driveway and a minute later, Lorie came in. "Hi," she said with a big smile, giving Wyck a hug and kneeling to greet Mandy.

"I didn't know you were coming," Wyck said. "I haven't seen you in weeks."

Lorie shrugged. "David just said to come, so I came."

"Well, I asked you both to come here tonight," said David, "because we're celebrating. I got a new job!"

"David!" Lorie exclaimed, springing to her feet to give her brother a hug. "That's wonderful! Where?"

He gestured to Wyck. "You did it," he said, grinning. "Whatever you said to Joyce Manning, it worked. She called me in for a very intense interview and gave me a job with her medical billing company."

Lorie flung her arms around Wyck again. "Thank you," she said tearfully.

"I didn't do anything," Wyck protested. "She's a client. All I did was say I knew of someone if she had an opening."

David looked at her. "She told me you did a little more than that. I know she had some reservations about all the extra work hiring me might make for her, and she said she wouldn't have even considered it if you hadn't talked to her."

Wyck blushed. "I was glad to do it," she mumbled.

"So anyway," David said, leading them into the small kitchen, "I made dinner to celebrate."

The back door stood open and, through the screen, they could smell the aroma of whatever was cooking on the grill. Within a few minutes, they were seated at the table enjoying a meal of chicken, steak, salad and fresh roasted corn while Mandy had her own bowl of chicken and rice.

As David talked excitedly about the new job, Wyck realized how abnormally quiet he had been when she first met him. She could near the relief in Lorie's voice as well.

"So, have you heard from Margaret?" David asked Wyck.

Lorie's ears perked up. "Who's Margaret?" she asked immediately.

Wyck could feel herself turn red. "She's... she's someone I'm hoping will be more than a friend," she said. "And yes, I had a couple of e-mails about a month ago, but she's in a part of England now where she didn't know what kind of Internet access she might have, so nothing recently."

Lorie frowned in puzzlement. "What are you doing getting involved with someone in England?"

"She's only there for a few months," Wyck explained.

"Wait," Lorie said. "Is this the woman you brought to the Biltmore? I thought she was married?"

Wyck nodded. "Her husband died, leaving her trapped with all the social expectations of being his widow." She held up both hands. "Here's me. Not exactly an even swap," she said wryly. "And there, as they say, is the crux of the matter."

Lorie reached over and took Wyck's hand. "If she's smart, she'll latch onto you and hold fast."

"She stands to lose a lot," Wyck said quietly.

"But she stands to gain more," David replied.

"If she believed that," Wyck said with a rueful smile, "she wouldn't be in England."

Chapter 24

WYCK SIGHED AS SHE scrolled through her e-mail. Nothing from Margaret. Not that she had expected anything, but... She went back through the new messages, replying to a few, deleting several and then turned to the stack of mail she had picked up from her post office box that morning. Several bills, some checks and – a letter, the envelope bordered by the red and blue signifying international mail. Flipping it over, she saw Margaret's return address, the cottage she was renting. She held it for several seconds and then set it aside, forcing herself to take care of bills first. Half an hour later, she left the office, walking a couple of blocks to the bank and dropping her envelopes into a mailbox on the way. Only then, did she allow herself to think about Margaret's letter.

Seated at a small table in a café – the same café where Margaret used to come to write, she realized with a smile – she ordered a chicken salad sandwich and iced tea. "Unsweet," she said firmly.

Her server paused as she wrote the order. "You said unsweet?"

Wyck glanced up at her, and was given a dazzling smile by a pretty twenty-something, her sandy hair cropped very short.

"Uh, yes," Wyck said.

"Be right back," said the waitress, returning a moment later with the tea. "Your sandwich will be right up. I'm Ashley. Just call if you need anything."

"Thanks," Wyck said, waiting until Ashley moved on to another table and then eagerly prying open the flap of the envelope.

My dearest Wyck,

Alas, (can you tell I am immersed?) the cottage I am renting not only does not have Internet, it doesn't have a telephone or electricity except in the kitchen. I am writing to you by oil lamp with an inkbottle and a nibbed pen!

My landlords, Mr. and Mrs. Hopson, are very nice and are taking good care of me - too good, I'm afraid, as they think I need frequent company, but they are sweet people. Mr. Hopson is a sheep farmer with a Border collie you and Mandy would adore, and Mrs. Hopson is a gardener. You would love the roses on my cottage. I think of you whenever I smell them, which is all the time.

I hope you don't mind, but I sent my mother your name, address and phone number in case something happens. I should have asked you first, but it slipped my mind before I left the country. If something should happen, it would take me a few days at least to get word and return to the U.S., so I wanted her to have someone closer she could call. Her name and information are below for you as well.

I hope you and Mandy are well and not working too hard. Please know that I miss you and think of you constantly.

All my love,

Meggie

Wyck started to read the letter over, but was interrupted by Ashley returning with her sandwich.

"Do you go to school here?" she asked as she set the plate down.

Wyck's eyes narrowed slightly and she hid a smile at the clumsy attempt at flattery. "No," she said slowly. "I have an office downtown."

"What do you do?" Ashley asked brightly.

"Landscape architecture," Wyck replied, wondering if Ashley was even old enough to understand what that was.

"So you design?" Ashley asked, surprising Wyck.

"Design and do most of the work," Wyck said.

"Excuse me, miss?" called a customer from another table.

Ashley gave an apologetic smile and went to wait on him.

Wyck re-read Margaret's letter over and over while she ate, becoming more buoyant with each reading. Not one mention of Gavin. The roses made her think of Wyck. She had given Wyck's contact information to her mother, not Amanda's or Jeffrey's. What did that mean? Most tellingly, she had signed the letter "Meggie".

"Don't read too much into this," she said to herself.

"But –"

"Just don't set yourself up," she cautioned.

"A letter from a friend?" Ashley asked curiously, peering over Wyck's shoulder as she brought the check.

"Yes," Wyck said, folding the letter and laying a protective hand on top of it.

"Well, here's your bill," Ashley said, sounding as if she wanted an excuse to linger. "Ask for me the next time you come in."

Wyck nodded. "I'll do that. Thanks." She gave a small snort of laughter when she turned the check over and saw that Ashley, in addition to writing up her total, had left a blank check with her telephone number.

"Hello," said a middle-aged couple passing in the opposite direction, each of them laden with a backpack and using walking sticks.

"Good morning," Margaret returned, feeling underequipped as she walked back toward her cottage carrying nothing more than a bottle of water.

Wearing shorts and a loose top, she completed a five-mile loop she had discovered within the system of walking trails that transected most of the area. She had been doing this hilly walk each dry morning for the past three weeks. At first, she had barely managed to complete the loop, fearing she might actually have to ask for assistance, and collapsing in exhaustion when she had at last reached her cottage. But gradually, her fitness had improved until she felt invigorated at the end of the five miles.

Pausing to catch her breath, she took in the magnificent view spreading out below her as the couple walked on. Uncapping her water, she raised the bottle in a toast. "Happy birthday to me," she murmured, thinking this was the last place on earth she would have expected to pass her fifty-third birthday.

Back at the cottage, she sat down to a large bowl of oatmeal and resumed writing. The manuscript was flying along. She was hopeful she would have a first draft transcribed to her laptop by the time she returned to the States. If she could just get this book under contract to be published, maybe it would loosen St. Aloysius's stranglehold on her....

She was interrupted by a knock on the open front door.

"Good mornin', dear," called Mrs. Hopson. "How are you this beautiful day?"

"Just fine, Mrs. Hopson," said Margaret, forcing herself to smile. "Won't you come in?"

"Just for a minute, then," said Mrs. Hopson. "I've brought you some summer flowers and a few early beans." She stepped inside with a wrapped bundle of cut flowers. "These are delphinium, and astilbes, and bougainvillea," she said proudly.

"They're beautiful," Margaret said sincerely, going to the kitchen to get a jar and filling it with water at the tap. "I don't know how you do it."

"Oh, tut," Mrs. Hopson said, arranging the flowers in the jar. She placed them on the table where Margaret's manuscript pages were scattered about. "You are a writer, then. Archie thought you was a poet."

"Not a poet," Margaret said. "A novelist."

"Really? Braithwaite... Braithwaite," Mrs. Hopson intoned, trying to place the name.

"You're more likely to have heard of my husband's books about the American Civil War," Margaret said. "Gavin Braithwaite?"

Mrs. Hopson shook her head. "No, dear. Can't say as I've read any of those. I like a good love story meself. Not shenanigans, mind, but a real story about broken hearts mended by findin' true love." She immediately looked stricken. "I'm so sorry, dear. That was unkind, you so recently widowed and all." She peered at Margaret shrewdly. "Do you miss him?"

Margaret opened her mouth, and then closed it, not sure how to answer.

"It's all right, dear. There's many a marriage as the couple is more friends than... you know, all lovey-dovey."

"Yes," Margaret said, choosing not to elaborate.

Mrs. Hopson sighed. "Mind you, though, a heart does long for poetry and roses, don't it?"

Wyck thought she would never be so glad to see a job finished as she would the Branche project. The aggravation of dealing politely with Sandra's unwanted advances was almost more than the money was worth. It seemed that Sandra was taking Wyck's refusals as a personal challenge. Her flirtations were becoming more overt, and the closer Wyck got to the end of the job, the more desperate Sandra seemed to get.

"Has anyone ever refused her?" Wyck mumbled, using the handle of her trowel to tap a paver into place. "Might actually be less work to just give her what she wants."

She didn't even bother to look up as she heard Sandra dive into the water, certain that she was skinny-dipping again. This had become Sandra's latest ploy, apparently hoping the sight of her nakedness would drive Wyck to give in to the lust she must no doubt be struggling to control. Wyck chortled to herself as she tried to imagine what could possess someone to work this hard for something so meaningless. Wyck turned her back on the pool and continued the monotonous task of laying the last section of pavers.

She shook her head as she tried to figure out what was spurring all the attention from women recently – Sandra, Ashley the waitress, even the dyke who worked at the Stone and Block where she ordered all her patio supplies seemed more attentive lately. *None of this was happening two or three years ago*, she thought as she tapped a slightly oversized paver into place. *The only thing that's different now is that I'm in love. Maybe it's like some kind of pheromone.* She smiled, wondering for probably the millionth time how Margaret was doing.

She straightened up with a groan as the last paver slid into place. Standing up stiffly, she looked around at the expanse of newly laid stone, pleased with her work. Turning, she was startled to find Sandra there, water dripping from her naked body, no lines marring her perfect tan. Sandra stepped up wordlessly and mashed her lips against Wyck's.

Wyck was so startled, it took her a second to react. Placing her hands on Sandra's shoulders, she pushed, perhaps a little harder than she had intended. Sandra reeled backward, arms windmilling and, for a terrifying moment, Wyck was afraid she would fall onto the stones, but as she backpedaled, she came to the edge of the pool and fell in.

"You bitch!" Sandra sputtered furiously when she surfaced.

Pushed beyond enduring by Sandra's brazenness, Wyck said, "You really don't get the art of seduction, do you? And just in case you still think any part of this has tempted me, Mrs. Branche, I've got to tell you, the sight of you falling just now, all floppy and naked, was not attractive. I'll be happy to keep that as my last image of you."

"Well, well, what's this?" said a male voice.

Bob Branche had come around the corner of the house and was standing on the patio, taking in the strange scene.

Wyck had no idea how much he had seen and heard. Flushed in her anger, she retrieved her tools and said, "I'll be finished here tomorrow,

Mr. Branche. I'll expect your check for the second half of the job at that time."

She stalked away, tossing her tools into the bed of the truck and left, still fuming. Driving home, she kept shaking her head, muttering angrily to herself. If Branche tried to stiff her over this... She was startled by the ring of her cell phone.

"Hello?"

"Is this Wyck Fitzsimmons?" asked a woman's voice.

"Yes," said Wyck cautiously.

She nearly drove off the road as she heard the woman say, "This is Muriel Collins, Peggy's mother."

"Is Margaret okay? Are you all right?"

"Oh, yes, nothing like that," said Muriel. "But I think you and I should talk. Can you come to Richmond?"

Wyck reached over to where Mandy lay curled up on the seat next to her, freshly bathed and soft and fluffy. Her warmth comforted Wyck who was more than nervous as she drove. In the week since Muriel Collins had called, Wyck had fretted about what in the world she could want.

"I have some work I need to finish here before I could go," Wyck had said. "And I have a dog –"

"A golden retriever, yes. Peggy told me," Muriel said. "You're welcome to bring her. Several people here have dogs. I have a pullout bed that Peggy sleeps in when she comes to visit. Whenever you can clear your schedule will be fine."

Wyck called as she neared Richmond, and, finding her way to the assisted living facility with no trouble, sat in the parking lot, trying to calm herself. "I don't know about this," she muttered to Mandy as she clipped her leash to her collar, wondering if Margaret would approve of this unauthorized meeting. Muriel was waiting for them in the lobby at the sign-in desk. Mandy politely sat and greeted her.

"Mrs. Collins," Wyck said holding out a hand.

"Please, Wyck, call me Muriel," she said, taking Wyck's hand and staring at her curiously.

Wyck could see much of Margaret in her mother, especially the eyes. Muriel chatted animatedly as she spryly led the way to her apartment, greeting nearly every person they passed by name. She asked Wyck how the traffic had been, if she had any trouble with the directions. Wyck answered, gazing around as they passed a hair salon, a chapel, a library, even a small branch of a bank.

"Oh, yes," Muriel said, noting her interest. "We have everything we need. We can be entombed alive for years and never have to surface for anything except groceries. We don't even get to leave for the funerals. That chapel gets more use than any other part of the building."

Wyck choked on her laugh. "Didn't you want to live closer to Margaret – I mean, Peggy?"

"Oh, I considered it," Muriel said, punching the button for the elevator. "But Frank – he was my husband – Frank and I never were all that chummy with Gavin, and it just seemed better to keep some distance. But after Frank died, I agreed to move here. I'm close enough for Peggy to come for weekends. Here we are," she said, as the elevator opened on the third floor. She led the way to a light, airy apartment with a balcony that gave her a distant view of the James River.

"This is very nice," Wyck said as Mandy sniffed and explored.

"It is," Muriel conceded. "It was just a hard adjustment, knowing it's a one-way trip coming here."

Wyck looked at her appraisingly.

"What? Too honest? Not what you expected?" Muriel asked slyly.

"No," Wyck said. "Just, from some of the things Margaret said, I got the impression you were more... passive."

Muriel laughed. "That was very diplomatically put. But, you're right," she admitted. "When Frank was alive, I was more passive. I shouldn't have been, but... there you are. How about some lunch?"

Presently, they were seated at the table, munching on sandwiches and salads, Mandy lying under the table with her head resting on Wyck's foot.

"So," Muriel said, picking up where they had left off, "about my passivity while my husband was alive. I'm afraid Peggy has fallen into the trap we all dread – she has become her mother."

Wyck tried to swallow a bite as she laughed. Choking a little, she took a drink of her water.

"You know," Muriel said, staring off into the distance, "we were so proud of her when she was a girl. Smart as a whip, stubborn, independent. Frank worked like mad to make sure she could do anything she wanted. Not many steel workers' daughters went to Wellesley, I can tell you. When they fought –" she paused and looked sharply at Wyck. "You do know about that, don't you?"

Wyck nodded, not really sure how much Margaret had told her mother about Julia or about her. She felt as if she were walking on quicksand, having to tread carefully to avoid saying the wrong thing and falling into a quagmire she wouldn't be able to pull herself out of. She had quickly decided that saying as little as possible would be prudent – at least until she knew how much Muriel knew.

"When they fought," Muriel continued, "I suspected, but didn't know for certain what it was about. In those days, we were so ignorant about those things. I think for Frank, it tore him apart to think that Peggy might be a pariah."

Again, Wyck wasn't quite sure Muriel was talking about Margaret's relationship with Julia, until Muriel said, "We didn't know any homosexuals personally, and anything you ever saw portrayed was so horrible..."

Muriel looked at Wyck with her bright, black eyes. "I don't think I knew until just this past few months how hurt Peggy was at being torn away from Julia. When she married Gavin, I thought maybe the thing with Julia had been an infatuation that she had gotten over, but... it wasn't. Not until Peggy told me about you, did I realize how much she's been hiding all these years."

Wyck sat, her forgotten sandwich still held in her hands, her eyes fixed on Muriel's.

"She told you about me?" Wyck repeated in surprise, a sudden tightness in her throat to think Margaret had taken such a step.

Muriel nodded. "Yes, but..."

Wyck's heart sank.

"...it wasn't a happy telling. She's changed. It's as if life with Gavin has beaten something out of her. She cares too much what people think now."

Wyck's heart buoyed back up, just a little.

"That's why I asked you here," Muriel said.

"I'm sorry, I don't understand," Wyck said slowly.

Muriel peered into her eyes, and Wyck had the feeling she was searching for something. "In case you think I'm sneaking around behind my daughter's back, I know her. Peggy wouldn't have given us each other's information if she didn't want us to meet," she said. "I want her to be happy. I think it was a good idea for her to get away to a place where nobody knows her, and no one expects anything of her, but she'll be back soon, and she's going to have to decide how much she's willing to risk for someone she loves. I'm not naïve enough to think - and neither should you be - that she'll be able to do this without a few stumbles. She'll need support, I think, to trust herself again." Muriel's gaze seemed to lose some of its intensity, as if she was satisfied by what she had seen. "And before she gets home, I wanted to know whether you were worth sticking my neck out."

Margaret hummed as she walked, smiling as she remembered what a struggle the six miles to and from Coniston had felt like just a couple of months ago. Her small backpack was loaded with fresh groceries and toiletries - a much easier way to carry them than bags dangling from her arms. Her legs, toned and lean, churned up and down the hills effortlessly, and her breathing was deep and even.

As she approached the cottage, she saw Mrs. Hopson working on the roses.

"Hello, dear!" Mrs. Hopson said brightly when she saw Margaret. "I hope you don't mind, but the roses are so heavy, I had to get them tied up a bit more."

"Not at all," Margaret said, shrugging off her pack. "Let me take care of these and then I can help if you'll teach me."

She quickly put her groceries away and rejoined Mrs. Hopson outside. "How can I help?"

Mrs. Hopson showed her how to use strips of ribbon to tie the roses to the lattice-work of stout cords fixed to the wall of the cottage. "In the fall, after they've finished bloomin' for the year, we'll prune them back," Mrs. Hopson said.

Margaret worked, trying to control the floppy branches, heavy with aromatic flowers, as she tied them to the cords.

"Ouch!" she said, catching her finger on a thorn for the third time. "How do you keep from getting stuck?"

"Oh, you don't," chuckled Mrs. Hopson. "I've been caught many a time. But everything as is worth havin' is like that, isn't it? If there wasn't thorns, we wouldn't hardly appreciate the flowers, now, would we?"

Privately, Margaret thought she could have gladly appreciated the beauty of the roses minus the thorns, but Mrs. Hopson's words stuck in her head.

"Would you mind teaching me a bit more about gardening, Mrs. Hopson?" she asked as they worked.

"I'd love to," Mrs. Hopson said delightedly. "But you must call me Julia."

Funny, Margaret thought later, *I've never known another Julia. It's as if I banished the name from my mind when I banished her from my life.*

Julia Vargas began coming to mind more and more often as Margaret wondered what she was doing now. She even thought about trying to track her down.

"What for?" demanded that other voice.

"To apologize. To make amends."

"Some things you can't make amends for. Maybe the past is better left in the past."

But none of Margaret's past was staying in the past. Her novel, even though it was fictionalized, had been dredging up so many memories of her father – and her mother. Funny how many years she had thought her mother had been clueless about Julia, about the conflict between Margaret and her father... only to realize her mother had seen everything. Seen, but not acted.

"Would things have been different if she had?" Margaret wondered aloud, a habit she'd developed, living alone in the cottage. "If she'd spoken up then, supported me, would it have changed things? Given me the courage I lacked?"

It was easy to feel brave here, where she had no daily responsibilities to anyone but herself, where no one knew her as Gavin's wife – or Wyck's lover. She found she liked being just Margaret. But could she stay just Margaret, could she continue to be herself, once she was back in Asheville?

It was impossible not to think of what was going on back there as the summer passed and everyone back at St. Aloysius was starting a new semester. She found she didn't miss it one jot. Forced to let go of things like e-mail and television, she'd gradually grown to not miss them, either.

Her evenings were spent with a glass of wine outside under the lingering English twilight if it wasn't raining. Some evenings, she went in to read by oil lamp, or simply went to bed if her eyes were tired, rising with the sun – something else she had not been accustomed to doing.

I wish Wyck and Mandy and I could live like this always, she thought one evening, staring up at the stars. *No worries, no one to bother us.* But she smiled as she thought what Mrs. Hopson would say to that. "Everything as is worth havin' is like that, isn't it? If there wasn't thorns, we wouldn't hardly appreciate the flowers, now, would we?"

Chapter 25

WYCK AND MANDY WANDERED through the Braithwaite house, making sure everything was clean and in order. Though Wyck had been given a key, she hadn't entered the house since Margaret left. She knew Margaret had arranged for the cleaning lady to continue to come weekly to vacuum and dust, so the house was as expected. She bumped the thermostat up against the September chill and put away the groceries she had brought. Upstairs, she paused at the door to the room where she and Margaret had... Shaking herself, she found the linen closet and set about putting fresh sheets on that bed and the bed in Gavin's room. Midway through that task, she heard a loud knock as the front door was opened with a call from downstairs.

Mandy raced downstairs eagerly and Wyck followed.

"Hello!" said Muriel, standing in the foyer with her friend Iris, a petite woman with short-cropped salt and pepper hair.

"Hi," Wyck said, hugging both of them. "How was the drive?"

"Piece of cake," Iris said. "It was beautiful. The trees are just starting to turn."

"I'll get your suitcases," Wyck offered.

"I'll help," said Iris, following her back out to the driveway. They pulled two small suitcases from the cargo space of Iris's Honda CRV and carried them back to the house.

"This way," Wyck said, leading the way up to the bedrooms. They helped finish making up the second bed and then all went back downstairs.

"This is a lovely house," Iris said admiringly.

"It is," Wyck agreed. "And the grounds are even nicer. I'll show you around if you like."

"Oh, yes," Iris said eagerly.

They went out into the back yard where Wyck acted as tour guide as they wandered the paths through the garden.

"Oh, Jan would have loved this," Iris said, clasping her hands. "She was the gardener, not me. I know she missed our house when we moved to Wildwood, but I just couldn't keep it up once she got sick."

Muriel wrapped an arm around her shoulders. "What was Jan's favorite?" she asked.

"She had no one she could talk to about Jan," Muriel had confided to Wyck a few weeks earlier during her visit to Richmond when she had been introduced to Iris. "Now, she can't seem to stop."

They lost track of time as they wandered the gardens, Wyck making sure to pause at places where Muriel could sit and rest. By the time they got back to the house, it was mid-afternoon.

"I've got a few errands I need to run this afternoon," Wyck said. "There's food in the house. Make yourselves a snack and rest. I'll be back later and we'll have dinner. I hope you brought comfortable shoes for the Biltmore tomorrow."

"Are you sure you have time for us?" Muriel asked. "We don't mean to take you away from your work."

Wyck grinned. "I cleared my schedule for the next few days just for this. I've been looking forward to it."

The following days were a blur of activity. If Wyck had been worried about whether the two older women could keep up, she was soon wondering if it was she who was going to give out first as they seemed to want to cram as much as possible into their visit. "Plenty of time to sleep once we're dead and buried," Muriel joked. They spent an entire day touring the Biltmore house and gardens, staying for lunch and dinner. The next morning, Wyck came to the Braithwaite house and drove them in Iris's car out to the barn.

"Misselthwaite?" Muriel turned to look at Wyck as they passed a hand-carved sign Wyck had fixed to a post just as the barn came into view.

Wyck smiled. "Not exactly a castle, but it's my Misselthwaite."

"That was one of Peggy's favorite books when she was a girl."

Wyck, recalling Margaret's disdain the first day she'd met the Braithwaites, said, "I don't think she thinks of *The Secret Garden* the same way anymore."

As Wyck pulled up, Mandy happily greeted everyone, her feathery tail waving like a banner as she pranced around them.

"Oh, Wyck," both Muriel and Iris gasped as they entered the barn and looked up into the vaulted space above.

Wyck showed them around the main level and then took them upstairs.

"And you did all this?" Iris asked in wonder, looking around at the master bedroom.

Muriel, though, was no longer looking at the room, but at Wyck. "You did this for Peggy, didn't you?"

Wyck, blinking rapidly, simply nodded.

Muriel took Wyck's hand as they went back downstairs.

"I hope you're hungry," Wyck said, stirring the contents of the crockpot. "I'm not much of a cook, but I'm a whiz with this thing." She placed a baking sheet of rolls in the oven while Muriel and Iris set the table and poured drinks.

"Are you going to tell Peggy about our being in touch with one another?" Muriel asked as they ate.

Wyck nodded. "I already have. I wrote her last week."

"Me, too," Muriel sighed. "I figured it wouldn't do to have her find out about it after she got back."

Wyck looked askance at her. "Do you think she'll mind?"

Muriel's bright bird eyes fixed on Wyck. "Oh, I think we can assume she'll have something to say about it," she said with a wry smile.

Birds flitted from tree branches and bushes down to the freshly dug earth, pecking for insects. A few squirrels chattered and chased one another around the garden, pausing now and then to dig. Margaret sat back on her heels and smelled the fall smells of Mrs. Hopson's garden.

"These bulbs will all pop up in the spring," Mrs. Hopson said, "leastways, the ones as the squirrels don't get."

She was showing Margaret how to bury the bulbs in the earth at the right depth. "Crocuses don't like to be so deep," Mrs. Hopson corrected, filling in Margaret's hole a bit so that the tiny bulbs sat closer to the surface.

"But won't the squirrels get them for sure then?" Margaret asked. "Can't you protect them with wire mesh or something?"

Mrs. Hopson looked at her as if she were speaking another language for a moment. "But the squirrels are part of the garden," she said as if this should be obvious. "Same as the birds and the bees and the worms and the moles. It all goes together. If you want naught but flowers as is perfect, you'd best grow them in pots in a greenhouse."

Margaret smiled sheepishly. "Just like taking the thorns with the roses?"

Mrs. Hopson beamed. "Exactly. We can try to create a perfect world as has no troubles, but what joy is there in that? The happiness comes when it all works together, the good and the not so good, the waitin' to see what will come." She glanced at Margaret in her shrewd way. "Kind of like us, isn't it? We can hide ourselves away in some remote place where none of the worries of the world can touch us, but humans is a funny lot. Sooner or later, we'll find a way to bring troubles in, just like Adam and Eve. We need a healthy dose of good, tempered with a little bit of bad to keep the balance just right and remind us what's important."

The garden gate opened and Mr. Hopson limped in with Wisp at his heels. She trotted over to nuzzle Margaret as he waved something. "You've got some letters, Miss Margaret," he announced. "I took the liberty. Hope you don't mind. Didn't know when you was like to go to town next."

Margaret sat up, wiping her hands on her pants. "Of course I don't mind, Mr. Hopson, thank you."

"You go and read your letters, dear," Mrs. Hopson. "We can continue this another day."

Margaret imagined this was what it felt like for Elizabeth Bennett receiving letters from her sister, Jane, as she hurried back to her cottage where a few late roses were still blooming, warmed by the sun on the cottage's stone wall. Her heart thumped as she saw whom the letters were from. Sitting down on the stone stoop, she pried open the letter from her mother first. Her mouth opened as she read and a curious flush came to her cheeks. Turning to the other letter, Wyck wrote a similar account of the activities taking place without her back in the States.

Her mother and Wyck, getting to be friends. She sat back against the cottage wall, the letters fluttering in her hand. She didn't know whether to feel annoyed or gratified. "They seem to like one another," she said in surprise. "That could make things easier... or weirder..."

She had always felt caught between her parents and Gavin. There had never been any outright animosity - at least not face to face - but her parents' disapproval over the age difference had been clear, and Gavin, in his turn, had never felt he needed to treat Frank and Muriel - chronologically his contemporaries - as his parents-in-law. "It's preposterous," he had grumbled.

As a result, most of her visits to them after she and Gavin married had been solitary trips, making excuses for him - book signings, appearances, classes. "Tell them whatever you like," Gavin had said.

When her father died, there had been a brief discussion of bringing her mother to live with them, but Muriel had settled that when she refused to move farther south than Richmond. But now... if her mother and Wyck were getting to know and like one another....

Suddenly, she sat up straighter. "What are they saying about me?"

She went inside where the completed first draft of her manuscript sat, the penned pages neatly stacked. Her laptop sat on the cooker, plugged into an adapter to charge the battery in preparation for beginning to type up the novel from her handwritten draft. This sabbatical had ostensibly served its purpose, allowing her the solitude she needed to write, but "it served other purposes as well," she mused. For the past four months, she had felt perfectly content to be here by herself with only occasional company from the Hopsons. She missed Wyck, but she had felt absolutely no desire to be back in Asheville. When she had thought of wanting to be with her, it was here, in England, away from everything and everyone.

But now, she felt more... "rested isn't big enough for what I feel," she would have said. It went deeper than that. She felt replenished – full to the brim – and she only realized now that she was, how truly empty she had been. She'd thought of herself as a dried-up shell, but even she hadn't seen how desiccated she'd become – her mind, her body, her soul. "Dried up and used up," she muttered. She closed her eyes and felt – felt her heart beating, her lungs breathing, and other, non-physical things. She felt an inner quiet and confidence that she hadn't known since she was a young woman. And she felt the first stirrings of any kind of desire to be back home – kind of like the itch when a wound begins to heal. Her eyes fluttered open and she realized with a smile that she was homesick.

Chapter 26

MANDY, FEELING FRISKY IN the cold air, leapt into the large pile of leaves Wyck was raking, scattering them everywhere. Wyck opened her mouth to scold the dog, but Mandy bowed down, her butt in the air, eyes dancing, mouth open in a doggy smile, begging Wyck to play with her.

"Oh, well." Wyck dropped her rake, picked up a huge armful of leaves and threw them on top of Mandy's head. Mandy barked and jumped aside and pounced back into the leaves from a different angle. Laughing, Wyck jumped in with her, the two of them rolling through the fallen pieces of red and gold and orange until they were both covered with bits of leaf and twig.

At last, they lay back, both breathing hard, Mandy's tail thumping the ground. Wyck turned her head, looking at the house, dark and lonely looking. Four more weeks until Margaret would be home, just before Christmas. She felt torn - part of her wanted Margaret back so much it hurt, but the other part didn't want to have to face the possibility of what her being back might mean. Margaret's last letters had been hard to interpret – she sounded good, happy even, but no matter how many times Wyck read them, she couldn't tell where Margaret was in terms of their being together.

The brightest spot on her horizon was that she and Mandy had been invited to spend Thanksgiving with Muriel and Iris. She'd felt a little bit guilty at having to tell the volunteer coordinators at the church that she wouldn't be helping out this year, but "I've spent every holiday for the past few years volunteering," she reminded herself.

Wednesday afternoon of Thanksgiving week, they locked up the barn and headed out for Richmond, Mandy freshly bathed and smelling good. "I know," Wyck had laughed as Mandy looked longingly at another pile of leaves, "you'd rather smell like a dog, but we're going visiting, and this is better."

It did feel a bit strange, Wyck thought as she drove, to be spending Thanksgiving with Margaret's mother, but she knew that Margaret had always spent this holiday with her mother and reasoned that she would rather Muriel not be alone.

"This will be extra nice," Muriel had said when she called to issue the invitation, "because last year, Iris was alone while I was with Peggy. This way, none of us has to be alone."

Wyck hadn't told Muriel about her estrangement from her family, nor did she know if Margaret had said anything, but Muriel seemed to have guessed. Whatever had prompted the invitation, Wyck was grateful – grateful to be wanted somewhere.

There had been no telephone calls or invitations home from her parents this year. "Why should there be?" she reminded herself. "You've declined for four years. You can't expect them to keep asking when you're just –" Just what? Waiting for an apology? For some indication that they knew how deeply they had hurt her? Waiting for what seemed unlikely to ever come....

"Wyck?" Iris asked, laying a concerned hand on Wyck's shoulder as they sat down to their Thanksgiving meal, having filled their plates from the buffet. "Are you all right?"

Wyck smiled sheepishly, losing the stony expression she had worn as her thoughts drifted to New Hampshire. "I'm fine."

"You know," Iris said, "Jan and I spent forty Thanksgivings and forty Christmases with her family. We watched her nieces and nephews grow up, have kids of their own. We were always there, but... I guess I was always just Jan's roommate in their minds. I don't know." She dabbed at her eyes with her napkin. "Now, they don't call or come by. It's as if I died when Jan did."

Muriel reached for her hand. "You didn't die," she said firmly. "There is a lot of life left to be lived, and," she focused her bright eyes on Wyck, "we have new friends - new family - to spend holidays with."

Margaret sat at her table, still cold despite wearing two sweaters as she typed on her laptop, the oil lamp positioned to throw its meager light onto her handwritten pages. The cottage had lost a considerable amount of its charm in her estimation as the weather grew colder and wetter. The tiny furnace could not produce enough heat to keep her warm and the fire, while cheery, only threw its heat a few feet, so that she often found herself with one of the armchairs pulled close to the flames, her laptop on her knees with her longhand pages balanced on the arm of the chair as she typed.

Just two more weeks, and she would be going home. She sat back, staring into the flame of the lamp. Her time in England had crawled and flown by all at the same time. She longed to see Wyck, but she hadn't missed the university or Gavin - his presence, his shadow hovering over her life. The people she'd met here hadn't a clue who he was, and so she had been simply Margaret - complete in and of herself. "You can't know how freeing that is," she had written to Wyck, "unless you have known what it is to be less than yourself, to be diminished by someone else." Wyck, she thought, had never been that - probably never could be that. She was too complete, too self-contained, to be diminished by anyone else.

"Not true," Wyck could have told her. "I spent a long time diminished, driven, by the incident with Carla's family, and mine. And then, after the attack, I was completely controlled by my fear – more powerful than the most forceful personality."

Margaret read the page on her computer screen. She was happy with the book, happy with her work – something else she hadn't felt in a very long time. She felt it was better than anything else she had written. She smiled. Wyck had said she needed to find Meggie to be able to write like she had – "wrong again," she murmured with a smile. This book, so tied to her love for Wyck, was a blend of Meggie, true enough, with a good bit of Peggy, but tempered by Margaret's maturity and perspective.

"Try explaining that to anyone, and they'll lock you up," she muttered with a droll smile.

"Is that everything, then?" Mr. Hopson asked as he closed the boot of the car.

"Oh, my dear, it will seem so lonely here without you," Mrs. Hopson said tearfully, giving Margaret a hug. "You're such a lovely girl. We wish you every happiness back in America." She reached into her apron pocket, pulling out a well-worn book. "I want you to have this."

Puzzled, Margaret looked at the cover. It looked like an old romance. "Thank you," she said uncertainly.

Mrs. Hopson pulled her into another hug.

"Come now, Julia, or she'll miss her bus," said Mr. Hopson. "Stay, Wisp."

Margaret got into the passenger seat as the car started with its usual bang, belching a cloud of black smoke and, with a grinding of gears, began rolling toward town. She drank in the views of the valley, knowing her photos could never recapture for her the feeling of being in this countryside for the past months – *the memories are part of me now,* she thought, *in the miles I walked, in the air I breathed, in my very skin.*

Mr. Hopson chatted as he drove, Margaret responding every now and again. He saw her onto the bus that would take her to the nearest train station, insisting on carrying her luggage despite his crooked leg. Doffing his cap as he had done the first day, he wished her well. Smiling, Margaret gave him a kiss on his grizzled cheek and climbed onto the waiting bus to begin her journey back to London, "back to my real life," she might have said. "But what kind of life will it be?"

Not until the train was beginning its journey south did she remember Mrs. Hopson's book. Pulling it from her bag, she flipped it open. There, pressed and dried in the pages, was a rose. Looking closely, she smiled as she saw that the stem still had thorns.

Wyck was out in the shop, boxing up all the leftover ribbon and bows and wire from the wreaths she had made for clients that season. Everything she had made, all the trees she had cut – all had been delivered. She carefully hung the dried berries and flowers that could be used at some later point and began sweeping up all the detritus of the wreath-making process.

"I hate having a messy workspace," she said to Mandy as she swept the debris into a dustpan and threw it away, and then ran the shop vac over the floor to clear the last bits of pine needles.

The air as they left the shop was sharp with a dry, biting cold. Stopping on the back porch to gather another armful of firewood, she entered the kitchen in time to hear her cell phone beep, indicating a text. She deposited the wood in the cast iron rack next to the woodstove and came back to check her phone. It was from her sister, Melissa.

"Dad had a stroke. Doctors say it's bad. U should come home."

Chapter 27

THE AIRPORT SHUTTLE DRIVER deposited Margaret's bags in the driveway and pulled away, leaving her standing there. Looking up at the empty house, she fought a momentary bit of panic. *Don't be stupid*, she thought. *It's your home.* She hadn't told Wyck or anyone else in Asheville when her flight was getting in - in fact, she had sent only one e-mail, to her mother, once she was back in London. She'd refrained from opening her inbox, though "you're only delaying the inevitable," she argued with herself. After so many weeks at her little rose cottage, living almost monastically, she was dreading getting pulled back into the rush and noise of everyday life here. Though she knew it was irrational - "how was she to know?" - Margaret felt a twinge of disappointment that Wyck wasn't here to greet her. She picked up her bags and carried them to the front porch. Her heart lifted when she saw the Christmas wreath hanging on the door.

Inside, the house was quiet. She set her bags down and wandered through the rooms on the main floor. Everything was clean, orderly - just as she had left it. In the den, to her delight, Wyck had put up a small Christmas tree, decorated simply with ornaments of dried fruit and strings of berries. In the kitchen, the answering machine light was blinking. "Why didn't I turn it off?" she said, and her voice sounded unnaturally loud in the stillness of the house.

She put the kettle on and stepped out onto the patio while she waited for it to boil. Out here, as well, everything was neat and tidy. Wyck had gathered all the leaves; bushes and trees were pruned, everything quiet and resting for the winter. Back inside, she made herself a cup of tea and sat at the kitchen table, where she was surprised to see an envelope she hadn't noticed. It was a note from Wyck. Apprehensively, Margaret unfolded the paper inside and read,

Dear Margaret,

I'm sorry I won't be here to greet you when you get home, but I received a message that my father has had a stroke. I've got to go – I think you know how hard this will be. It will be even harder as I so want to see you. I have no idea what cell phone reception is like up there now – it was terrible the last I was there, but please try and call me when you can.

I hope you are well and that your time away was all you'd hoped it would be.

The note was signed simply, "Wyck," but Margaret could feel all the unexpressed sentiments there, "because she has no idea what to expect from me." She sat, her hand resting on the note, listening to the silence of the house and watching the arrival of the early mid-December twilight. Gradually, darkness fell. The remaining tea in her cup had grown cold, and still, she sat.

While in England, she had re-read *Persuasion* four or five times, taking to heart as she never had before Anne Elliot's regret and heartbreak at having been talked into giving up her love out of a sense of obligation to her family's wishes. She had meditated long on Mrs. Hopson's advice and her own mother's assertion that she should follow her heart and she had returned to the States knowing at last what she must do – "Now, there remains only the doing of the thing," she muttered to herself. "Maybe it's a good thing Wyck isn't here until it's done."

Feeling that there was no sense in delaying, she reached for the phone and called Jim Evans.

"Jim, this is Margaret Braithwaite. I need to speak with you –"

"Margaret! Thank God! I've been trying to reach you for weeks," he said impatiently. "This damned sabbatical of yours, I didn't realize it was going to turn you into a recluse. I've e-mailed; I've called. Didn't you get my messages?"

"I haven't checked –"

"Well, never mind that now," he interrupted again. "The Board of Trustees decided to hold off on Gavin's memorial until you were back. They just felt it wasn't right for you to not be there. But in the meantime, it gave us time to put together a surprise – a supporter of Gavin's work has made a very generous donation to begin an endowment in Gavin's name. He wants it to fund a fellowship for a post-grad student and a scholarship for an undergrad, and – here's the best part – he wants you to help oversee the entire thing!"

He waited, presumably for some expression of delight on Margaret's part. She could almost hear him frown. "Margaret?"

"Um..." She squeezed her eyes shut. "We'll need to talk. I just got back."

"Of course," he said effusively. "Let's meet tomorrow. Can you do lunch? We want to announce everything as soon as everyone is back for the new semester."

Margaret hung up and sat, her fingers pressing the bridge of her nose. She had only just returned and already, he was pulling her back in. Like a many-tentacled octopus, Gavin was reaching out from the grave to ensnare her and keep her tied to him, to his memory.

"I wanted the damned memorial service to be over with," she longed to scream. "And the last thing I want is to be involved with some foundation that chains me forever to Gavin and his work!"

Shoving her chair back angrily, she went to gather her suitcases from the foyer and unpack.

"Dad, you're slouching. Let's get you straightened out," Wyck said, grasping her father under his arms and trying to help him shift in bed. "Use your left hand," she said, placing his hand on the bed rail, where it promptly fell back to the mattress. "Can you push with your leg?" she asked, bending his left knee and bracing his foot against the mattress. "Now push." The leg flopped sideways.

"Leave him alone," said Melissa said irritably.

A nurse came in to deliver a fresh cup of juice, thickened to slow it down as he drank it so that it wouldn't slide into his lungs before it could be swallowed. "Mr. Fitzsimmons, you're all crooked here," said the nurse. "Let's get you back where you belong."

Fighting the urge to give her sister a look, Wyck helped the nurse get her father repositioned in bed, smoothing his covers.

Her mother, Bobbi, came to the other side of the bed as the nurse left. "Gene," she said very loudly, "do you want some juice?"

Gene Fitzsimmons blinked, or at least his right eye blinked. The left one only partially closed, as he turned toward his wife's voice. She held the cup for him as Wyck propped him more upright, but he couldn't close his lips completely around the straw and some of the thickened liquid dribbled down his chin.

"Oh dear," Bobbi said, pulling a tissue from the box on the bedside table and wiping up the mess.

Melissa grimaced in disgust and Wyck turned to look out the window with a sigh. She'd had to break the trip to New Hampshire into two days – her body just wouldn't take eighteen hours' driving non-stop now. Mandy was at her parents' house in Bethlehem – "I don't have anywhere to leave her down here," Wyck had told her mother. "I'm bringing her with me."

Her reunion with her mother had been tearful, and *thankfully*, thought Wyck, *it had been private*.

"I've missed you so much," Bobbi said, wiping her eyes with an ever-present tissue. "I'm so worried about your father. I don't know what we'll do."

As her mother told her what had happened in halting phrases interrupted by more crying, Wyck had slowly gathered that her father had been neglecting to take his blood pressure pills, preferring to take a natural supplement touted, and sold, by her sister-in-law, Felicia - the Bible-beater - who eschewed anything to do with traditional medicine, apparently feeling that prayer and natural substances were enough to take care of any ailment.

"What, she doesn't think God's plan for us includes seeing doctors and taking real medicine?" Wyck longed to retort, but held back.

"Wasn't anyone checking his blood pressure?" Wyck did ask, trying to keep the anger out of her voice.

"Well, he checked it sometimes," Bobbi said in a small voice. "But he wouldn't tell me what the numbers were."

It was at the hospital in Littleton that Wyck had her first encounters with the rest of her family as they gathered in an atmosphere that could only be described as tense. Only Michaela, almost ten now, launched herself joyfully into her aunt's arms. Melissa gave her sister a perfunctory hug while her husband, Eric, shook Wyck's hand with a grin and a "hey". Felicia and Wyck's brother, Brian, didn't acknowledge her at all, opting to pretend she wasn't even in the room.

The hours in the hospital passed slowly, marked mainly by diaper changes, meals and visits from doctors, therapists and nurses.

"Come on, Dad," Wyck said. "Let's do some of your exercises," she insisted in between therapy sessions, helping him move his left arm and leg, trying to get him to move them on his own, but with little response.

"I think he's tired," Bobbi said worriedly as Gene's slack face turned to her and he moaned. "I think you should stop."

Trying to keep her voice even, Wyck said, "Mom, I know he doesn't want to do these exercises, just like he didn't want to take his blood pressure medicine, but this isn't a time to do what he wants. If he doesn't move now, the therapist said he'll miss his window for improvement. We need to push him."

"Do what Mom said and let him rest," Melissa said irritably.

Wyck turned to her. "If you guys don't step up and make him do more, he's going to get a lot of rest. Like in a wheelchair for the rest of his life."

Eric pursed his lips as if determined to keep out of this, but Melissa said, "You haven't been around here for years, and now you come marching in all important and just take over."

Wyck stared at her. "Were you listening when the doctor said his CT scan showed evidence that this wasn't his first stroke? Maybe," she said pointedly, "if he had listened to his doctors instead of quacks, we wouldn't be here now."

Felicia bristled at this. "I knew you would blame me," she said in a high voice.

Wyck raised one eyebrow, but didn't deny that she did, indeed, blame Felicia. Biting back all the things she longed to say, she left the room, pacing the hallway in agitation. Michaela followed her aunt.

"Let's go downstairs," Michaela said, taking Wyck by the hand and leading her to the elevator.

She led the way through the lobby on the ground floor to a little sunroom where patients could come to enjoy the plants, now mostly seasonal poinsettias and tiny pine trees in pots decorated by local school children with handmade ornaments.

She pulled Wyck down onto a bench where they sat side by side, Michaela's orange Converse high-tops catching Wyck's eye as she swung her feet.

"Nice shoes," she said, her mouth twitching into a grin.

Michaela beamed up at her. "Remember when you bought me my first pair?"

Wyck nodded. "The purple ones."

"Mom was mad."

Wyck chuckled. "Yes, she was."

They sat for a while in silence. Wyck reached into her pocket.

"Why do you keep checking your phone?" Michaela asked.

"No reason," Wyck said, seeing that the screen was blank and tucking it away again.

Michaela said, "Mom and Dad think it was wrong, too. What Aunt Felicia was doing with Grandpa."

Wyck looked down at her. With her auburn hair and freckles sprinkled liberally across her nose and cheeks, she looked like Pippi Longstocking. "Why didn't they say anything?"

Michaela shrugged. "I guess they didn't want to start an argument. Like the one with you before you went away."

Wyck sat very still. She'd never been sure how much Michaela knew.

"No one will talk about it in front of me, but Aunt Felicia and Uncle Brian don't like you because you're gay, right?" Michaela asked.

"Well," Wyck said slowly, "they think it's a choice to be gay and they don't agree with it."

Michaela frowned. "But haven't you always been gay? How could it be a choice?"

Wyck laughed. "You're smarter than all the rest of us put together, you know that?"

"Our family doesn't talk about things, do we?"

"Nope."

"That's dumb," Michaela said, frowning. "When kids fight, we yell and then it's over with."

Wyck smiled as she wrapped an arm around her niece. "Maybe it would be better if we did that, but I think sometimes, grown-ups have held onto things for so long, they're afraid if they start yelling they won't know when to stop, and they might say things that can't be fixed by saying sorry."

"Like what happened when Uncle Brian and Aunt Felicia yelled at you when you and Carla broke up?" Michaela looked up at her.

Wyck blinked hard for a few seconds before asking, "What do you know about break-ups?"

Michaela shrugged again. "Some of my friends' parents have broken up and got divorced. It makes everyone sad."

"It does," Wyck agreed. "It makes you very sad when you loved someone and realize you can't be together anymore, for whatever reason."

Michaela looked up at her. "But... isn't that when your family is supposed to stick together?"

"It would be nice if it happened that way," Wyck said with a quick swipe at her eyes, "but it doesn't always."

"Is that why you don't come home anymore?"

Wyck nodded. "Yes. No one has ever said sorry, and I don't want to fight anymore. I miss you, but I don't miss anything else."

Michaela wrapped her arms around Wyck's waist and said, "I miss you, too, Aunt Wyck."

Chapter 28

ANDREW JACKSON DUCKWORTH WAS a man accustomed to getting what he wanted – whether by buying it, cajoling others or bullying if need be. A.J., as Jim Evans introduced him, took every opportunity, Margaret noticed, to bandy about his full name, as if being named for the seventh president somehow bestowed upon him some special powers.

"I'm sure you'll agree this is a phenomenal opportunity," he said confidently as they had coffee in Jim's office, "to honor your husband's memory and his legacy."

He sounds like he just walked off the set of Gone with the Wind, Margaret thought, and wondered if the accent was an affectation or if it could possibly be genuine. She also noticed with some distaste that he wore a Confederate flag pinned to his lapel and she wondered vaguely if they would be having this conversation if she were African-American. "Of course not," she answered herself, "because Gavin would never have married a black woman," – not because he was bigoted, but because he could never see things from any point of view other than his as a privileged white man. The hours of research she had done for him had opened her eyes to the utter misery of every poor, common person touched by the war - the foot soldiers dying from exposure to disease and weather and malnutrition, the women left behind to try and feed families after fields had been burnt and ravaged, the blacks - free and slave - who fought, even Native Americans who were in the process of being displaced during the conflict. Gavin had never wanted to use those bits. *No, he and men like A.J. only want to glorify the military strategists and talk about this blunder and that brilliant countermove. It's all like a big game of chess to them, with every move known in advance.*

"Margaret?" Jim prompted. "What do you think?"

She blinked and looked up at him. "What do I think about giving up my career to manage this trust? To be enmeshed - entombed - forever under a monument dedicated to Gavin?" But she did not say this. They wanted her to give up her academic position and move to an administrative position in the Development office where overseeing this endowment would become just one of her responsibilities.

She glanced out the window and saw that it was snowing lightly. She was leaving for Richmond after this meeting and *I wonder what the roads are going to be like?* she thought vaguely.

"Margaret?"

She looked back at both men. "I just finished the first draft of my next book," she said vaguely. "I've got plans -"

"I'm sure your book is very nice, Dr. Braithwaite," said A.J. patronizingly, "but surely you can see how much more important your husband's body of work is."

Jim, seeing something in Margaret's face, hastily said, "I know this is a lot to think about, Margaret, and you just got back yesterday. Why don't we get together again after the holidays, and in the meantime, you think over what we've talked about."

"I don't have to think!" she nearly blurted, but didn't. This was not going at all as she had planned. She had come back to the States with her decision made, knowing what she wanted. She'd spent days and weeks rehearsing what she needed to say to Jim, explaining that she'd met someone - though somehow, she'd never been able to envision the actual blurting out that the someone was a woman - and that she hoped he wouldn't see the need to use the morals clause against her. That part of her visualizations had always been rather foggy... like her imaginings of bringing Wyck to faculty functions and introducing her as... what? Her friend? Her lover? Partner sounded so impersonal... so business-like, but she knew, for herself, "I never want to be anyone's wife ever again."

Her mind was in turmoil, mulling all these things over as she left Asheville. Fortunately, the drive to Richmond soon demanded all her attention as the snow began to stick to the highways, swirling toward the windshield so that it became hypnotic after a while. She was exhausted and she had a headache when at last she got to her mother's place. She pulled her cell phone out of her purse and stared at it. She pressed her forehead against her steering wheel. She couldn't call Wyck. Not yet. She dialed her mother to let her know she had arrived.

Muriel met her in the lobby. "Let's have lunch before we go up," she suggested as she gave Margaret a tight hug. "We can leave your bag here behind the reception desk."

To Margaret's surprise, her mother had also invited Iris, who had a table waiting for them.

"So, Peggy," her mother said as soon as they had filled their plates from the buffet and sat down, "tell us all about England."

And so, Margaret spent several minutes describing the Lake District, and the cottage and the Hopsons and Mrs. Hopson's garden.

"It sounds beautiful," Iris said wistfully.

"It was," Margaret said, avoiding her mother's sharp gaze.

"Remember the gardens Wyck showed us at the Biltmore?" Iris asked, and, to Margaret's dismay, this launched a series of stories about the days Wyck and Mandy had spent with the two older women. Margaret felt a deep ache somewhere in the vicinity of her heart - *a reminder I still have one*, she thought miserably.

Her thoughts were interrupted by her mother and Iris discussing something about a museum.

"What?"

"We were talking about our shift at the Holocaust museum to-morrow," Muriel said. "We're docents there," she added at Margaret's bewildered expression.

"Since when?"

"Since Wyck," Iris said happily. "She showed us around the Bilt-more, and we thought, why are we just sitting around here, letting time pass us by? Jan's mother was a prisoner at a Nazi prison camp in Norway, so we thought the Holocaust museum was a good place to volunteer."

Margaret stared at them. "I didn't know Richmond had a Holo-caust museum."

"Well, it does," Muriel said. "You'll be okay by yourself for a few hours, won't you?"

Margaret shrugged. "Uh, sure."

When at last they got up to Muriel's apartment, Margaret waited for the inevitable, "Have you talked to Wyck since you got back?"

"Not yet," Margaret said, trying to sound casual. "There was a note from her that she had to go to New Hampshire - something about her father's health."

Muriel didn't say anything more on that subject, but only, "You must be tired. Why don't you go to my room and rest?"

If Margaret had thought the offer was meant to be innocent and kind, she scoffed a moment later as she spied a card on her mother's nightstand. She recognized the garden image immediately as a view of the Biltmore and opened it to read a note from Wyck thanking Muriel for having her and Mandy for Thanksgiving.

It left her feeling queer - "a curious choice of word" - to realize that her mother had a relationship of her own with Wyck, one that Margaret wasn't part of. *This should make everything easier,* she said to herself as she recalled that one of her worries when she first realized she was falling in love with Wyck had been what her mother's reac-tion would be.

"You're running out of excuses."

Why was that in her mother's voice?

Christmas that year was forever a blur for Wyck. Her father was moved to rehab on the 23rd. He was transported by ambulance and the family was allowed to see him later that day. To her relief, the rehab setting mandated therapy - physical, occupational and speech - five times a day, as PT and OT were done morning and afternoon, except for Christmas Day and weekends, when he only had to go once each. Excuses weren't tolerated and the onus of pushing her father was removed from Wyck's hands. No matter how her father moaned and resisted, and how her mother fretted that he needed to rest, the therapists gently but firmly insisted he work. Family was allowed to observe the sessions from across the gym as he took his first tentative steps in the bars with two people supporting him.

"See? He can do things for himself," Wyck pointed out to her mother as they watched the occupational therapists teaching him how to dress and feed himself. All the therapists emphasized to the family the need to allow Gene the extra time it would take him to do things for himself. "Don't jump in to do it for him just because it's slow and it frustrates him. He has to practice these things," they said over and over and Wyck knew they were accustomed to dealing with people like her family. "We don't treat just the patient," they would have said.

"Your family is easy," laughed Sue, the social worker, after her first meeting with the clan to help them arrange whatever equipment Gene would need when he came home. "We see some really dysfunctional families. Yours mean well, I think they just don't know how to handle things that rock their boat."

"You have no idea," Wyck said drolly.

Wyck had brought Michaela's present with her - a complete set of Madeleine L'Engle's A *Wrinkle in Time* series, but, as she had done the past four Christmases, she hadn't bought gifts for any of the other members of her family. *Not that I expected to be seeing them.* She and her mother had a quiet breakfast before going to the hospital on Christmas morning. Mandy, missing Wyck during all the hours she was away, was leaning against her, staying glued to her side as Wyck's hand ran over the silky head again and again. Bobbi slid a card across the table to Wyck. Inside, Wyck knew, would be a check. At home was an envelope with all the uncashed checks her mother and father had sent each Christmas and birthday since she'd moved away. She'd scoffed at such an impersonal gesture, wondering why they bothered – *but it's more than I've done,* she realized with a hollow feeling.

"I don't really know what you need anymore..." Bobbi said uncertainly.

Dismayed at the sudden tightness in her throat, Wyck blinked rapidly as she stared at the Christmas scene on the card. "Thanks, Mom," was all she could say as she gave her mother a hug.

Later, at the hospital, Michaela excitedly told her aunt all about the presents she'd had waiting for her that morning. She was delighted with her new books and pushed a badly wrapped package into Wyck's hands. "I'm not very good at wrapping," she said apologetically.

Wyck peeled the paper back to reveal a hand-made collage of old photographs of Wyck and Michaela up to about age five – Wyck holding an infant Michaela, pulling her in a wagon, making a snowman together, teaching her to hold a bat, sitting next to her on the pier at the lake while they fished. Wyck's jaw worked back and forth as, for the second time that morning she fought tears. "You made this?" she managed to ask through a tight throat.

Michaela nodded, leaning against Wyck. "I don't have any newer pictures." She didn't have to say, "because you haven't been here."

Wyck kissed the top of her head. "I know."

"What did you get from Grandma?" Michaela asked.

Wyck told her about the card and the check. "We just don't know each other anymore," she shrugged.

Michaela looked up, her big blue eyes searching her aunt's. "It doesn't have to be like that."

Wyck nodded. "You're right."

She was relieved that there was no Christmas dinner to have to sit through, as the family spent most of the day at the hospital while her father slept the afternoon away, exhausted from his morning therapy sessions.

"I'll stay here," she insisted. "You guys go to the cafeteria and get something to eat."

She could hear her father's roommate visiting with his family through the pulled curtain. The families here all kind of got to know one another, sitting for hours, watching therapy sessions, fetching fresh drinks and snacks, encouraging each other.

She watched her father, his slack face drooping as his mouth hung open and he snored, his left hand lying on the covers, already exhibiting some wasting of the muscles. How different he looked from the robust highway worker he had been when she was younger, his ruddy face sunburned and windburned from hours on mowers or plows, so different from the frail old man lying here now....

Wyck was startled by the vibration of her cell phone in her jeans pocket. Her heart leapt into her throat as she saw who it was.

"How is she?" Muriel asked as Margaret came out of the bedroom.

"How did you –?"

Muriel gave her daughter a look. "I heard you talking. Who else would you call on Christmas Day? And who else could put that light in your eyes?" she asked as if this should be obvious. "How is she? I hope you wished her a Merry Christmas for me."

"I did," Margaret said, frowning. Was this astuteness on her mother's part something she had recently acquired, or was it, perhaps, that Muriel had always been this way, but had been so overshadowed by Frank – "the same way I was overshadowed by Gavin" – that Margaret had never seen it before?

"She's fine," she added at her mother's questioning glance. "Her father did have a stroke. She's in New Hampshire with her family."

It had been hard to tell from Wyck's voice how things with her family were going. She said it was fine, but there had been a tightness to her voice that indicated otherwise. It had sounded as if she couldn't talk freely – or maybe she doesn't want to talk to you, Margaret realized.

"She never said much," Muriel's voice cut through Margaret's thoughts. "But I got the feeling she doesn't get along with her family."

"Well, there was a confrontation a few years ago," Margaret said hesitantly, wondering if she should be discussing this. "She was going through a break-up and her family was less than supportive."

"That's a shame," Muriel shook her head as she helped herself to another Christmas cookie. "And now," she said, sitting down in an armchair opposite Margaret, "what about you?"

"Well," Margaret began, expressing to someone for the first time the conclusions she had come to while in England, "I thought I'd like to try introducing Wyck to some of my colleagues, you know, go places together, let people see us –"

"– so they'll accept her," Muriel finished for her.

"Exactly," Margaret said, frowning a little at the tone of her mother's voice.

"And maybe they'll leave you alone so you can have your relationship and your home and your career," Muriel continued.

"Why not?" Margaret asked testily.

"No reason," Muriel shrugged. "But what if that isn't what Wyck wants?"

Margaret stopped. It hadn't occurred to her that her mother might know some sides of Wyck better than she did. *Why did I allow them to get in touch with one another?* she asked herself, angry that her mother seemed to be challenging her on this after all the soul-searching and questioning it had taken to reach this point.

Perhaps Muriel sensed Margaret's resentment, for she said soothingly, "It might all work out the way you hope."

Margaret's gut churned queasily as she recalled that, even as she and her mother were discussing these plans, Jim Evans and A.J. Duckworth were busily re-arranging her life into something she didn't want at all. She couldn't help wondering what else wouldn't go according to plan.

Chapter 29

"IS SOMETHING WRONG, AUNT WYCK?"

Wyck blinked and turned to Michaela. "No. Nothing's wrong." The family was gathered in Gene's room while he finished his morning therapy sessions.

"I have to go see Jeffrey and Amanda," Margaret had said apologetically on the phone. "I'll spend New Year with them and then come home."

"I should be able to leave here by then," Wyck had said, though she knew her departure would probably spark another argument.

Michaela looked up at Wyck now. "You're getting ready to go, aren't you?"

Wyck nodded, wrapping an arm around Michaela's shoulders. "I have to get back."

Melissa sat up straighter. "You're not staying until he goes home?"

Wyck snorted. "He's not going home for four weeks. I have a home and a business I have to get back to. I don't live here anymore," she reminded her sister.

Felicia bristled. "And who do you think is going to help your mother with him when he does get home?" she asked waspishly. "I know you all think it will be me because I don't work, but I won't!"

"Why not? You helped get him in this condition," Wyck so wanted to retort, but bit the words back. There was a twinge of guilt at the thought of leaving her mother to deal with her father in his compromised condition, but he was walking now with one person's help in the bars; he was feeding and dressing himself – badly, it was true – but he was doing it if left alone. Gene, though, was very good at looking helpless and Bobbi, any time the therapists weren't around to stop her, would jump up to take over for him, despite Wyck's protests that he needed to do things for himself. Wyck was under no delusions that her father would maintain his independence, such as it was, once he was home, and "I don't want to be here to see it," though she didn't say that.

Struggling to keep her voice neutral, she said, "I know there will be some adjustments when he gets home, but I have obligations in North Carolina that I have to get back to."

"I hope more than obligations are waiting for me when I get back," but she didn't say that, either.

Saying good-bye to Michaela was the hardest part. "I'll talk to your mother and see if you can come down for a visit this summer," she promised a couple of days later as Michaela hugged her tightly.

At last, with one last hug for her mother and a promise to call frequently, Wyck and Mandy were in the truck headed home.

Wyck let out a relieved sigh as they got underway. She reached a hand out to Mandy who settled on her seat with a soft whoof as if she, too, was more than ready to get back home.

"Damn," Margaret cursed as she saw the flashing blue lights in her rear-view mirror. She pulled over on I-40 as other westbound cars slowed to get by them. She rolled down her window as the highway patrol officer approached.

"Ma'am, do you know how fast you were going?" he asked as he leaned down to peer at her through the car window.

"I know I was speeding," she admitted as she dug in the glovebox, already resigned to the ticket she knew was coming.

He looked her license and registration over. "Travelling back home after the holidays?"

"Yes," Margaret said in such a harassed tone that he smiled.

"My in-laws just left this morning. Longest week of my life," he said as he handed her documents back to her. "Please slow down and get home safely."

"Uh, thank you," she stammered, thanking him again and again in her mind as she pulled back out onto the highway, setting the cruise control at a more reasonable speed.

She'd gone straight from Richmond to visit with Amanda and Jeffrey and their families. She loved getting together with them. Cecilia, Jeffrey's wife, had become a close friend over the years. She had a wry sense of humor and often confided to Margaret how Jeffrey was becoming more and more like Gavin - "and that really scares me," she would whisper.

It had been wonderful to see everyone again, but *I hadn't realized how accustomed I've become to peace and quiet*, she thought, and there was precious little of that with the kids running around. Still, she was their grandmother - "not a role I ever saw for myself," she had once admitted wryly to Wyck.

Jeffrey was indeed more like Gavin than ever, "pretentious and arrogant," Margaret mused as she drove, remembering Cecilia's roll of the eyes. More troubling had been Amanda's coolness toward Margaret - until she got a little tipsy on New Year's Eve. The drunker she got, the more emotional she became.

"I miss him so much," she sobbed against Margaret's shoulder. "I know you must, too," to which Margaret didn't respond, but fortunately, Amanda was too drunk to notice. "You're... you're not with anyone else, are you?" she asked, holding tightly to Margaret's arm.

Margaret, to her immense relief, was rescued by Jeffrey who raised his glass in an impromptu toast to Gavin. *You are such a hypocrite*, she said to herself as she silently sipped her champagne.

"To Dad," Amanda hiccupped, holding her glass up also, apparently forgetting her unanswered question to Margaret.

Though she doubted Amanda would remember much from that night, it was clear to Margaret that introducing Wyck to them would be problematic. "This might not be as easy as I had envisioned," she muttered as she neared Asheville.

Back home at last, she breathed a deep sigh of contentment as she stood in the foyer, enjoying the quiet. She deposited her suitcase in her bedroom and went back downstairs where she turned on the lights of her little Christmas tree in the den and went to make herself a cup of tea.

While she waited for the kettle to boil, she checked the messages on the answering machine. One was from Jim Evans.

"Margaret, Jane and I are having a little pre-semester gathering Saturday evening at seven. I hope you'll be able to attend, and if there's anyone you would like to bring, please do. We hope to see you then."

Saturday. She couldn't be sure Wyck would be back by then, but this could be the perfect opportunity to introduce her to some of the university people. "If only she'll agree."

Unlike her trip to New Hampshire, Wyck pushed straight through the entire eighteen hours back to Asheville, stopping only for food and bathroom breaks for herself and Mandy. It was nearing two a.m. when they got home to the barn. Dropping her suitcase in the middle of the bedroom, she undressed, letting her clothes stay where they fell and collapsed immediately into bed while Mandy did the same.

She didn't wake until Mandy nudged her arm, whining a little. Glancing at the clock, she saw it was after ten.

"Oh, I'm sorry," she mumbled, getting out of bed and pulling on the same clothes she had left piled on the floor. She stumbled downstairs and let Mandy out back where she squatted for a very long pee. Unlocking the dog door so Mandy could come back in when she was ready, Wyck put some coffee on and went upstairs for a quick shower.

Back downstairs a few minutes later, wearing clean clothes, she put some bread in the toaster and scooped some kibble for Mandy. Just as she was buttering her toast, her cell phone rang.

"Wyck?"

"Margaret," Wyck said warmly. "Are you home?"

"Yes. You?"

"Yeah. Late last night, or early this morning. I feel kind of jet-lagged," she said, running her hand through her damp hair.

"Can you - are you available to come over later today?" Margaret asked.

"Sure. How about after lunch?"

"That sounds good," Margaret said. "I'll see you then."

When Wyck rang the bell a couple of hours later, the gong had barely sounded when the door was yanked open by Margaret.

"Hi," Wyck said simply.

"Hi." Margaret's expression was radiant as her eyes drank in Wyck's face.

Mandy, refusing to stand on ceremony, wriggled in to say hello, bouncing happily around Margaret. She trotted into the den where her bed still lay and plopped into it, rolling on her back to make it smell like her again.

Wyck stepped inside, waiting uncertainly as Margaret closed the door and turned to her. Wordlessly, Margaret stepped close and kissed Wyck, their arms wrapped tightly around one another.

"I can't believe you're home," Wyck murmured, her hands caressing Margaret's face.

Margaret nodded. "I'm home." She led Wyck into the kitchen where her laptop sat on the table next to a thick manila envelope.

"What can I get you?" she asked.

"Um, coffee if you have any," Wyck said, taking a seat at the table.

"That, I have," Margaret said. "I picked up a few groceries this morning. I hadn't been home long enough to have any food in the house."

"Does it feel strange to be home after such a long time away?" Wyck asked.

"It does," Margaret admitted. "I was so looking forward to getting back here, to you..."

"...but?" Wyck asked apprehensively.

"No," Margaret said quickly. "It's just that as soon as I got back, there were university things to deal with, and then leaving right away to spend the holidays with my mother and the family, it's been more hectic than I had hoped."

She brought two cups of coffee and a plate of cookies to the table and sat. Her eyes shone as she looked at Wyck. "It is so good to see you." They looked at each other for long seconds. "There's so much to talk about. I don't know where to begin."

Wyck reached for her hand. "Let's begin with England?"

"Oh, Wyck, it was wonderful," Margaret said feelingly. "It was so good. You and Mandy would have loved the place I stayed..." and she launched into a description of the cottage and the Hopsons and the surrounding Lake country. "I can understand why Wordsworth and Beatrix Potter fell so deeply in love with the region," she said. "I'd love to go back there with you some day."

"That... that would be..." But Wyck wasn't sure what to say, how much of a future to give voice to. Other than the statement she had just made about going to England together someday, Margaret still hadn't given any indication of how she was feeling about them, together, here and now.

"What about you?" Margaret asked with a squeeze of her hand. "How are things with your family?"

"Oh," Wyck said, expelling a deep breath. "That was just weird. My dad's stroke is serious. He should be able to go home, though they say he won't ever regain full function. But it's going to mean a lot of work for my mother, and my brother and sister, if they'll help. They clearly resented my being so far away and leaving them to deal with things, partly because they aren't dealing with things. They won't make him do the exercises and activities he's doing with his therapists, and he's very good at being pathetic, which my mother just can't stand." She shook her head. "I'm glad I won't be there to have to watch it." Her face lit up a little. "The best part was seeing my niece, Michaela. She's a great kid. I want to get her down for a visit this summer. I'd like her to meet you."

Margaret smiled in surprise. "Really?"

"Yes, really," Wyck said. "How's your mother?"

"She's fine," Margaret said drolly. "I hadn't considered that the two of you would strike up a friendship in my absence. I'm feeling a little ganged up on."

Wyck grinned. "I like her."

"Apparently, it's mutual."

"Is that okay?" Wyck asked, her head tilted to one side.

Margaret nodded. "Yes, actually. It's a bit of a relief that she likes you, that she's okay with the thought of us. That was a huge surprise."

"I think her getting to know Iris and seeing through her eyes everything she's had to deal with since Jan died has made your mother more aware," Wyck said thoughtfully.

Margaret considered. "She told me that she'd known I was in love with Julia all those years ago," she said quietly. "And she saw how... different I was with Gavin."

"Were you unhappy?" Wyck asked.

Margaret sat back, staring out at the garden – Gavin's garden – and thought about all the things she'd come to understand about her and Gavin over the past several months. "I wasn't unhappy per se. I mean, Gavin was not unkind or abusive; I had anything I wanted materially."

"You sound like Charlotte Lucas defending her decision to marry Mr. Collins," Wyck pointed out.

Margaret gave her a rueful smile. "I guess I do. And no jokes about my maiden name." She sighed. "I've had a good career, even if it wasn't the career I'd envisioned for myself when I was young. It's just that there was never a spark of romance, never that kind of happiness with him. Even my mother saw that." She looked at Wyck. "I had thought I didn't need that, but I was wrong. I do need it. I need you."

Wyck lifted Margaret's hand to her lips, her eyes closed as she heard for the first time the words she had longed to hear. "I love you so much," she murmured.

Margaret's face was radiant. "And I love you."

Wyck opened her eyes as she released Margaret's hand.

"And," Margaret said happily, "I've finished my book. At least the first draft." She slid the large manila envelope across the table. "I've sent a copy to my agent, but I'd like you to read it."

"Really?" Wyck asked. "I'm honored. And I'll be honest," she added at the look on Margaret's face. She fingered the metal clasp fastening the flap of the envelope. "You mentioned university things. What kind of university things?"

"Why didn't you just tell her what they're planning?" Margaret asked herself later.

"The same reason I didn't tell my mother or anyone else," she replied.

"And what is that? You think if you pretend it isn't happening, it won't?"

Instead, Margaret said, "There's a gathering this Saturday at Jim Evans' house. He encouraged me to bring someone if I wanted, so...?"

Wyck pulled back a little. "That seems like an awfully drastic first step," she said apprehensively. "It wasn't all that long ago that you couldn't introduce me to him when we were just having lunch together. Now you want to take me a party at his house? How about we go out to dinner a few times?"

"No," Margaret said emphatically. "No. I'm ready to do this. I want to do this," but "I need to do this," she nearly blurted. She didn't know how to explain her need to hang onto the person she felt she had become while in England, but she was afraid if that person didn't assert herself right from the start, she might slip away, no more than a souvenir of her time there.

"And who am I going as?" Wyck asked, still doubtful.

Margaret frowned. "Why do you have to have a title?"

"Margaret," Wyck said, "people are accustomed to thinking of you as Gavin's wife. He hasn't been gone that long, and you haven't been with anyone else as far as they know. You can't just bring me to something like that without expecting questions about who I am in your life."

Margaret continued frowning at her coffee cup. "Why do I have to explain myself to everyone?"

Wyck sat back. "Because it isn't just us. You function as part of a broader community – the university, Gavin's children. Have you told them about us?"

"No," Margaret said, squirming uncomfortably as she recalled Amanda's emotional questions at New Year's.

"Don't you think that might be a good place to start?" Wyck asked gently.

"No," said Margaret stubbornly. "I think this get-together is the right place to start. So, will you come?"

Wyck searched her eyes, still not totally convinced, but she could see the determination in Margaret's gaze. "All right. I'll come."

Margaret's face relaxed and her eyes took on a different kind of light. "Good." She tugged a little on Wyck's hand. "And now, will you come upstairs?"

Wyck grinned wickedly. "Over and over, I hope."

Chapter 30

WHY DID I EVER think this was a good idea? Margaret asked herself nervously a few nights later as she drove to Jim Evans' house, Wyck in the passenger seat beside her. She glanced over at Wyck, who looked very nice in dress slacks and a blazer under her winter coat.

Wyck, sensing her anxiety, said, "You can still change your mind. I won't be offended."

Margaret felt braver as she took Wyck's hand. "I don't want to change my mind. Just..." She swallowed. "I've never done this before."

Sooner than she would have liked, she was parking in front of the Evans home, lit up welcomingly, with Christmas wreaths still hanging in the windows. Together, the two women walked to the house, Wyck trailing behind a step.

The door was answered by Jane Evans who exclaimed, "Margaret! We're so glad you could come," as she gave Margaret a hug.

Margaret introduced Wyck and Jane shook her hand warmly. She invited them inside where perhaps a dozen people were already gathered.

Jane took their coats as Jim Evans came over to greet Margaret with a kiss on the cheek.

"Jim, this is a dear friend of mine," Margaret said. "Wyck Fitzsimmons, Dr. James Evans, the president of the university."

Wyck could see the curiosity burning in his eyes as he shook her hand.

"Jim, get them drinks," his wife prompted as she returned.

"Ladies?"

"White wine, please," Margaret said.

"The same," said Wyck.

Jim returned a moment later with two glasses.

"I want to introduce you to some people," Margaret said as she accepted her glass, cutting off any opportunity for Jim to ask questions as she steered Wyck toward a small knot of people.

For the next hour, Margaret introduced Wyck to various colleagues, so many that Wyck couldn't remember all their names. Wyck could see polite curiosity - "mostly polite," she would have said - in their faces as they chatted with her. Invariably, those same faces registered some degree of surprise at her ability to converse with them about their varied areas of study. *They don't expect that from a landscape architect,* she thought wryly as Margaret beamed.

She could feel Margaret tense at the sudden intrusion of a loud male voice with an ante-bellum accent.

"Who is that?" Wyck asked in amusement, watching Jim Evans greet the newcomer.

"Andrew Jackson Duckworth," Margaret said grimly.

"You're kidding."

"Unfortunately, I'm not," Margaret replied.

"But who -?"

"Margaret!" A.J. said, spotting her and approaching with a toothy smile.

Jim deftly wedged himself between Margaret and Wyck, engaging Wyck as A.J. steered Margaret to an empty alcove.

"So..." Jim said, forcing Wyck to look at him, "how long have you known Margaret?"

"About a year and half," Wyck replied warily, glancing quickly toward the alcove where Margaret was in conversation with Duckworth.

"And how did you meet?" Jim persisted.

Wyck looked him in the eye and said, "We met when Gavin hired me to take over the grounds at their house."

"I see," he said, looking down at her with a smile that didn't quite reach his eyes. "You know that Gavin donated the house to the university in his will?"

"Yes," said Wyck coolly. "Which is why there will be no further improvements to the garden, at least not by me. Only maintenance. When Margaret is ready to give it up, you can do whatever you wish."

Jim continued to stare at her appraisingly for a few seconds. "Gavin was pretty particular about his garden," he said.

"Yes, he was," Margaret said, reappearing at Wyck's side. Jim turned quickly and looked at Duckworth who was frowning in their direction. "Which should say a good bit about how much Gavin trusted Wyck's vision and knowledge, and why she became such a close friend of ours."

Wyck had the feeling she had become a pawn in some unspoken power game she didn't quite understand.

"Miss Fitzsimmons," said a distinguished-looking man with a silver goatee whom Wyck recalled taught French. He took Wyck by the elbow, saying, "We need you to settle a dispute about the best method for propagating orchids."

With a quick backward glance, Wyck allowed herself to be pulled away to a small group of men engaged in heated debate. Only half-listening, Wyck tried to hear what Jim Evans was saying to Margaret, catching only snippets of their conversation.

"– a landscaper?"

"She's not a landscaper," Margaret corrected. "She has a Master's in landscape architecture. There's a difference."

"But still –" and his voice lowered so that Wyck couldn't hear what he was saying as he leaned over Margaret trying to make some point. Margaret's voice suddenly rose.

"She was also a Rhodes scholar, Jim," she said hotly. "She's probably the most intelligent person in this room."

Wyck could feel the heat rise in her face as Jim pulled Margaret into the kitchen where she could no longer hear what they were saying.

"Miss Fitzsimmons?"

"Sorry, what?"

"We were asking whether aerial cutting was preferable to keiki," said the French professor.

"Um, I prefer dividing the plants, myself. It's much simpler for novices." At the disappointed expressions on their faces, she quickly added, "But for those, like you, who know what they're doing, keiki and aerial cuttings work equally well." She backed away. "If you'll excuse me –" but the orchid enthusiasts were already engaged in further argument.

She made her way toward the kitchen where she was nearly bowled over by Jim who spared her the briefest glance before returning to Duckworth who was sipping his Scotch over near the fireplace.

Margaret followed him out of the kitchen.

"What was that all about?" Wyck asked.

Margaret watched the two men talking, her eyes narrowed.

"Margaret?"

"Duckworth wants to make a donation to create an endowment in Gavin's name," Margaret explained. "And Jim is kissing his ass to make it happen."

Wyck watched her closely. "What does that have to do with you?"

Margaret's jaw clenched for a moment. "They want me to take an administrative position and oversee the whole thing."

Wyck stared at her. "Why didn't you tell me about this?"

"They just hit me with it when I got back from England," Margaret said. "I haven't really had a chance to take it all in."

"Is this something you want to do?" Wyck asked incredulously.

"No," said Margaret firmly, "but they don't want to take no for an answer. I never had a chance to tell them about my book or about my ideas for new classes I'd like to propose." She looked down at her wine glass. "I'll never get out from under Gavin's shadow if I do what they want."

"Can we leave?" Wyck asked hopefully.

Margaret nodded. "Let me say good night to Jane."

In the car a short while later, Wyck asked quietly, "Why did you tell Evans about my Rhodes?"

Margaret glanced over and saw the hard set of Wyck's mouth. She reached for Wyck's hand. "I didn't do it because I was embarrassed by what you do," she said, correctly interpreting Wyck's attitude. "He was implying that it was beneath me to be socializing with –"

"– the gardener?" Wyck quipped.

Margaret smiled. "Yes, basically. I told him because I'm proud of you. What you did was a tremendous accomplishment, something he never achieved, and he tried." She squeezed Wyck's hand. "I know you don't feel like you have to brag about it, but it's also not something you need to pretend never happened."

Wyck thought about what she'd said. "It just feels like it belonged to a different person's life."

She looked around at the scenery as they drove and realized Margaret was not taking them back to her house. "Where are we going?"

Margaret lifted Wyck's hand to her lips. "I thought tonight, we could spend the night at the barn."

Wyck woke to find Margaret sitting up in bed, her arms wrapped around her knees as she stared out at the mountains, their tops tinged with pink from the sunrise.

"You okay?" she asked, rubbing Margaret's back.

"Mmmm," Margaret responded, half-turning. "I was just thinking... for so long, I thought I'd never see the dawn from this room you built."

"I did it for you," Wyck reminded her softly.

"I know," Margaret murmured. "You put so much love into everything." She shifted and looked down at Wyck. "You put so much love back into me. I feel like a different person when I'm with you. A better person."

"I can't think of a higher compliment than that," Wyck said.

Margaret opened her mouth and then paused before saying nervously, "How... are you okay with... I mean, is everything okay for you, when we're together?"

Wyck smiled at Margaret's shyness. "Are you asking me if the sex is good?"

Embarrassed, Margaret nodded.

Wyck sat up and wrapped an arm around Margaret's shoulders. "Couldn't you tell by my response?"

Margaret frowned. "Would you tell me if you wanted me to do something different? I don't know what you like..."

"And I'm learning what you like," Wyck said. "Why would you think I know better or more than you?"

"It's been so long for me, with a woman, and... we were so young back then," Margaret said lamely.

"I don't think things have changed that much," Wyck joked. At Margaret's serious expression, she added, "This is something we'll learn about each other. It's only the beginning, and it will get better, for both of us."

"It's just that, you're so beautiful, so young," Margaret said haltingly, "and I'm -"

"Hey," Wyck interrupted, pulling Margaret back down, and gently tugging the sheet away from her clutches. "You are beautiful, too. Don't you know that? You will always be beautiful to me," she said, lying down atop Margaret.

Margaret looked at her dubiously. "I'm so much older -"

"Shhh," Wyck commanded. "That is not something I even think about."

"Really?" Margaret asked, her eyes still doubtful.

"Really."

There was a soft whine and a scratch at the door.

Wyck grinned. "The kids are up."

She slid out of bed and walked naked to the door where Mandy bounded in playfully. Wyck yelped and jumped back. "Cold nose!"

"Margaret! I've been hoping to run into you," said Cindy Wilson as Margaret approached the faculty parking lot. She gave Margaret a hug. "How are you?"

"I'm good," Margaret said, thinking back to the last time she'd run into Cindy, at the grocery store on Christmas Eve - was that really Christmas a year ago? *I felt like a character in a Dan Fogelberg song. God, that was a horrible Christmas,* she thought, recalling the endless hours in Gavin's hospital room.

"We missed you last semester," Cindy was saying. "Did you have a good sabbatical?"

"I did," Margaret said. "It was very good. I finished a new novel."

"Did you?" Cindy replied. "That's fantastic! I can't wait to read it. How about coming home with me for dinner tonight? Jerry is cooking, so I can't promise anything," she laughed.

"Oh, thank you, Cindy, but I can't. I've got my first set of papers to get started on," Margaret said. "Maybe another time?"

"All right. Have a good evening."

"You, too. Hi to Jerry."

Margaret drove, eager to get home, but not to grade papers. Pushing the button on the garage door opener, she smiled as she saw Wyck's truck parked inside. She had sold Gavin's Lincoln a few weeks ago. That evening, she had pressed the garage door control, along with a house key, into Wyck's hand.

"Are you sure about this?" Wyck had asked hesitantly.

"I'm sure," Margaret said. "You're here almost every night anyhow."

It was true. Through the dreary days of January and February, they had begun spending most of their evenings together, at Margaret's house during the week and out at Misselthwaite on the weekends - "our secret garden," Margaret joked as she lounged about in jeans and over-sized corduroy shirts, "things Gavin would never have let me be seen in," she said.

She could never recall feeling so completely happy - "not the wild intoxication of being with Julia, making love in all kinds of forbidden places, and not the staid contentment of being married to Gavin," she tried to explain to Wyck. "I needed to be on my own for a while after Gavin was gone. And if you weren't here, I probably could have been content to be by myself. After thirty years of marriage, it felt good to be alone," she admitted. "But just being with you, sharing little things, everything feels so much more... I don't know. I feel whole, when I didn't even know part of me was missing."

Sometimes they watched television or a movie, but more often, they spent the evenings in companionable silence as Wyck read and Margaret worked on a new book – "I want to write about my time in England."

"It's okay if you want to work in your study," Wyck had repeatedly said, but "I want to be with you," Margaret said simply. "I can be myself with you, in ways I never could with Gavin."

"Mmmm," she said now as she entered the mudroom from the garage and smelled dinner cooking. "It smells wonderful. How nice to have a wife," she quipped as Mandy trotted over to greet her.

Wyck came to greet her as well, but with a hug and a long kiss. "Don't get too used to it," she warned. "It probably won't happen often once my season picks up again." She turned back to the stove where a pot of chili was simmering. "How was your day?"

Margaret hung her coat and scarf on a peg in the mudroom, saying, "Oh, it was fine. Got another e-mail from Jim about the new position, pushing for a meeting."

Wyck turned to her. "You can't keep putting this off."

"I know," Margaret said, rubbing her eyes tiredly. She poured glasses of ice water for each of them. "If I can just get through the memorial for Gavin next month, then I can deal with this."

Wyck retrieved two bowls from a cupboard. "I thought they wanted to roll the announcement of your new position and the whole endowment thing together as part of the memorial?"

"They do," Margaret sighed. "But the memorial feels overwhelming enough as it is."

"Have you heard back from Jeffrey and Amanda?" Wyck asked as she set bowls of chili on the table.

"Yes," Margaret said. "They'll be here. And they'll be staying," she added apologetically.

"It's okay," Wyck said, carrying a loaf of bread and cutting board to the table as well. She dished some food out for Mandy and joined Margaret at the table. "I wasn't planning on being around while they're here."

Margaret frowned. "But I want them to know you."

Wyck smiled grimly. "That would be nice, but I wouldn't hold my breath if I were you."

Margaret ate a couple of bites as she thought. "They'll have to get used to the idea eventually. They can't expect that I would never be in another relationship."

"I think that's exactly what they expect," but Wyck kept that thought to herself.

Chapter 31

"COME ON, JUST ONE more push," Wyck groaned as she stretched her left arm to make a few more passes with her saw on one last dead branch high in a tree.

A chill March breeze blew, and she swayed with the movements of the tree. Her cell phone rang, startling her. She looked down just as the saw ground through the last bit of wood connecting the branch. As the branch and saw gave way together, Wyck's arm was suddenly pushing into thin air, throwing her weight to her left. Her injured thigh, unable to support her weight, buckled, toppling her into empty space. She let go of the saw, her arms flailing as she tried to grab onto another branch. Other branches whipped at her as she fell... ten, fifteen feet before her safety rope stopped her with a spine-breaking snap.

Dangling from the rope fastened to her climbing harness - the rope she hadn't bothered to move and re-tie to get up to that last branch - Wyck swung in mid-air as her heart raced.

"You knew better, you stupid, stupid bitch!" she whispered along with a few other expletives, berating herself as her terror made her furious with herself. "How could you be so careless?"

When she could finally breathe again and her trembling subsided enough for her body to obey her, she pulled herself onto the nearest branch, untied her anchor rope and climbed down. Once on the ground, her legs turned to jelly and she collapsed, breathing hard and continuing to cuss herself as she inspected her jeans which now had a few rips and spots of blood where branches had torn at her. Reaching up, she could feel similar scratches on her face as her fingers pulled away, sticky with blood. Retrieving her cell phone from her pocket, she saw she had a voicemail from Margaret.

"Lunch? Call me."

Wyck flopped back on the ground with a bark of mirthless laughter, trying not to think about how close she had just come to never calling Margaret again.

An hour later, somewhat calmer and cleaned as best as she could manage, she joined Margaret at the little café downtown near her office.

"Hi," Margaret said as Wyck came in and sat. She peered more closely at Wyck's scratched face and her torn jeans. "What happened to you?"

Wyck shook her head. "Nothing. A tough morning fighting with a stubborn tree. How's your day going? Everything all set for tomorrow?"

A shadow fell over Margaret's features. "As much as it can be, I guess. I really had hoped they would do this memorial service while I was in England. I –"

"Hi, Wyck."

"Ashley, hi," Wyck said, looking up at their server.

"You haven't been in lately," Ashley said, placing a familiar hand on Wyck's shoulder.

Margaret's eyebrows raised questioningly as Wyck blushed.

"I've been busy on other jobs," Wyck said. "I haven't been downtown much."

Ashley glanced curiously at Margaret. "What can I get you to drink?" she asked, pulling out her pen and pad.

She left a moment later to fill their orders, watching them curiously from the drink station.

"I think you have an admirer," Margaret teased.

Wyck blushed a deeper red. "She's uh... she's just very friendly."

Margaret chuckled. "With you, I think."

"Anyway," Wyck said, changing the subject, "you were saying? About the memorial service?"

"Oh. I'm expecting Jeffrey and Amanda this evening sometime."

Wyck nodded. "I'll come for the service, but I'm not staying for the reception after."

They were interrupted by Ashley returning with their drinks. "The usual?" she asked Wyck, jotting before Wyck could answer.

"Uh, sure, that's fine," Wyck said as Margaret covered a smile.

"And your mother?"

Margaret's expression froze. "A chicken salad on wheat," she said in a strained voice.

Wyck waited until Ashley left with their orders, before leaning forward. "Margaret," she began.

"Don't," Margaret said tersely.

"She's twenty," Wyck said. "What does she know?"

Margaret kept her eyes downcast. "Maybe more than we do."

"She doesn't know anything about us," Wyck said defensively.

"No, she just stated the obvious," Margaret said, her tone curiously flat. "The thing everyone else will think, but be too polite to say."

"That's ridiculous," Wyck said. "Didn't you tell me before that you always heard those kinds of whispers about you and Gavin? Did it bother you then?"

Margaret's knuckles were white as her hand held tightly to her glass of iced tea. "That was different."

"The only thing that was different was that you were the younger one in that relationship," Wyck pointed out reasonably. "That's how I feel now. It doesn't matter to me."

Margaret's eyes filled with sudden tears. "But it matters to me."

Abruptly, she pushed away from the table, grabbed her purse off the back of her chair and rushed from the café.

"Here are your sandwiches," Ashley said brightly, setting two plates down.

With a withering look, Wyck threw money on the table and went after Margaret. Standing helplessly on the sidewalk, she watched the Audi pull away from a parking space with a squeal of the tires.

"Dr. Braithwaite?"

Margaret blinked and looked up. "Sorry?"

Her graduate students were watching her from their armchairs gathered in a loose circle. She realized one of them had been reading and that she hadn't heard a single word.

The students glanced worriedly at one another. "Why don't we call it a day?" one young man suggested.

"Yes," the others murmured at once. "We'll see you tomorrow," they said and Margaret knew they all assumed her preoccupation was due to the upcoming memorial service.

Wordlessly, she nodded without correcting them as they shuffled from the room. She sat there for several minutes, staring out the window at the still-bare tree branches rattling in the breeze.

"You're just being stupid about this."

"Maybe."

"She said it doesn't matter to her. Why can't you accept that?"

"I could now. Thirty-five and fifty-three doesn't seem so bad. But when she's sixty, I'll be seventy-eight. Maybe I'll still be able to keep up with her, but at some point, I'm going to drag her down, keep her from living the way she'll want to."

"There's something else, though."

Margaret sat there, unwilling to admit, even to herself, how hurtful the waitress's comment had been.

"How many times did people assume Gavin was your father? Even Wyck did at first."

"I know, but..."

"So, this is about your vanity?"

262

Yes, Margaret realized. To a certain extent, it was. *How does this happen?* she wondered. *I still feel like I did when I was thirty. I'm not ready to be thought of as old,* and it occurred to her that most her students were the same age as Ashley. *They must think of me just as she did.*

She went to the small mirror hanging on one wall of the classroom and lifted her hands to her face, feeling the slight sag of the skin on either side of her mouth, examining the crow's feet at the corners of her eyes, the furrowed lines etched between her brows.

Cruelly, the voice said, "Ready or not, you're going to have to find a way of accepting it."

Still pensive, she gathered up her things and went to her office where she shut her computer down and prepared to go home.

She drove slowly, in no hurry to have to deal with Amanda and Jeffrey this evening. To her surprise and indignation, Jeffrey's car was already in the drive when she arrived.

"What the –?"

Hurriedly, she pulled into the garage and entered the house to find Jeffrey seated at the kitchen table.

"Where is Dad's car?" he asked in a voice of forced calm.

"What?" Margaret could hear footsteps running down the stairs.

"There's an extra towel and toothbrush in the bathroom –" Amanda stopped short as she came into the kitchen and saw Margaret. "Who else is staying here? With a dog," she added, "and this." She held up a glass case in which Margaret had placed Mrs. Hopson's rose. Amanda had obviously retrieved it from its place on the mantel in the den. "Where did this come from?"

Knocked off-balance by the accusatory tone of their questions, Margaret turned her back on them to hang her coat and briefcase in the mudroom.

"What are you doing here so early?" she asked rather than answering them.

"Why? Were you going to have all the evidence cleared away by the time we got here?" Amanda asked.

Margaret stared at her. "Evidence of what?"

"Where is Dad's car?" Jeffrey repeated.

"I sold it," Margaret said, "not that it's any of your business," she wanted to add, but didn't.

"Sold it."

"Yes," Margaret said. "Why shouldn't I?"

Amanda glared at her. "It's like you've removed all signs of Dad from the house. You tore apart his den. You just shoved all his stuff into his office." Her chin trembled.

Trying to calm herself as she realized the extent to which they'd gone through the house, Margaret quickly did a mental inventory, trying to remember whether there really was anything of Wyck's that she hadn't wanted them to see.

She went to the stove to put a kettle on to boil. "I redecorated the den to update it and make it more comfortable. And I put your father's things in his office so you could go through them to see if there's anything you want."

Turning to face them, she crossed her arms and said, "I don't appreciate the tone of these questions. And I don't appreciate your letting yourselves into the house before I got home."

They glared at each other, and Jeffrey said, "It's our home. We've always had a key. Why is that a problem?"

Margaret, fighting to keep her voice neutral, said, "Jeffrey, you are forty-nine years old and your sister is forty-six. You haven't lived here for decades. This is not your home. It's my home now. Your father has been gone for nine months. I can understand that the changes around here are difficult for you to accept, but my life has moved on."

There was a very strained silence, before Amanda said, "So you are seeing someone else?"

Oh, God, Margaret thought, totally unprepared for this. Stalling, she turned to the kettle, which mercifully began to whistle at that moment. "Tea?"

"I need something stronger than tea," Jeffrey grumbled, going to the bar and pouring himself a Scotch.

"Pour me one, too," Amanda said.

Jeffrey glanced at her in surprise, but poured a second crystal tumbler half-full of the amber liquid.

They all sat at the kitchen table.

"Well?" Amanda demanded.

Margaret took a sip of her tea and realized her hands were trembling as the cup rattled a bit when she placed it back on the saucer. "There is someone."

"Someone we know?" Jeffrey asked.

"You've met," Margaret said vaguely.

Amanda opened her mouth, but Jeffrey laid a restraining hand on her arm. "Tell us about him," he suggested calmly, taking a drink of his Scotch.

Margaret's mouth opened and closed as she quailed, trying to find the words. "Well... it's... she is the landscape architect your father hired to take over his garden and the grounds."

A thick, heavy silence followed those words, a silence prickling with energy, like static electricity waiting to be set off - *it just depended on what kind of spark*, Margaret would realize later.

Jeffrey sat, digesting this revelation, and Margaret wished that he had spoken first - *it might have changed everything* - but "I knew it!" Amanda shrilled. "I knew there was something between you when I saw you clutching each other at the hospital!"

Instantly, Jeffrey's eyes blazed. "At the hospital? So before Dad was even gone -"

"No!" Margaret cut in. "It wasn't like that. Wyck was just comforting me. Nothing happened while Gavin was alive -"

"Oh, please," Amanda said scathingly. "You expect us to believe she was around here for months, while Dad was sick and couldn't defend himself -"

"Defend himself?" Margaret asked in shock.

"Defend his home! Defend his marriage!" Amanda said dramatically.

Margaret held up her hands. "It wasn't like that," she repeated. "Your father and Wyck respected each other, they were friends -"

"That makes it even worse!" Jeffrey chimed in angrily.

"Makes what worse?" Margaret asked, wondering how this had gone so badly so quickly.

Jeffrey set his Scotch glass down hard, his eyes narrowed. "You were Dad's wife. He stood for something. And for you now... with a woman. It's just..."

"How could you?" Amanda said. "You'll make Dad a joke. A laughingstock."

"How does this affect your father in any way?" Margaret asked in amazement.

"You can't be serious," Jeffrey said, leaning forward. "Even if, as you say, nothing happened while Dad was alive, no one will believe that. You may as well have cheated on him while he was on his deathbed. Amanda's right. You'll make a laughingstock of his memory. This will be what people remember him for... 'the man who wasn't man enough to hold onto his wife.'"

"That's ridiculous," Margaret gasped. "I was never unfaithful to Gavin."

Amanda waved a hand dismissively. "Who will believe that? I wouldn't, if we were talking about someone else."

Margaret stared at her. "You don't believe me now."

Amanda stared back. "No. We don't," she said coldly.

"Amanda," Jeffrey said uncomfortably. "You're going too far."

"It doesn't matter," Amanda insisted, ignoring him. "Just the fact that you're fooling around with a woman now after you were Dad's wife for so many years, it makes a joke of your entire marriage."

Margaret slumped back against her chair, looking from Amanda to Jeffrey. "You won't even give Wyck a chance, will you?"

"She's beside the point," Amanda said coldly.

"But I love her," only Margaret couldn't bring herself to say those words to them. "You don't even know her," she whispered.

Amanda stood. "I don't need to know her. If you insist on continuing to see this Wyck person," she said, "we will never see you again. You won't see the kids again. No holidays, no birthdays."

"Amanda," Jeffrey said again, more startled this time.

"I mean it," Amanda said, her voice getting shrill again. "Don't you see that this rubs off on us as well? We'll all be tarnished by this scandal."

"What scandal?" Margaret asked in bewilderment. "I'm a fifty-three-year-old widow who fell in love with someone else after my husband died. Where is the scandal in that?"

"There wouldn't be a question if you were with a man," Jeffrey said. "But this... this..." he faltered, unable to find the words to describe Margaret's relationship.

"You have a choice to make," Amanda said. "Your family or your fling."

Chapter 32

WYCK STARED AT HER phone, one line of text splayed across the screen. "Please don't come today."

She sat on the side of the bed, half-dressed for the memorial service. A cold emptiness filled the space where her heart should be and her mouth was dry and her ears buzzed with memories of hateful words.

"If you ever come back here, I'll kill you."

"What did you expect me do? I couldn't ruin my mother's Thanksgiving."

"This is for the best. It's God's way of showing you your sin. Now is the time for you to accept Jesus Christ as your savior and turn from your life of perversion."

Wyck closed her eyes. "This isn't like that," she whispered to herself. "Something happened and she needs to handle it, that's all. She'll call when she can."

She took off her dress slacks and changed into jeans and a sweatshirt. Mandy followed her out to the shed behind the barn where she resumed work on a set of bookshelves she was building.

She had to keep blinking to clear her eyes of the tears she couldn't stop, tears that kept blurring her vision, dripping with dark spatters onto the board she was planing. No matter how she told herself Margaret would call, she couldn't help feeling like she was back in the empty parking lot of the mall, waiting for someone who wasn't coming....

Margaret couldn't remember later more than scattered scenes from the memorial service, like flashes of memories of dreams. It was held in the university's chapel, and she recalled Jim Evans giving quite a lengthy speech, praising Gavin's contributions to St. Aloysius over a fifty-year career. He introduced A.J. Duckworth and announced the Gavin Braithwaite Endowment, though he shot Margaret a cold look as he did so. She still hadn't agreed to take the administrative position he was offering. Others got up to speak, and then it was Jeffrey's turn. Amanda cried into a handkerchief as Jeffrey eulogized their father – *he sounds as if he's beatifying him for sainthood,* Margaret thought miserably as she sat there.

For herself, she felt as if she had come to peace with Gavin. The realization while she was in England that he had asked for her forgiveness had changed everything – "but only for me." No one else knew about that, nor did they understand the dynamic that had played out among Gavin, Wyck and herself.

I suppose it could look like a sordid triangle to others, she thought as she only half-listened to Jeffrey.

"Triangles always look sordid to others," said that other voice, the one she couldn't silence.

"But we waited. Nothing happened while Gavin was alive. It wasn't like that."

"That's what people inside the triangle always say."

The service was followed by a reception in the hall off the chapel. Margaret shook multitudes of hands, hugged many people offering her their condolences and support and remembrances of Gavin. It was almost as bad as the funeral, except when she looked out and scanned the room, there was no Wyck. She had stayed away as requested.

Suddenly, she smelled a familiar cologne and turned to find Taylor at her elbow, looking as handsome and dapper as he had before "the fall," as he had so dramatically called it.

"What are you doing here?" she gasped as she hugged him.

"Well, you can guess it's not to praise the bastard or his minions," he said sarcastically, casting a poisonous glance in Jim Evans' direction. "I came for you," he said in a low voice.

His appearance had been noticed and there were a few whispers as people saw that he was present. Margaret, oddly touched by the selflessness of Taylor's return to hostile territory, hugged him again. He steered her toward a quiet corner where there was a sofa against the wall.

"Where are you now?" she asked as they sat.

"UNC-Asheville," he said, his eyes shining. "It's great. Better than I would have expected. I am so glad to be out from under St. Asshole's thumb. That's part of why I'm here. We have an opening in the English department. I think you should apply."

"What?" Margaret asked, startled. "Leave St. Aloysius?"

"Why not?" Taylor asked. "You know you'll never be completely yourself here. They'll always accept you as Gavin's widow, but you'll never be recognized for your work independent of his influence."

Margaret's eyes filled with sudden tears. Taylor, guessing at the turmoil behind them, said, "Walk outside with me."

He took her by the arm and guided her toward a side door, which opened onto a grassy enclosure. They walked and Margaret found herself pouring everything out to Taylor – her argument with Jeffrey and Amanda over Wyck, her concerns about the difference in their ages, Evans and Duckworth pressuring her to give up teaching to take over the administration of the endowment.

Taylor listened – much more attentively than he would have before, Margaret would realize later when she thought back – and let her talk herself out.

"Where is Wyck today?" he asked.

Margaret looked down. "I asked her not to come," she admitted shamefacedly. "I didn't want a scene."

Taylor pulled her to a halt. "She is the best thing that could have happened to you. Don't let them rip the two of you apart. As for the endowment –"

"Margaret?" Jim Evans had come looking for them. "People are asking for you inside. Don't you think it's time you came back where you belong?"

Taylor drew himself up, but as he was only five-foot-nine to Jim's six-four, it wasn't a very impressive move. "She doesn't have to answer to you. And I don't have to kiss your ass anymore, Dr. Evans," he said bitterly.

Jim, using his height to his advantage, came closer so that he towered intimidatingly over the two of them. "As I recall, it wasn't kissing asses that got you into trouble in the first place, Dr. Foster," he said in a quietly menacing voice.

Margaret laid a restraining hand on Taylor's arm as he bristled. "It's all right. I should go back."

She started to accompany Jim back inside.

"Think about what I told you," Taylor called after her.

She turned to look back at him. "I will."

Wyck sat at her computer in her office, trying to catch up on bills and get tax information ready for the accountant. Her cell phone rang and her heart leapt as she looked, but then just as quickly plummeted as she saw who was calling.

"Hi, Melissa," she said to her sister. "What's up?"

Her sister and mother called frequently now, since her visit back to New Hampshire – "but I'm not sure that's a good thing," she would have said ruefully. Usually, her sister called only to complain. Today was more of the same.

"Dad won't do anything for himself," she began. "Mom won't make him walk; she wheels him around the house, dresses him, practically feeds him..." All the things Wyck had predicted would happen were coming true.

"It's getting to the point where Mom needs help with him," Melissa said resentfully, "and guess who gets that job."

"I know," Wyck said sympathetically. "The therapists said he would regress quickly if he wasn't made to keep doing things for himself."

"We could use some help," Melissa said, and Wyck wasn't sure if that was another hint that she should move back home to help out more, but *like hell*, she thought.

"Talk to Mom about hiring someone to come in for a few hours a day," she suggested, and then half-listened as Melissa went on for a long time about why that wouldn't work. Every suggestion Wyck had made over the past few weeks was met with resistance. Stifling an impatient sigh, she listened a while longer until, "well, I've got an appointment with a client. I'll talk to you later," she said as an excuse to get off the phone.

She transferred her bank and accounting files to a flash drive, gathered up some folders and walked everything to the accountant's office two blocks away, staring at the concrete in front her as she stumped along. *The memorial service was only yesterday*, she reminded herself. It felt much longer. Wyck still had not heard from Margaret and wasn't sure how long Jeffrey and Amanda had planned to stay, so she didn't feel she could call or go over, even under the pretext of doing some garden work.

She got out of the accountant's office quickly and walked back to her truck, feeling tears stinging her eyes again. *You have got to stop doing this to yourself*, but telling herself that hadn't stopped the bad dreams and the constant sick feeling in her gut. She felt she was reliving that horrible Thanksgiving and Christmas over and over, but this time, there was an added layer of - what? *It feels like more than sadness*, she thought. It was a deeper feeling of grief, as if someone dear to her had died.

Margaret drove to the barn, not noticing the trees beginning to bud or the early flowers - crocus and forsythia and daffodils - forcing their way up along the rows of trees and fence posts lining either side of the road.

Jim Evans, sensing that he needed reinforcements to convince Margaret to accept the new position, had enlisted Jeffrey and Amanda during the memorial service.

"We've been trying to convince her that this is a wonderful opportunity," he said with a forced joviality, "but she is being stubborn."

Amanda turned to her. "This is a fantastic way to honor Dad," she said pointedly. "You owe it to him as his wife."

"That's exactly what I said," said A.J. Duckworth, joining the conversation. "Gavin's legacy deserves to be preserved. No one has given us anything that compares to the body of work he left behind."

"And," said Jim in a deceptively casual voice, "I've been thinking about the curious wording of Gavin's bequest to the university, wondering why in the world he would have stipulated things the way he did."

Margaret, feeling a blotchy flush of anger rising in her cheeks, turned away, searching for someone, anyone, whom she could latch onto and get away from them, but Jeffrey hadn't let it drop there.

"You aren't seriously thinking of declining Jim's offer?" he asked, as he drove them back to the house. "It's an important opportunity to keep Dad's work alive."

"That's what I think, too," Amanda chimed in from the back seat. "And I could come out and help when you start cataloguing all his notes and letters."

They seemed to have decided to act as if the prior argument had never happened, and were taking Margaret's silence on the topic of Wyck as a sign that she was willing to relinquish the relationship as they plowed ahead with plans - "plans for my life."

"You need to come see us over spring break," Amanda said, as she and her brother packed to leave the day after the service. "The kids want to see you and I think we may have a surprise to announce by then."

Margaret had seen them off, feeling as if she might throw up. Miserably, she turned back into the house, pausing at the door to the den, spotting Mandy's bed and missing her and Wyck like a physical ache. From the fireplace mantel, Mrs. Hopson's rose sat in its glass case, a reminder to Margaret of - "what?" she asked herself harshly. "The person you thought you had become? A person strong enough to hold onto the woman you love, no matter who stood in the way?"

Making up her mind, she'd grabbed her car keys.

Pulling into the lane leading to the barn, she saw that Wyck's truck wasn't there, but Mandy, hearing the car approach, raced from behind the barn to greet her. Margaret rubbed her silky coat and let herself in with the key Wyck had given her. Together, she and Mandy waited for Wyck to come home.

Wyck stopped the truck abruptly in the lane when she spied the Audi through the trees. Taking a deep breath, she slowly drove the rest of the way to the barn and got out.

Margaret opened the door at her approach. "Hi," she said.

Wyck couldn't tell anything by looking at her face. "Hi."

Mandy circled behind her, using her body to nudge Wyck through the door. Wyck entered, hanging her jacket on one of the pegs near the door while Margaret stood by silently.

"Can I get you anything?" Wyck asked.

"I made some tea," Margaret said, pointing to the cup and saucer on the coffee table. "Would you like some?"

"No," Wyck said flatly. "What I would like is an explanation," but she didn't say it.

Margaret sat on the sofa, leaving room for Wyck, but Wyck sat in her armchair and waited, stroking Mandy's head, which was resting on her knee.

"They left this morning," Margaret said. Still Wyck said nothing.

"I told them about us," Margaret said nervously. "Actually, I came home to find them already there. They'd let themselves in and had gone through the house, picking up on every sign of you and Mandy there. They were livid."

Wyck, who had been absently running her fingers over Mandy's ear, looked up. "Why?"

Margaret, her hands clasped tightly between her knees, said, "They think I'm erasing all signs of Gavin from the house, and they were surprised to realize I was seeing someone," she said lamely.

Wyck tilted her head. "Someone?"

"Okay, you," Margaret admitted. "They're upset because - well, that you're a woman and... they don't believe nothing happened between us while Gavin was alive." She leaned toward Wyck and said, almost pleadingly, "They're really hurt over this. They see it as a betrayal of their father, of his memory. They're worried that he'll become a butt of people's jokes and scorn..." Her voice trailed off.

Wyck's eyes narrowed slightly as she waited. "What do they want?"

Margaret shifted on the sofa so that she was nearer Wyck's chair. "Well, they want me to stop seeing you, but... I think if we could just give them time to get used to the idea..."

Wyck's jaw worked back and forth a couple of times. "How much time do you think that will take?" she asked softly.

Margaret shrugged a little. "It hasn't even been a year that Gavin has been gone. They just need time to get used to the idea of us," she said.

Wyck nodded slowly. "And what does that mean for us in the meantime?"

Margaret tossed her hands. "I don't know. Probably not living together, not spending as much time together as we have been..."

Wyck rubbed her fingertips across her furrowed brow. "I see. So basically, we go back to hiding, not being seen together in public, living separately, but you'll agree to see me every now and then for a quick fuck? And that will placate them?"

Margaret winced. "Don't be like that."

Wyck's mouth dropped open. "Don't be like what, exactly?"

"They've threatened to never let me see the grandkids again, Wyck. They've been my family for thirty years. I can't just ignore that. I don't want to hurt them."

"And what about me?" Wyck asked, but her voice cracked with emotions she couldn't hold in check any longer. The question sounded pathetic and she knew it, but she couldn't help it.

"I don't want to hurt you, either," Margaret said in anguish.

Wyck swiped angrily at her cheeks. "That's good of you."

"Can't you see how torn I am?" Margaret asked in frustration. "I'm trying to do what's best for everyone. It won't be forever."

Wyck took a calming breath and said, "Margaret, I love you. I don't care how old you are. I don't care that you were married to Gavin Braithwaite. I love you with everything that I am, but I don't know how to make everything enough. This should be simple, but it isn't. What you don't see is that it will always be something – the family, the university, whatever. I am not giving up on us, but you are torn. You always will be until and unless you can find some way to separate yourself from Gavin."

Stricken, Margaret whispered, "I can't do that."

Wyck's chin quivered as she said, "I know."

A short while later, Wyck and Mandy were alone, listening to the throaty exhaust of the Audi as Margaret drove away. Mandy nudged Wyck's arm with her nose.

"Stop it!" Wyck shouted, raising a hand in frustration and anger. Mandy cowered, her ears back and her tail tucked as she dropped to her stomach.

"I'm sorry," Wyck murmured immediately, falling to her knees and reaching for Mandy who crawled to her, still cowering on her stomach. "I didn't mean it; I'm so sorry," Wyck cried, burying her face in Mandy's neck.

Chapter 33

"MORE SALAD?" MURIEL COLLINS passed a bowl to Margaret who took it wordlessly. Muriel watched her daughter's expressionless face for a moment. "How long can you stay?"

"I thought I'd stay with you three days and then go visit Jeffrey and Amanda," Margaret said. "Amanda said something about an announcement."

"Is she pregnant?" Muriel asked in surprise.

Margaret shook her head. "I don't know. I wouldn't think so. She and Matthew always said they only wanted two children."

Muriel smiled. "Children have a way of coming, whether they're wanted or not."

They ate in silence for a few minutes before Muriel said, "I thought Wyck might come with you."

Margaret kept her eyes glued on her plate. "No. She –" Her voice cracked and she dropped her fork, covering her face with her hands.

Muriel let her cry, waiting patiently for her daughter to tell her what was wrong. Once Margaret could talk, it all came gushing out –

how strange that my mother has become my confidante, she would think later - as Muriel listened thoughtfully.

"And now," Margaret sniffed, "I think I may have lost her for good."

Muriel reached for her hand. "Peggy, I don't think Wyck will give up that easily."

Margaret shook her head. "It's not her. She said she won't give up on me, but she also said I would always be torn unless I could find a way to separate myself from Gavin. She's right." She looked up at the ceiling, blinking rapidly. "Every time I turn around, Gavin or his family or the university has found some new way of entangling me."

"Hmmm," said Muriel. "It's not easy, being threatened with not seeing the grandchildren."

Margaret looked skeptically at her mother. "You don't blame me for not telling them I would see Wyck no matter what they said?"

"Oh, honey, no," said Muriel. "They put you in a horrible position, having to choose between your family and the person you love."

"For the second time in my life," Margaret said bitterly.

"Oh, yes," Muriel frowned. "I'd nearly forgotten."

"Lucky you," Margaret wanted to retort, but didn't.

"What are you going to do about the university?" Muriel asked.

Margaret closed her eyes and shook her head again. "I'm probably going to take the position."

Muriel's eyebrows raised in surprise. "Is that what you want?"

"No!" Margaret said emphatically. "But," she said, remembering Jim's veiled threat at the memorial service, "I don't think I'm being given a choice any longer."

"What's the worst that could happen if you say no?" Muriel asked.

Margaret expelled a frustrated breath. "They fire me. Take my house."

"Exactly," said Muriel. "They fire you, take your house. And then... what? You still have to deal with Amanda and Jeffrey, but you're free. Free to do what you want. Be with the person you love.

Work somewhere else. Write your books. Do what *you* want for the first time in your life."

Wyck ran a measuring tape around the perimeter of the property, jotting the dimensions she would have to work with if she got this new job. She made notes as she went, ideas for planting beds and, surveying the trees she would have to work around, how much sun the new plants were likely to get. After about an hour, she knocked on the door.

"I think I've got everything I need to come up with a design and an estimate, Mrs. Carter," she said to the woman who answered. She held out a card. "Call me if you think of anything else you'd like, but I'll be in touch in a couple of days to go over the design and see if it meets your needs."

The woman nodded and thanked her, and Wyck went back to her truck. As she had expected, spring was bringing a slew of new jobs as homeowners got the itch to improve their yards. Once again, she had almost more work than she could handle herself – "No," she reminded herself harshly. "That's not true anymore." She kept forgetting she didn't need to budget so much of her time for the Braithwaite house any longer. She and Margaret hadn't discussed it, but she had no intention of going back there, and she knew Margaret wouldn't ask.

Glancing at her watch, she put the truck in gear and headed to a restaurant where she was meeting Lorie Brooks for lunch. She hadn't seen Lorie for a few weeks, not since the last time she had worked at the Biltmore, helping get the spring flower display ready.

She arrived at the restaurant first and got a table. Lorie arrived within a few minutes, and greeted Wyck with a hug and then held her at arm's length, peering intently into her face.

"What's wrong?" she asked. "You look awful."

Wyck gave her a look. "Let's order and then we can talk."

A few minutes later, their orders placed, Lorie said, "So tell me what's going on."

"You know that I was involved with someone –"

"Margaret Braithwaite," Lorie recalled, nodding. "She was in England the last we talked about it."

"Well, she came back at Christmas," Wyck said. "Things were really good for a while, a short while."

"What happened?"

"Her husband's family - kids and grandkids - threatened to cut her off and never see her again if she continued seeing me," Wyck explained.

"That's awful," Lorie said, reaching out to lay a hand on Wyck's arm. "She's doing it?"

Wyck shrugged. "She's not cutting me out of her life entirely, but she wants us to hide our relationship, hoping everything will blow over if they just have enough time to get used to us..."

"And you're not willing to do that?" Lorie guessed.

"I just -" Wyck swallowed. "It's not the first time I've been with someone who was forced to choose between me and family." She managed a pained smile. "So far, I'm zero for two. We haven't spoken for a few weeks."

Lorie looked at her sympathetically. "I wondered."

"What?"

"Why you don't sing anymore."

Wyck frowned. "What do you mean?"

"You always used to sing when you were working," Lorie remembered with a smile. "We all used to listen."

Wyck blushed. "I didn't realize -"

"No," Lorie hastened to say. "It was nice. We enjoyed listening to you. But you don't sing anymore. I wondered why."

At that moment, their server arrived with their plates and Wyck took the opportunity to change the subject.

"How's David?"

Lorie chewed and swallowed before saying, "He's enjoying his new job, thanks to you."

"How's his arm?"

Lorie shook her head as she ate a fry. "It still hasn't healed completely. He's not on antibiotics any more, but the doctors have warned him that the bone will never be healthy – there was too much damage."

Wyck stared at her plate. "Another proud piece of Gavin Braithwaite's legacy," she mumbled.

"Grandmother, you're not listening."

Margaret blinked and looked down at six-year-old Kaila who was sitting next to her, reading a story she had written about a little girl who found a pony in her backyard – a not-so-subtle hint to her parents that she very much wanted a pony.

"I was listening, Kaila," said Margaret.

"Yes," said Cecilia. "I think we were all listening – again," she said pointedly. "Why don't you go play with Thomas and Annie and your cousins?" she suggested. "The grown-ups need to talk about grown-up things."

Everyone was gathered at Jeffrey and Cecilia's house. With the kids playing down in the basement rec room, Amanda nudged her husband to get a bottle of champagne out of the refrigerator. *Not pregnant, then,* Margaret thought. Matthew popped the cork on the champagne and poured for all five of them.

"We have some news," Amanda said, barely containing her excitement as Matthew handed the glasses out. They grinned at each other and Amanda continued, "Matthew applied for a research fellowship and we just found out he got it!"

"Congratulations," the others said, raising their glasses in a toast.

Amanda shivered in excitement as she said, "We'll be going to Portugal. For three years!"

For Margaret, the lights seemed to dim and the voices suddenly sounded as if they were coming through an old gramophone as "when are you leaving?" and "sometime in May" and "we'll be leasing the house" were said from somewhere very far away.

"Margaret, I really don't think you should travel if you're not feeling well," Cecilia said in concern the next morning.

"Yes," said Jeffrey. "You were supposed to be here until Saturday anyway. You should spend as much time with Amanda and Matthew as you can before they leave."

Cecilia looked at him. "Jeffrey, for once in your life, would you please shut up?"

Jeffrey looked bewildered as Cecilia wrapped an arm around Margaret's shoulders.

"Jeffrey," Margaret said in a strained voice, "don't you understand what I gave up? What I did because Amanda threatened to keep the kids from me? And now, they're not even going to be in the country..."

He frowned, looking shame-faced. "You shouldn't have let her – I guess I should have spoken up. But, surely this... relationship wasn't so important to you?"

Margaret covered her face with her hands, her shoulders shaking as she cried. Cecilia gave him a withering look.

"I'm sorry, Margaret," he said, his hands shoved into his pockets as he stood awkwardly for a moment before mumbling about something he needed to do. His office door closed a few seconds later.

Cecilia gave Margaret a squeeze. "Go to her. There's still a chance to make things right."

Margaret took a deep breath, wiping her cheeks dry. "No, there isn't. Not as long as I'm tied to Gavin, and that means I can never make it right."

Chapter 34

MARGARET PULLED ANOTHER HANDFUL of books off one of her shelves and placed them in the cardboard box sitting open on her desk. Glancing out her office window, she noticed again the campus's landscaping, bushes and trees bursting with blossoms. *I never noticed things like that before,* she thought, *and now, I can't not notice.* She wondered, as she had done a million times, what Wyck was doing. Probably up to her ears in work now that the April weather had warmed for good and spring was in full bloom.

She maneuvered around behind her desk to her computer, looking up at a knock on the door.

"Packing already?" Jim Evans said, his head and shoulders appearing around the door, which would only partially open, blocked by more boxes already packed with books and stacked in piles on the floor.

"I don't believe in waiting until the last minute," she said.

Jim, if he heard the iciness in her voice, ignored it. "I don't, either," he said. "I've got your new office all set. I'll put in a work order for maintenance to get some guys over here to move your things as you get them packed." He paused. "This will be a good move, Margaret, you'll see."

"I guess you're right," she said in resignation.

"I'll see you later," he said, backing out of the doorway.

Sighing, Margaret dropped into her desk chair. Her bookshelves were half-empty. The room looked sad. With a shock, she realized she'd never packed up Gavin's campus office and wondered what had happened to all of his things. "A.J. Duckworth has probably turned his office into a shrine," she muttered.

The campus community had been surprised at the announcement that Margaret Braithwaite would be heading up the newly formed Office of Endowments and Gifts. There had been many congratulatory notes and e-mails, but it felt to her as if she was already separated from her colleagues. The promotion had brought a substantial increase over her academic salary, and she kept telling herself this would be a good thing, but again, as she sat at her computer, she opened an e-mail from Taylor. She had read it probably a hundred times. He, as she would have expected, had urged her not to take the new position, but he had also attached the vacancy announcement in the English department at UNC-Asheville that he had told her about. She had memorized it, she had read it so many times. It was stupid to keep it. Her finger hovered over the Delete button, but still....

"Come here, you," Wyck said in a playful growl as Mandy danced around her. They'd just returned from a long walk through the woods. Wyck was trying to jog again, but her leg wouldn't take the stress for more than a couple hundred yards. Still, she persisted, jogging as far as she could and then slowing to a walk until she felt she could jog again. Mandy, though, had found a creek and decided a swim sounded like a good idea. She had dropped into the water, grinning up at Wyck as she happily lay submerged in the cool running stream. By the time they got home, they were both wet and stinky.

Wyck managed to get hold of Mandy's collar and ran the hose over her before sudsing her up with shampoo. Mandy stopped moving and stood as if hypnotized as Wyck's fingers worked through her thick coat, massaging the shampoo in. When Wyck got the last of the shampoo rinsed out of the heavy, wet coat, Mandy shook, sending a drenching spray of water everywhere.

"It's a good thing I'm already wet," Wyck said, laughing as she picked up a bath towel, rubbing and rubbing to get the dog as dry as possible.

"Oh, no you don't," she said as Mandy made for the back yard to rub in the new grass growing there. With the interior of the barn done, it was time to tackle her own landscaping. "Inside you go." Wyck stripped down on the back porch and left her wet clothes in a pile as she padded nude through the house to take her own shower.

Standing under the shower, she let the water rinse away the accumulated sweat and dog spray. Without opening her eyes, she reached for the shampoo bottle, and squirted some into her hand. As she raised her hands to her hair, she caught the scent on them and realized she had accidentally grabbed Margaret's shampoo. Holding her hands to her face, she inhaled the scent. For long minutes, she stood there under the shower, just breathing in a bit of Margaret, her tears mixed with the rivulets of water running down her face.

When at last she stepped out of the shower, she toweled off and grabbed the trashcan. Reaching into the shower, she took the bottles of Margaret's shampoo and conditioner, her toothbrush and face creams from the vanity – every vestige of Margaret that remained, she placed in the trash and shoved it back under the sink. "Enough of this," she muttered.

She went to the bedroom to get dressed, and then went to brush Mandy before her coat got matted and tangled.

Working patiently, she combed out the blond coat, using a hair dryer to speed up the drying process.

"That's better," she said at last, stepping back, satisfied with the results.

She stood there staring at the floor for a few minutes, and then stomped upstairs, retrieved the trashcan from under the sink and replaced every one of the items she had just put in the can. Mandy watched her, her head tilted to one side.

Wyck shrugged. "They're not really in my way, and... she might want these back..."

Margaret pulled into the driveway. A truck with a trailer was parked on the curb and a slightly built man wearing a battered, brown Fedora was running a riding mower on a diagonal across the front lawn. He pulled the pipe from his mouth and waved, stopping the mower when he got near the driveway.

"Does it look okay, ma'am?" he asked as Margaret emerged from the garage.

"It looks fine, Mr. Martinez," she said, going to the front porch to collect the mail.

He took off his Fedora, mopping his forehead with the bandana draped around his neck. "It's warm for April, but everything's growing like crazy. Oh, I did a little work out back, " he said, putting his hat back on and starting the mower again. "I hope you like it."

She'd hired him a few weeks ago when it became apparent Wyck wasn't going to be back. "What did you expect?" she asked herself harshly. "She's not good enough to pass muster with your family, but 'oh, by the way, could you still mow the lawn?'"

"You don't want nothing done with the garden?" Mr. Martinez had asked curiously when she interviewed him to get his price for keeping the lawn mowed. He pointed with his pipe. "Someone done a lot of work back there."

"No, Mr. Martinez," Margaret said curtly. "As I said, I only want you to mow the lawn and keep the weeds and hedges under control."

"Yes, ma'am," said Martinez, doffing his hat. "I'll be out every Tuesday, then."

The garden was an area Margaret never went to any longer. It held too many memories of Wyck - "why doesn't it remind me of Gavin?" - and it was just too painful to wander those paths alone. She mainly stayed in the house as "my world becomes smaller and smaller..." but she didn't like to think about that.

She entered the house, depositing the mail on the kitchen table. Pausing to leaf through the envelopes, she glanced out the window and froze.

The hedges had all been trimmed. They stood rigidly at attention with freshly cut square, straight edges - just the way Gavin would have wanted.

She had no idea how long she stood there, remembering the care and time Wyck had put into gently freeing them from their constraints - "them and everything else," Margaret realized. "The hedges, the garden, me. Allowing everything room to grow, to be..." She closed her eyes.

A crash from another room scared her to death. Racing through the house to find the source, she came into the den where the glass case holding Mrs. Hopson's rose lay in pieces on the floor. "I will never know what knocked it over," she would think later, as the rose lay, fragile but undamaged, in the midst of the brokenness. Kneeling, Margaret picked it up and jerked her hand away to find a single drop of bright red blood surrounding the thorn embedded in her finger.

With a sharp intake of breath, she whispered, "What have I done?"

Wyck wiped her sweaty face on her t-shirt sleeve and surveyed her work. This back yard design had come together beautifully - tiered planting beds surrounding some very old trees, a flagstone patio formally arranged in a rectangle with urns placed at the corners, softened by small boxwoods.

"Oh, Wyck, it's wonderful," said Mrs. Carter, coming out to inspect her progress. "It's exactly the look I wanted. You are a genius."

Wyck grinned and thanked her. "I'll be back tomorrow to finish up," she said.

She packed up her tools and wheeled them all out to the truck. Leaving the windows down to catch the May breeze blowing down from the mountains, she felt the sweat cooling her face as it evaporated. She contemplated calling her mother, but wasn't in the mood to hear the latest on her father's toileting habits. She was eagerly looking forward to getting home for a walk with Mandy as she negotiated her way through traffic, eventually making her way out of town to the tree-lined road that led to her lane.

Early columbine was blooming along the fencerow, and honeysuckle and trumpet vines were growing in profusion, but not yet in bloom. She turned onto her lane and stopped the truck at the Misselthwaite sign, thinking for the hundredth time she should take it down. "It was a stupid dream," she muttered. "I'll come back later with some tools." She put the truck in gear and continued on her way. As she neared the barn, she spotted a familiar car parked there and her breath caught in her throat.

Mandy galumphed out to greet her, barking happily as she jumped about in excitement, clearly trying to tell Wyck something.

Wyck slid out of the truck, looking around. Mandy took her by the hand, keeping her mouth soft, and pulled Wyck around behind the barn where a very strange sight met her eyes.

Margaret was kneeling in a patch of freshly dug earth near the shop. Half a dozen small rose bushes sat gathered there, waiting to be planted.

At the sight of Wyck, she got to her feet, brushing off the dirty knees of her jeans.

"Hi," she said uncertainly when Wyck just stood there looking at her.

Margaret gestured toward the roses. "I hope you don't mind, but this seemed like a lovely spot - lots of sun and a beautiful view from the kitchen..."

"Margaret, what -?"

Margaret took a deep breath, and Wyck could see the cords standing taut in her neck. "I've left - everything. The house, the university, everything."

Wyck stared at her, not sure she understood. "What do you mean, you left?"

"You were right," Margaret said, her voice trembling in her nervousness. "I couldn't bridge my two lives, one with Gavin and one with you. I had to make a choice. So I left."

Wyck's mouth opened, but no sound came out at first. "You... you quit your job?"

Margaret gave a funny sideways twitch of her head. "I resigned from the university. I've applied for another position at UNC-Asheville, but I may not get it." She gestured toward the driveway where the vehicles sat parked. "My car is stuffed with boxes - just my clothes and my books. I was hoping you wouldn't mind building some more bookcases. Oh, and I took that." She pointed to a wrapped parcel leaning against the shed. "It's the Jedediah Hotchkiss map. You liked it and I want you to have it." She swallowed. "I didn't take anything else."

Wyck sat down hard on her chopping block.

"It had to be like that," Margaret said fast, as if she needed to explain before her courage failed her. "Every thing, every piece of my life with Gavin was like an anchor, holding me down, keeping me in place."

"What about Gavin's family? Your grandchildren?" Wyck asked.

"Oh, well... Amanda and Matthew and the kids are in Portugal for three years. Hopefully, that will give Amanda time to get over herself," Margaret said. "Jeffrey, I think, will come around more quickly, but that's up to them now. I've left the door open."

"But the university," Wyck said, still not quite believing this was real. "I saw in the paper... you took the other position."

"I did," Margaret admitted. "Jim basically blackmailed me, forcing me to take it. After I brought you to his party, he put two and two together and figured out what Gavin meant by the wording of the will, so... we could never have..." She looked as if she might faint.

Wyck went to her and took her by the hand, leading her to the shade of the back porch. There, she made Margaret sit on a bench. Wyck sat beside her, still stunned by the enormity of Margaret's decision, everything she had given up, knowing how hard it must have been to let go of that security. Wyck looked down at Margaret's hand, still held in her own. For long minutes, they sat in stupefied silence.

When Margaret spoke at last, her eyes were filled with tears. "I know I have no right... after everything I've done. I don't have a job. I don't have a house. I literally don't have anything to offer you except my love. A love I promise I will never again be afraid of." She squeezed Wyck's hand and held on tightly. "But if it's too late, I will understand. I've put you through hell. I'll leave if you want me to."

Margaret released her grip on Wyck's hand, but Wyck grabbed hold and raised Margaret's hand to her lips, blinking hard as her own eyes stung with tears. "You know," she said, looking up at Margaret, "this is not how Jane Austen would have ended a story. All of her heroines ended up marrying for love and fortune. Like you, all I have to offer is my love."

Mandy squirmed in between them, looking from one to the other as her tail thumped the floorboards.

"And a dog."

Margaret laughed, her tears spilling over. "My dearest Wyck. This is the perfect ending, where the foolish heroine follows her heart at last and marries the poor, but honorable, gardener. I think that's exactly the kind of happy ending Jane would have written."

THE END

Author Biography

Caren was raised in Ohio, the oldest of four children. Much of her childhood was spent reading Nancy Drew and Black Stallion books, and crafting her own stories. She completed a degree in foreign languages and later another degree in physical therapy where for many years, her only writing was research-based, including a therapeutic exercise textbook. She has lived in Virginia for over twenty years where she practices physical therapy, teaches anatomy and lives with her partner and their canine fur-children. She began writing creatively again several years ago. Her debut novel, *Looking Through Windows*, won an award from the Golden Crown Literary Society and most recently, *Miserere*, *In This Small Spot* and *Neither Present Time* all won or placed in the 2013 Rainbow Awards. *She Sings of Old, Unhappy, Far-off Things* is her sixth novel.